Never the Bride

Never the Bride

PAUL MAGRS

headline
review

First published in 2006
by HEADLINE REVIEW

An imprint of Headline Book Publishing

1

Cataloguing in Publication Data is available from the British Library

Hardback 0 7553 3286 5 (ISBN-10)
Hardback 9 780 7553 3286 1 (ISBN-13)
Trade paperback 0 7553 3287 3 (ISBN-10)
Trade paperback 9 780 7553 3287 8 (ISBN-13)

Typeset in Garamond by Avon DataSet Ltd,
Bidford-on-Avon, Warwickshire

Printed and bound in the UK by
CPI Mackays, Chatham ME5 8TD

Headline's policy is to use papers that are natural, renewable and recyclable
products and made from wood grown in sustainable forests.
The logging and manufacturing processes are expected to conform
to the environmental regulations of the country of origin.

HEADLINE BOOK PUBLISHING
A division of Hodder Headline
338 Euston Road
London NW1 3BH

www.reviewbooks.co.uk
www.hodderheadline.com

for Sherry Ashworth

Chapter One:
The Deadly Boutique

I love it here. It's the only place I could have settled down. I've never found a town like it, never in my long, long life.

My name is Brenda. Hello!

Since the beginning of summer I have lived here, deliciously inconspicuous: just one more bed-and-breakfast lady in a resort that teems with them. Here, the streets are narrow and intricate, the rooftops are ramshackle and the wind is biting. The seagulls are as big as Yorkshire terriers and, for a good nine months of the year, the town is steeped in a thick sea mist . . . and that's probably a good thing.

There are things here that you don't necessarily want to see.

Keep your head down, Brenda. That's what I tell myself. Fry those sausages, eggs and bacon. Make those beds. Be welcoming. Be at home.

Now it is autumn. I have settled into the gloomy, doom-laden, chintzy Gothic atmosphere of the place.

And I love it.

*

I am a woman of a certain age who is ready to settle down. In the past I have had to pick myself up, time and again, and reinvent my life from scratch.

Now I want a quiet one.

I have known adversity, disaster and dodgy relationships. I have moved around from place to place, all over these islands. Sometimes I have even had to go on the run.

Now I want a quiet life. A respectable life.

I have no family. No ties.

I want to look after others.

I want to keep everything immaculate and just so, making sure that the breakfasts and teas are on time and that the rooms are exact, with the correct number of towels, flannels and little bars of soap. My guests are quite particular. My establishment attracts a certain class of person, I would say, though I'm not a snob.

My friend Effie, who owns the junk shop next door, is a bit la-di-da and she says I'm obsessed with getting things right for my guests. She used the word 'mania'. She says no one else running a B-and-B in this town goes to the same trouble. For all her airs and graces, Effie is a bit slapdash about her own place. She's the arty type, very literary. The only books I have are the Bible, Milton and Shelley, of course. I make sure there are copies in each of my three rooms, in the drawer of the bedside cabinets, and two fresh bath towels laid out, two flannels for every basin. The curtains are always opened exactly a foot wide, to let enough sunshine in but not so much as to make the room look bleak. Effie says I fuss, but it's like someone once said, 'God is in the details.'

But don't get me on to the subject of God. Effie tried once and I had to stop her. She understands now that my God and her God are not quite the same. That was as far as the conversation went. Effie is a good friend to me but, like everyone else in Whitby, she knows nothing about my past.

No one living knows about my past.

I always wanted pretty things. I wanted sofas and chairs, and nicely patterned curtains in light fabrics. I wanted colourful, dainty crockery. And I wanted to please people, to serve them tasty, wholesome, well-cooked food. I've got a craze for cleaning. I wait until the guests go out in the mornings, and leave their rooms all a-tumble, strewn with seaside-holiday bric-à-brac. And then I creep in, clutching cloths, yellow dusters and a tin of baking soda. I crouch in bathtubs, sprinkle on the powder and scour to my heart's content. Everything has to shine.

My livelihood depends on the excellence of my establishment.

Despite everything, I am, in the end, more or less, a self-made woman.

Mondays, I take my afternoon off. Effie and I stroll along the prom, up the hill, to the Christmas Hotel for afternoon tea. It isn't the swishest of places, as Effie says. But I like it. I like its deep, cavernous interior and its ancient, unchanging clientele. I love to sit in the conservatory at our usual table, overlooking the craggy, inhospitable bay. I like to sip too-hot tea, crumble biscuits and stare at the jet-black cliffs, the ruined abbey and the fathomless sky.

Effie grumbles and moans, of course. As I say, she puts on airs and wishes she was somewhere altogether nicer. Yet she has been coming here since she was a child. She has lived in the town all her life, inherited the house and her belongings from her family, which has always been rooted here. I envy her that much. She could no more think about leaving this town and her usual days than she could sprout a second head.

She's neat and slim, Effie, in a pale grey woollen suit, little ruffles round the neck of her lilac blouse. She takes a twist of lemon in her tea and her mouth is pursed much of the time. Appraising. Watchful.

That Monday afternoon her eyes were narrowed as she gazed round the conservatory at the Christmas Hotel. Neither of us bothered to comment on the party hats the decrepit hotel guests wore, the crackers they struggled feebly to pull or the dusty swags of vulgar tinsel strewn everywhere. This hotel is frozen for ever on the cusp of Christmas Eve. That is its selling point, its gimmick, and it is the way its eccentric proprietress likes it to be.

So it wasn't the festive lavishness that was attracting Effie's frown of intrigue. She was staring at our waitress, Jessie, who invariably served us our afternoon tea on Mondays. She was approaching with the trolley and its usual freight of gleaming, tinkling china, squashy cakes, mounds of golden cream and precise geometrical arrangements of egg and cress sandwiches.

'What on earth has Jessie gone and done to herself?'

I peered over my glasses. 'She looks all right to me. In fact, she looks rather well.'

Effie's mouth squinched up even tighter. 'Exactly. She looks better than she has any right to.'

Jessie was breezing along between the tables. Her usual tread was listless and heavy. She had worked here eighteen years and she despised her job. She had told us so on many occasions. We had speculated repeatedly on what kept her tethered to a job she hated. Maybe it was a blackmail thing, and the proprietress of the Christmas Hotel *had* something on Jessie. Or maybe Jessie was a timid person who feared leaving a situation she loathed because the thought of the outside world was even more terrible. Who knew? We were too polite to ask her. As it was, we were used to Jessie's quietly corrosive despair. Today, though, she was positively jaunty.

'She looks twenty years younger!' Effie cried.

Surely she was exaggerating, I thought. But it wasn't like Effie to resort to hyperbole. I waited until Jessie and our afternoon tea arrived and then I could properly stare at her.

And it was true! Where were her deeply etched wrinkles? Where was her scraggy old chicken neck?

'Ladies!' She grinned. 'How lovely to see you.'

Where was her surliness, her migrainey frown?

'What on earth has happened to you?' Effie demanded crisply.

Jessie shook out her golden (golden!) perm and treated us to a dazzling (dazzling!) grin. 'Ladies . . .' she announced. 'I have had a make-over.'

Her complexion was marvellous. She had a kind of glow. We basked in it, incredulous, as she wielded her tongs, popping cakes on to plates, then slid teacups before us.

Effie could restrain herself no longer. 'But it's impossible!' she burst out. 'No beauty parlour is *that* good.'

I winced. Usually it's me who's tactless like that. Jessie gave a carefree laugh. This in itself was alarming. We had never heard her sound carefree before. She let out a volley of shrill guffaws that rang out and bounced off the glass of the conservatory. Pensioners at the other tables glanced up from their tea, sherry and Christmas pudding. Jessie? Chortling? In a carefree fashion?

'It's all right.' She smiled down at Effie and me. 'I don't mind. You can say it – it's impossible that I should look so much better. No one could have made the old, careworn Jessie look like this. What a feat! It's amazing, I know. Last time you saw me I was like a wrung-out old dishrag, all disappointment and bitterness. I know that better than anyone.'

She gave the teapot an energetic swirl and poured our tea. We leaned in closer to hear her secret.

'Even I don't quite believe this miraculous transformation,' she said, lowering her voice. 'I woke up on Saturday morning and dashed to my mirror. I did the same on Sunday, and again this morning. Just to check that it was true. I can't believe my luck. I've dropped twenty-five years as if they never even happened to me. I've dropped the worst twenty-five years of my life.'

'But,' gasped Effie, 'how?'

'It happened on Friday,' said Jessie. 'It cost a whole two months' wages. I went to that new place, up Frances's Passage. You must have noticed the adverts in the *Gazette*?'

'Adverts?' Effie hadn't seen the local paper. But I had.

'The Deadly Boutique,' Jessie said, giving us that glorious smile again, 'has just opened for business. I was one of the first.'

'"Deadly"?' sniffed Effie. 'Why's it called "Deadly"?'

I must say, the adjective had rung alarm bells with me when I clapped eyes on the advertisement.

'I don't know!' cried Jessie. 'Who cares? Look at me! I'm fantastic!'

That was as much as we heard about it, for now. Effie was keen to pump Jessie for more details, and I wouldn't have minded hearing more, but suddenly Jessie turned shifty. 'I'm sorry, ladies. I can't stand here gossiping all day.' She gulped. 'I keep getting into trouble for chatting with guests. Madam doesn't like it.'

'Madam' was how all the staff at the Christmas Hotel referred to the proprietress. To me, there was something old-fashioned and even sinister about this nomenclature. Jessie was perturbed. 'I can't go upsetting her. I've drawn a lot of attention already, due to my make-over, and she isn't very happy at all.'

'Hmm,' mused Effie, looking troubled. Then she smiled at Jessie. 'You run along then, my dear. We'll see you later.'

'Are you coming to the pie-and-peas supper on Wednesday evening?' Jessie asked. 'Shall I put your names down?'

Effie frowned. 'Is this a new thing?'

I could tell she thought it sounded rather common. 'It's bingo as well, isn't it?' I asked Jessie. 'What a delightful combination! Sign us up, Jessie. We'll be there!'

We received another dazzling smile, and then Jessie was off, shoving that tea trolley along the thick carpeting with a lot more vigour than she used to.

Effie sighed. 'Pie and peas and bingo.' She tutted. 'Honestly, Brenda.'

'At least we'll get a chance to quiz Jessie further,' I said, tapping my nose.

It was from that point onwards that I think you could say Effie and I were officially *intrigued*.

We both knew – in our water – that something strange was going on. No amount of primping, pampering and preening in some beautician's parlour could change a woman so much. Jessie hadn't been exaggerating when she said she'd shed twenty-five years. She'd slung off those years as Gypsy Rose Lee would fling off her long satin gloves.

Effie and I ambled along the breezy front, down the hill, walking off our tea, thinking about Jessie's transformation.

'She said it was like being mesmerised,' I shouted, above the crash and boom of the surf.

'Hm?'

'She let that much out,' I said. 'Being done up – being *titivated* at the Deadly Boutique was like being mesmerised. That was how she put it. She said she was in a lovely trance the whole time.'

'Yes,' purred Effie. 'I heard her. It was all most interesting, wasn't it?'

I could feel that we were at the beginning of a crazy adventure, at the still point before the storm.

One of the things that Effie and I had discovered about each other – early on in our friendship – was that there was nothing that either of us liked better than a bloody good mystery. It kept our minds active, kept us limbered up mentally, so to speak. No matter how trivial or earth-shattering, we liked something mysterious and – dare I say it? – spooky to keep us occupied in our spinstery decrepitude.

Right now, treading on the gold and crimson leaf mulch, tasting the stiff salt breeze off the North Sea, we knew we were on the brink of something grand.

I returned to my home, my glorious B-and-B, to get on with my work. Effie marched off to hers next door having issued a curt goodbye. There's nothing sentimental about Effie. She's not what you'd call a clingy friend, which suits me fine. She went in through her ground-floor junk shop, then to her echoing rooms upstairs.

It must be gloomy for her. Lonely, up there.

I think she prizes her solitude, as do I.

That Monday I had no paying guests. The season had wound down to a standstill and I had only a few bookings lined up over the next couple of months. However, that was no reason to let things slide. I anticipated a headily enjoyable evening scrubbing out the four bathrooms. Getting the old baking soda going. Sloshing around with the mop.

And maybe I'd have a lovely deep bath and pamper myself a bit.

As you can see, I was thinking about make-overs.

But there was no way I would visit the Deadly Boutique. I wouldn't let any beautician lay their hands on me, no matter how skilled or magical they were. I simply couldn't let them touch me.

I can't let anyone get that close.

In the eyes of the world I have to look like an unobtrusive woman. I have to draw scant attention.

How old am I?

In the eyes of the world, and the eyes of this town, I am coming up to pension age. Effie keeps asking when I'll be due for my bus pass. She's guessed it must be soon. She already has hers and she isn't too proud to get on the buses for nothing. Effie says that when I have mine, we'll go on trips together, up the wild north coast, and count the pennies we're saving. I haven't the heart to tell her my pension will never come. I can't bring myself to say that I'm not on the official records. Really, I don't exist. It's hard to explain that to your best friend.

Effie thinks I'm a marvel – she's told me so – for the way I've kept my youth and vitality. I know she means it must be compensation for being so plain. 'Rather plain' is the worst thing I've heard Effie say about a woman. She has no compunction about passing comment in public on people's looks, even within their hearing. She has the blithe air of someone who was beautiful in her youth, and can't understand how others may be upset by having their appearance remarked on. She's a subtle thinker, Effie, but she doesn't understand *feelings*.

And yet she has never asked about the scars on my face. Perhaps she is too polite. Not being the type to stare into mirrors, I forget they're there. For whole days at a time I can forget how I look. I enjoy running my fingers along their puckers and gathers, but I try not to do it in company, because people seem to find it disconcerting.

I have always used a lot of makeup. There is something satisfying about piling on layers of paint and grease, knowing that you're still the same person underneath, even in disguise. I have always found it steadying to know myself exactly.

These were the lines my thoughts were running on, that Monday evening, as I set about my chores. My hands were rough and crabbed with scrubbing and my knees ached from the lino. I had my bath in my claw-footed tub, up in my attic, and I relaxed at last, and found myself dwelling on these selfish and self-absorbed thoughts.

It was Jessie who had put me in this frame of mind, regressing herself and making herself over. She had become a better woman.

That's what I've spent my long, long life doing. Learning to be a better woman.

After I hoisted myself out of the bath, and when I was all cosy in dressing-gown and slippers, with some oily black jazz LP going round and round, crackling away, I allowed myself a little weep. It's not often I indulge myself like this, believe me. Sometimes it all catches up with me. My life's been quite harrowing. I'm so grateful that I've landed in this safe new harbour.

But sometimes I still have a little cry.

I am alone on this earth. No siblings or children to divert or confuse me. I have only ever been perfectly myself, alone. And that perfect self takes the eyelashes and sticks them on with glue; each black lash long as a spider's leg. And she washes, combs and fluffs up her various wigs. I have always wanted to blend in, to be one more barely visible woman.

I always imagined I could draw nearer to the world of human beings and believe myself part of it.

Here I am in Whitby. The homely, caring bed-and-breakfast lady with the air of quiet authority. When I first came here I listened to the screaming, wheeling gulls. From the jetty I watched the shot grey silk of the perplexing sea. I could smell the vinegary warmth of the fish and chips that the holiday people on the prom were eating. I might have thrown in the towel right then.

What am I? A freak of supernature. A thing of shreds and patches. I might have killed myself long ago. But I haven't.

As you may have guessed already, I'm extremely proud of my B-and-B. It cost me an arm and a leg. I'd been saving for years and years. I began with nothing: a few silver coins that I deposited several lifetimes ago, or so it seems. And I went wandering, looking for a place to settle. By the time I found this house, my savings had grown. I had sufficient.

I have three guest rooms, and my own small set of rooms in

the attic. This house and Effie's ancient family pile next door are set on one of the most sloping, perilous streets in our town. Effie is further down the hill and has a ground-floor entrance. My downstairs is a small grocery belonging to an Indian family. Quite handy.

I like being slightly higher up. I love living in the eaves – the old mad woman in her spruce, tidy attic. I have a tiny garden where I grow geraniums, and I can poke my head out of the skylight and get a glimpse of the turbulent sea, the rocks and the abbey.

This is my little queendom. Whole days can pass when I don't see anyone, and that doesn't bother me a jot. I'm quite happy entertaining myself and doing my chores.

That Tuesday was one of those distracted, solitary days. I polished, baked and hummed little tunes. And then, in the early afternoon, the phone rang. Guests!

It was a polite young woman, who said she was a researcher on a cable TV show.

'A TV show?' I frowned.

'Yes. I wrote to you, remember? I asked about booking three rooms for our crew at the end of the month.'

Of course. Now I remembered. The TV people at the end of the month. I hadn't replied to her letter. I'd let it slide. I didn't want showbiz people poking around in my place. Filming things and asking questions.

'You see, everywhere seems to be booked up that weekend,' the researcher girl was going on. 'It's one of the big pagan festivals or something, so all the B-and-Bs and hotels in your town are chock-a-block . . .'

'Well,' I said, 'they would be.'

'So we thought we'd check back with you to see if your place is available.'

I twiddled the phone cord. 'Oh, go on, then. I suppose I can fit you in. Three rooms, you say?' Business was business, I reckoned. I needed to make a living.

'Three rooms,' she said. 'There's the presenter, Eunice, and a girl who does hair and makeup. And Brian, the psychic.'

'The what?'

'The psychic. You know the show, don't you?'

'I'm afraid I don't.'

'We're on cable. It's the one where they spend the night in a haunted house and film themselves in infrared getting more and more scared, and trying to call up the spirits of the dead. *Manifest Yourself!* it's called.'

'What?' My heart was thudding alarmingly in my chest. 'You're not planning on doing . . . a whole lot of unsavoury practices round my house, are you?'

The researcher chuckled. 'To be honest, I think it's a lot of nonsense. Brian fakes it half the time when he cracks on he's possessed. But it's a popular show. There's a hunger for this kind of spooky stuff.'

'I know.' I nodded. 'But you didn't answer. I asked if you were investigating me . . . my house.'

'Oh, no.' She laughed. 'Next door. Some old junk shop that an old dear owns. She called us in.'

'Effie?' I exclaimed. 'She called you in?'

'Oh, yes,' said the girl. 'She was very keen. Quite a fan of Brian the psychic, she is. And she reckons there are some queer old spirits round her place.'

'I see,' I said. I wondered why she'd never told me about them as I took down further details in my green leather guest book. I made the researcher girl spell out every name, including the name of the show. *Manifest Yourself!* it was called, apparently. 'With an exclamation mark,' the girl prompted. 'It's important. It puts across the wonderful sense of urgency that Brian and the team conjure up.'

'Hm,' I said. 'I must say I don't hold with dabbling in this kind of thing. I've seen some nasty things happen in my time.'

The girl shrugged this off. 'Like I say, it's all faked. It's only showbiz.'

And then she was gone, having booked the team in for the end of the month. It was still a couple of weeks away. Maybe it was nothing to fret about.

I flung on a housecoat and hurried downstairs to the alleyway. I was going to beard Effie in her den. What was she up to, inviting TV shows and not telling me?

It was dusk. A fine, clinging mist was snaking up the cobbled alley, and when I turned into the sloping main street I saw that it was inching its way in thick scarves and smothering all in its path. I gave an involuntary shiver as I turned to Effie's front door and rapped on the thick glass.

The shop was dark. Was it closed? I'd lost all sense of time. I peered inside at the battered copper kettles, cracked ceramics and mottled books in tottering stacks. Filthy old place. I wished she'd get shot of it. It should have been a house make-over show she'd invited, not ghost-hunters.

As I thought that word, 'make-over', another shudder went through me, as if someone had walked over my grave.

Effie was out, that much was certain. I'd given her bell a good old ring. There was no way she'd not have heard it. She was out somewhere for definite. Out in the descending fog and the indigo twilight. I don't know why . . . but that made me a little nervous on her account.

And I was right!

I should trust my instincts after all these years. When my hackles go up, and all the hairs on my back stand on end, it's a sure sign that something horrible is going on somewhere close.

Poor Effie was having a terrible time just a few streets away, in premises hidden up an alley called Frances's Passage.

Effie had snuck out to visit the Deadly Boutique. She had gone investigating alone.

It was only much later in the evening that I got to hear about it.

I was dozing in front of my little fire that night when there came all this hullabaloo from the alleyway. Someone was banging at my front door, just about breaking it down. I came to with an almighty jolt and staggered, all befuddled, down the stairs. My dreams had been as lurid and odd as ever and I hadn't had a chance to wake properly.

I flung open the door on to darkness, and Effie was standing there, pale with shock, her eyes all red. 'I'm a vain, stupid woman,' she wailed, and burst into tears. 'I've only just escaped with my life, Brenda!' Then she fell into my arms. She was only the weight of a sackful of leaves.

Questions could wait. I hoisted her easily up to the attic, where she was soon installed in front of the fire. After some moments I had it blazing again, putting some colour back into those cheeks of hers. Effie slugged back the brandy I gave her and asked for more. I'd never seen her drink so much, and I'd never seen her cry.

Another shudder went through me. Foreboding. A not wholly unpleasant tingle of foreboding.

At last Effie glanced at me and fixed her watery eyes on mine. 'We must put a stop to them, Brenda,' she said. 'They're up to no good whatsoever.'

I already knew who she was talking about. 'You daft old mare,' I cursed her. 'You went there, didn't you? By yourself. That's why you called yourself vain. You went to the Deadly Boutique tonight. For a secret make-over!'

Effie stirred in her armchair. I'd given her the most comfortable seat in the house but I wasn't sure she deserved it. Sneaking about by herself like that. Investigating things on her own. I thought it was understood by now: we would only investigate these matters together. We needed each other to depend on. We needed back-up.

But then . . . This investigation wasn't the only thing Effie had planned alone lately. I was reminded, suddenly, of *Manifest Yourself!* and how she had arranged to hold a televised seance and ghost-hunt in her house – all without informing me!

What kind of friend was Effie turning out to be?

I could feel my battered old heart steeling itself against her. But then I looked at her pouchy, tear-smudged face and relented. Poor old dear. I think she'd realised she'd bitten off more than she could chew. Next time she'd make sure Brenda was with her. No fear.

'What happened?' I asked.

Effie gulped. 'Oh, Brenda. It was awful.'

For a moment I thought she was going to cry again, but she

swallowed it down. She was wearing her best woollen suit and had pinned her favourite brooch to the lapel. This added to the pathos somehow, as if she had wanted to look her best even when she arrived at the Deadly Boutique. 'What did they *do* to you, Effie?' I urged.

'I didn't give them the chance to do much at all,' she said. 'As you can see, they didn't have time to make me over and do whatever terrible thing they'd planned. I haven't suddenly shed twenty-five years, like poor old Jessie, thank goodness.'

'Start at the beginning,' I told her.

Effie drank the rest of her second medicinal brandy and considered. 'I didn't mean to go there. I hadn't made an appointment or anything. I just took a little wander down the prom this afternoon, before the sea mist came in, and I thought . . . well, it wouldn't hurt to have a look at the outside of the place. To check in case there was anything suspicious about it. You have to admit, Brenda, we were both pretty intrigued yesterday afternoon, what with Jessie and all. If you'd been out today, you'd have done the same as me . . .'

I harrumphed. 'I wouldn't have got myself into trouble. I'd have had more sense than that, I hope.'

'There was no escaping it!' Effie gasped. 'Really! The things they're up to! It's wicked. They won't rest until – until – every woman in town has had a make-over . . . and been put into the Deadly Machine.'

Effie was jumping ahead of herself again. I glugged us out another shot of the old brandy and found that it soon straightened out the narrative.

Effie told me how she had ventured up the shady, cobbled alleyway – almost unwillingly – as if she was acting under some weird influence. That put me in mind of what Jessie had said: that she had been mesmerised by the boutique's owner. Drawn away from the straight and narrow of her late-afternoon constitutional, Effie had strayed into Frances's Passage. On the way, she passed a young woman in a plastic mac. She was pulling the collar up round her ears and her rain hat down over her eyes. She was scooting past Effie as if she didn't want to be observed quitting the Deadly Boutique.

And there was the establishment. The black and gold enamel paint of its elaborate sign still looked wet and fresh. The front windows displayed nothing but an extravagant spray of tropical flowers. Effie peered through the distorting glass and found herself staring at a livid green caterpillar – a disgusting thing – inching its horrid way inside the dewy whorl of a lily. It was munch-munch-munching through the fleshy hood. 'I've never seen such unnatural-looking blooms,' Effie told me.

It was while she was thus bent over, peeping into the front bay, that the insinuating voice came over her shoulder: 'If Madam would like to step this way?'

Effie is susceptible to flattery.

That quiet voice went on: 'It is quite obvious that Madam takes great care with her appearance. Her grooming is immaculate. She looks splendid. However, there is always something that a humble artist, such as myself, can suggest. If Madam would like to step into my boutique . . .'

Listening to all of this, I was wondering if Effie wasn't building up her part. Immaculate grooming, indeed. Not that it wasn't true. But trust Effie to feed herself little compliments while she was still supposed to be traumatised.

She turned to see a dapper, quizzical little man standing in the alleyway, blocking her exit. He had thinning, sandy hair, gold-rimmed glasses and a weak chin. His lips, she said, were very wet. He wore a trimly cut suit and a tailor's tape measure hung round his neck. He looked harmless.

'I am Mr Danby.' He smiled, then bowed, which made Effie feel bizarrely powerful. She felt as if she towered above him. 'Welcome to my Deadly Boutique.'

'Why "Deadly"?' Effie found herself asking, as she allowed herself to be propelled into the dim interior.

'Oh,' Mr Danby chuckled, 'a silly whim of mine. It simply describes the effect of the new look we will give you. You will – as the saying has it – "knock 'em dead".'

Effie was glancing at her new surroundings. It was certainly elegant and plush, with more of those flowers. The sofas were leopardskin and the walls and floors were carpeted with shaggy black fur. It felt thrillingly decadent. There was, as far as she could tell, none of the usual paraphernalia associated with a beauticians': no mirrors or sinks, hair-driers or cupboards crammed with powders, paints and unguents.

'I'm not sure,' she said, to Mr Danby. 'I'm not at all sure why I came here. I was intrigued, you see. We met a friend of ours – Jessie – and she's been a visitor here, at the Deadly Boutique. Your, ehm, treatments, whatever they are, seem to have done her a power of good . . .'

'Ah.' Mr Danby was flipping through a book of handwritten notes on the glass-topped counter. 'Oh, yes. Mrs Sturgeon. I remember. She was one of our very first clients. We did a rather good job on her. I recall being particularly proud of Mrs Jessica Sturgeon.' He gave an oily laugh – whether at his own cleverness or at poor Jessie's unfortunate surname Effie couldn't be sure. 'I am pleased that Jessie is spreading the word,' he added. 'I shall have to arrange a reduction in price for her when she returns tomorrow for her next treatment.'

Effie was surprised. 'She isn't finished?'

'Not quite. She needs a few more sessions so that we can be sure that the work we have begun on her . . . achieves perfection.' He clasped his tiny, pink hands together and smiled at Effie. 'Now,' he said, 'I think we should stop talking about other people, Ms Jacobs. I think we should concentrate on *you*. You have seen what we are capable of here. Just imagine what we could make of you . . .'

Effie paused. She was trembling. 'Did you notice?' she whispered. 'He knew my name. He seemed to know all about me. He knew what I hate about my . . . body, and he also knew what I take a secret, foolish pride in. He was an insinuating little toad. And yet as he spoke to me – in these personal, intimate terms – about my nose and my neck, my complexion, my neat little ears, my legs and my . . . my bust, I felt lulled and drifted off . . . into a trance. I was being hypnotised, Brenda! Right there and then in the Deadly Boutique! That slimy little devil was putting me under!'

There were gaps in Effie's recollection of her bizarre experience at the Deadly Boutique. As she told me the tale, she twisted her face and pulled at her wispy hair with the effort of remembering. Try as she might, she couldn't fully penetrate the fog in which Mr Danby had ensnared her.

'It went wrong with me,' she said. 'Somehow the hypnotism didn't work. I came round too soon. I woke up and I was standing inside the machine! It was like a sort of tanning booth

– you know the type of thing. But it was different. It wasn't just lit up inside, it was pulsating, with flashing lights and clouds and— Oh, Brenda. It was like a nightmare. I was standing there swaying and it was like being on drugs or something. I screamed and screamed, right there inside the Deadly Machine, but nobody came. Nobody would set me free. I felt like I was going to die.'

'But what is it, Effie? What did it do?'

'I don't know! I could feel . . . tiny little hands all over my body, patting and stroking and primping me. They were kneading me and rolling me about like a lump of dough. I screamed and thrashed about, but to no avail. I was being spun round and round . . . and I remember thinking, This is it! I'm being . . . made over!'

I stared at her. She looked exactly the same as she always did. 'What happened? Why didn't the process work?'

'I wasn't docile and still enough, I suppose,' she said thoughtfully. 'That's why he mesmerises his victims. So they don't kick about and pummel at the doors in fright at the terrible things that go on inside that machine. Honestly, Brenda, it was like being inside the mind of a maniac!'

'You kicked your way out?' I gasped.

'I never knew I had that kind of strength.' She seemed rather proud of this. 'But that's precisely what I did. I was thrashing about so much that my foot connected with the heavy cubicle door and the thing flew open! And there I was, starkers, toppling out into the middle of this white-tiled, laboratory-type place.'

'Starkers!' I cried. 'He undressed you?'

'I suppose he must have,' she said, 'but there wasn't time to be embarrassed.'

21

I was amazed at Effie. Usually she was so prim. But here she was, relating her terrible nude adventure, barely even raising a blush.

'Mr Danby wasn't in the laboratory. That devil hadn't even stuck around to see how his handiwork turned out. But his helpers were there, his assistants in the beautifying process. They were milling around me, flapping their arms and shrieking. I don't suppose they'd ever known anyone to stagger prematurely out of the make-over machine before. They squealed and shouted, motioning me to get back into that dizzying deathtrap. But I wasn't about to take any of their nonsense. I demanded my clothes! I demanded to be set free!'

'But what did they say? Did they explain themselves?'

Effie frowned, concentrating. 'My impressions are pretty scrambled, but I don't think they were even speaking English. They were tiny, like children, in white plastic spacesuit things. They were squabbling and gibbering in some sort of foreign language. Nasty-sounding.' Her eyes widened as she pictured them. 'They were like little children, but they had awful, withered up ancient faces, like little primates.'

I tried to picture Effie surrounded by these panicked, unpleasant beings, bellowing for her clothes.

'I grabbed one and twisted its arm, hard and spitefully. Remember that ju-jitsu class I took in the summer? Came in handy. I was so riled, I could have broken the creature's arms. I must have looked a fearsome sight because they brought my clothes, all neatly folded, and stood back as I dressed. Then they showed me to the back door and pushed me out into the night, as peremptorily as their master had got me through the front. Evidently they knew that the process had gone wrong, and they wanted me off the premises. I stumbled out into the misty night and found myself in a very ordinary backyard in Frances's Passage. It took me just minutes to walk through the labyrinth of alleys back to the prom. I came straight here.' She held out her glass for more brandy. 'Brenda, can I stay tonight? I keep thinking about that man and his monkey-like women assistants. I fear they'll come after me in the night.'

'Of course!' I cried. 'I've three rooms, all clean and made up . . .'

Effie nodded, cradling her balloon glass in both hands. 'It was one of the most hair-raising experiences of my life.'

'What would have happened,' I said slowly, 'if the hypnotism had worked properly? If you'd stayed in the machine till the end of the process.'

'I suppose I'd have been the same as Jessie. A full twenty-five years younger.'

I nodded. 'You must be more strong-willed than her to withstand the mesmerising.'

She agreed. 'I've always known my own mind.'

'But what would be so wrong with regressing twenty-five years? Surely the process was only horrible because you woke up too early.'

Effie's eyes were haunted. She looked ghastly and drawn. 'I can't explain it, Brenda, but it was evil, whatever it was. There is something in that machine, and in that boutique, that isn't right. Whatever they're doing, it isn't for the good of their clients. The purpose of the Deadly Machine isn't just to give women make-overs. There's more to it than that. I could feel it.'

Then Effie declared herself exhausted. I swept into action. I was the dedicated and professional B-and-B lady, showing my guest to her room downstairs, making sure she had everything, making sure of her comfort. 'Tomorrow,' I promised her, 'we can start to get to the bottom of this business.'

She lay back in the clean, crisp linen of my best guest room. 'When I close my eyes . . . I can still see the swirling mist and lights inside that machine. It felt terrible, Brenda. I could feel it pulling and sucking at me . . . sucking away the time and the years and all my experience . . .'

I let Effie sleep in for much of the next morning. I knew it wasn't like her to stay in bed so late. Usually you can hear her rattling about in that huge house of hers next door, and she seems to rise even before I do. She doesn't half clatter around among all that dusty junk. It's odd, really: she sounds so careless and rackety within the privacy of her own four walls, yet when you see her out and about she's so proper and tidy.

On the Wednesday morning, however, she was sleeping placidly in my B-and-B, recovering from the shock of her make-over ordeal. At eleven I took in a tray with a modestly tempting breakfast of kippers. She seemed muddled but grateful.

I left her to it and, struck by a certain impulse, rang the Christmas Hotel. 'I'd like to be put through to the staff quarters,' I told the girl on the reception desk.

'Madam doesn't like the phone lines to be used by the staff,' I was told, quite frostily.

'I don't care about that,' I said. 'Madam will just have to lump it. This is an emergency.' I could hear grumbling in the background as I was put through to the relevant line. There was a snatch of a Christmassy jingle, then the phone rang for a good few minutes. At last I heard a male voice.

Young-sounding. 'I'm afraid you've missed Jessie,' he told me. 'She went out first thing. I'm her nephew, Robert. Can I pass on a message for you?'

'Oh,' I said, surprised. 'Robert! She's told me all about you. She said she'd got you a job for the autumn season. Have you just started? How are you liking it?'

He sounded sardonic in his reply: 'I'm not wholly convinced I'll make a career as a Christmas elf. But it's OK, I suppose. For a while. And it's nice to spend time with Aunt Jessie. We've always got on well.'

'I'm Brenda. I'm an acquaintance . . . well, a friend, really, of your aunt's.'

'Good,' he said. 'She could do with some sensible people unconnected to this madhouse. She needs people to talk sense into her.'

'Sense?' I said. 'What about?'

Robert the elf sighed heavily. 'This make-over business. She's taking it too far. It's like an obsession. I mean, fair enough, they've done an amazing job on her. She looks much, much better than she has done for years. But it's all she'll talk about! She's swanning round the hotel like a pin-up girl for the Deadly Boutique.'

'I know,' I said. 'We saw her. We were amazed. It's certainly impressive. It's almost uncanny.'

Robert snorted. 'Uncanny is exactly what I'd call it.' He sighed. 'Now she's got all the old dears stirred up about it and they've been trooping down to the place. They can't wait to get done! They're scraping their pennies together and making appointments.'

My heart-rate stepped up. I imagined queues of old women,

anxious to go through the same trauma as Effie. 'You know, Robert . . . they should be warned. I don't think anyone is doing themselves any favours by visiting the Deadly Boutique.'

'I think you're right, Brenda,' he said. 'I've tried to tell my aunt that – I tried this morning, first thing – but she won't listen. All she can think about is the good it's doing her. How, at the age of sixty-six, she looks forty-one and how, after her next appointment, she'll look even younger, in her twenties, perhaps. Well, that's not natural, is it? There must be a catch.'

I liked this Robert. He seemed a sensible young man. 'Exactly my thinking. We need to stop Jessie going back.'

'But,' he said, 'it's her morning off. She's already there. She's at the Deadly Boutique right now!'

For the size I am, I'm quite nimble on my pins. Even though the rest of me can seem a bit ungainly I can dash about when I want to. I can move quickly and stealthily, and that was precisely what I did when I'd finished on the phone with Jessie's helpful nephew. I didn't tell Effie I was nipping out. She'd only have wanted to accompany me and, despite her protests, I could tell she was still shaken up by her recent escapade.

It was too soon for her to return to the boutique.

So I went by myself.

I ran down our hill and through the narrow streets towards the prom. I ignored neighbours and acquaintances alike as I barrelled along, filled with ire and determination. When I came to Frances's Passage I took a deep breath and stepped bravely into its chilly confines. There was a waft of something clammy and evil down that ginnel. It was obvious to me, straight away. I surveyed the front of the boutique, and everything was as Effie had described it, down to the outrageous flowers flaunting themselves in the bow window.

The door was locked. A sign was hanging on the inside, claiming that the place was closed. I knew that couldn't be right: Jessie Sturgeon was inside, probably crammed into the Deadly Machine, having goodness knows what done to her. I rapped heavily on the shiny black door, then I pushed hard against the wood with my shoulder. Nothing. And when I pressed my ear to the glass panels, I couldn't hear a thing. Not a dicky-bird.

It wasn't the kind of silence that makes you think the interior is deserted, that everyone has packed up and taken a day off. It was the kind of silence that makes you think of creeping, underhand, untrustworthy things. Of foul deeds going on, just out of view. Of nefarious people hiding their wicked selves away . . .

I decided to sneak round the back. Effie had said they'd let her out of the back door into what appeared to be an ordinary yard. There was an elaborate network of back alleys and interconnecting yards, as there was in all of these Victorian warrens, but I was sure to find the right one in the end. It would just take perseverance.

I shivered when the church clock bonged out the hour. Eleven. Jessie's appointment had been for ten, her nephew had said. I was already too late.

All of those backyards looked the same, concrete and cobbles, lichen and moss, dripping grates and drainpipes, and cold, grey stone. I went creeping about, clattering past bins and hauling myself up to peep over crumbling walls. It's a wonder I wasn't mistaken for a burglar. But it was uncanny: there was no one about. No net curtains twitching, no one bringing out the rubbish. Not even an old moggy prowling about the place. Silence. No one.

Except . . . one building. It was as anonymous as the rest, but the back door was silvery. It was a new, solid-looking metal door. As I watched, perched half-way up a wall, it opened and out came three of the strangest-looking women I have ever seen. They were carrying large glass bottles filled with a variety of greenish liquids. They had a selection of hoses and funnels, too, and they were gabbling away to each other quietly in a strange tongue.

I shrank back so they wouldn't see me, and narrowed my eyes, appalled at the sight of them. All I can say is that Effie had been quite generous when she described Mr Danby's assistants as withered-up primates. To my eyes, they were the most peculiarly horrid creatures I have ever seen. Their flesh had turned white, like fish bellies, while their hair was colourless and stringy. They were the height of infants and wore bizarrely unflattering boiler-suits. They gibbered and whispered and they were pouring the green liquid down the drain. It ran, glistening and oily, into the sewers and the little women gathered to watch it go.

I couldn't guess what they were up to. It looked as if they were disposing of some by-product of their experiments.

Then, as soon as they had appeared, they hurried back indoors and the silver door was slammed shut.

There had been no sign of Jessie. For all my scrambling about, barking my shins and knees, I had learned nothing.

I hadn't liked the look of that green fluid, though. It was like bitterness and bile, and they were siphoning it straight into the water system . . .

*

Effie is the type to go pottering round auction houses and stately homes. To her, an evening's entertainment is a concert, some soothing and hummable classical thing. It isn't her idea of fun to go to a pie-and-peas supper, and suffer the tawdry thrills of bingo.

But that night we had to attend the Christmas Hotel. Effie muttered only a few complaints as we trip-trapped up the sloping streets to the smart row at the top of the town. That night the view out to sea was dramatic. The clouds were plumped up and tempestuous. The seabirds were weirdly quiet.

On the way I filled Effie in on my adventure in the back alley.

'Green liquids.' She frowned.

'Do you think they're trying to poison everyone?' I asked her. 'Pouring something nasty into the water system . . .'

'It doesn't sound like it to me,' she said. 'It sounds more like they're disposing of something they don't need. There'd be easier ways to poison us than chucking things in the sewers. With pies and peas, for example.'

'I do hope Jessie's all right.' I sighed.

'We'll soon find out, won't we?' said Effie, heartily. She was displaying a good deal more bravado than I'd expected. As she led the way through the hotel's grand entrance, I saw that her dander was up. She had been scared, mortally scared, the previous evening, and now she was determined to sort this business out. She had an enemy in her sights: Mr Danby. He had done something nasty to her, which made the business straightforward in Effie's mind. She had to sort him out.

Meanwhile . . . it was Christmas time at the Christmas Hotel.

Everything that could be had been well and truly trimmed with tinsel, holly, mistletoe and fake snow. Carols rang out through hidden speakers, three or four different ones at once, in a weird, festive cacophony. Party hooters and crackers were going off and we were offered, as always, a cup of mulled wine from the silver tureen on the reception desk as soon as we stepped inside.

Effie and I took some, relishing its spiced warmth. We'd need to be fortified indeed, if this macabre adventure carried on as it had begun. A tall, rather good-looking young man was wielding the ladle. He nodded at us knowingly. 'It's me,' he said. 'Robert. You *are* Brenda, aren't you?' His friendliness and searching glance made me feel self-conscious. I wasn't used to that degree of scrutiny.

'Yes,' I mumbled, 'and you're Jessie's nephew?'

He was dressed in one of the hotel's absurd elf outfits. The indignity of it! The boys were forced to wear skin-tight green felt one-piece suits with pointy green hats and stick-on pointy ears. The poor thing looked quite at home in his costume, even the two dots of red on his cheeks and the fake freckles across his nose. I introduced him to Effie.

'I knew it was you two, soon as you walked in. Auntie Jessie said you were unmistakable.'

Now I felt even more self-conscious. I felt lumbering, hideous, and my scarred, twisted flesh itched under the layers of makeup. I struggled to listen as the boy talked – so insouciantly. He was so handsome and young that, I found myself staring, in a trance of my own self-loathing.

'So Jessie's here?' barked Effie, breaking the spell. 'She returned safely from her appointment at the boutique this morning?'

'Oh, yes,' he said. 'She came back at lunchtime, ready for her afternoon shift. I saw her briefly and she seemed fine. Well, this time the treatment hadn't had such a dramatic effect. She'd only regressed another couple of years. Nothing as drastic as last time. She seemed disappointed by that.'

'She should think herself lucky she's still alive,' Effie said bitterly.

Robert looked shocked.

'Effie's been there,' I explained. 'She knows what—'

We were interrupted quite rudely then, by a raucous, hectoring voice that cut through our conversation from the direction of the old-fashioned lift cage. We turned quickly and guiltily to see who was calling.

Of course, we already knew.

There, in her motorised scooter, Christmas green and red, bedecked with tinsel, bows and mistletoe, sat the gargantuan form of Madam: the owner, manageress and genius of the Christmas Hotel. We didn't know her real name. We knew her only as Mrs Claus and, seeing her there, all thirty stone of her, clad in red velvet with a wreath of holly leaves crowning her snowy bouffant, no other name would have suited her. She advanced on us, flanked by a royal guard of elves, all uniformed as Robert, all solemn with yuletide responsibilities.

'Welcome! Welcome!' she bellowed at us. 'It's rare to see you two at one of my evening gatherings.' Her face was bright red. At first it looked like makeup – like the red spots on the elves' cheeks. But her complexion was crazed with broken veins. The reek of spirits wafted off her – very powerfully. 'Robert!' she yelled. 'I need you to call the bingo numbers. You've got the clearest and nicest speaking voice of all my elves.'

Astonished, we watched Robert scurry round the desk and away into the main dining room to do her bidding. All of the elves were over-anxious to please her. Effie and I exchanged a glance.

'Ladies,' Mrs Claus simpered, 'we must hurry and take our places. Otherwise we will be left with no dinner. That lot through there are like gannets.' She trundled off, the elves marching alongside her.

'They're scared of her,' Effie said.

'They certainly seem to be.' I frowned. 'Even Robert, and he's so sensible.'

'I wonder what's going on.' Effie shuddered. 'I hate this creepy place. It used to be so classy when I was a little girl. My father used to bring me for tea on my birthday. She's spoiled it. She's made it gaudy and sickly . . .'

I followed Effie into the dining hall, where the walls rang with false jollity and edgy jubilation. The heavy scent of gravy hung in the air as the waitresses went round with their trolleys. Effie was right. Under the gilt and the crêpe paper, something was rotten and wrong about the Christmas Hotel. But perhaps that was another mystery. For another day, maybe.

I enjoy a good game of bingo. I was well aware of Effie's scorn as I brought my dabbing-pen down on my numbers. I was within a whisker of winning one of the later games and, I must admit, I got quite carried away, wailing in disappointment when someone called, 'House!' just ahead of me.

'Well,' sniffed Effie, 'I'm glad that's at an end.' She had done nothing but complain all evening. The peas had been cold, the pie too hot so that she'd burned her mouth. The game had been simplistic, and then it had gone too fast so that, what with her arthritis, she couldn't hope to keep up.

'Didn't Robert do a good job calling out the numbers?' I nodded at him, still standing behind the glass tank of coloured balls.

'Is he a nancy-boy?' Effie asked loudly. 'I've nothing against them, mind you. He seems to be that way, doesn't he?'

I found myself blushing, and hushed her. 'Don't be so rude.'

'There's nothing rude about it,' Effie protested. 'It's just a statement of fact. I'm sure he wouldn't be offended.'

'Oh, I'm sure,' I said. 'Nancy-boy, indeed! What an awful thing to call the lad.'

Effie pursed her lips and glared at me. 'Not all of us are ashamed of what we are, Brenda,' she said, in a much lower voice. 'Not all of us keep a tin lid on things.'

I turned away from her abruptly. She was being very peculiar. I didn't know what she meant. Was she still talking about Robert? Or was she trying to tell me something about herself? Or . . . No. She was having a dig at me, wasn't she? She was referring to the way I don't talk about myself. Where I'm from. Who my people are. Who I really am.

Oh, Effie. I can't tell you. You wouldn't like it. You'd never believe it. You'd think you were best friends with a crazy woman.

I saw then that Jessie was coming over to us with her trolley. It was time for coffee and she had sought us out, bringing the silver pot and china cups. She had come to show herself off to us. Slinkier and younger than ever.

We gasped. She did a twirl, and the two of us sat there agog. We weren't faking it. We didn't have to pretend or flatter her. Our mouths hung open in shock and awe, and Jessie laughed. She tossed her head and laughed joyously.

'But . . . Robert said that, this time, there was less of a

change,' I stammered. 'He said he saw you when you came back from the boutique at lunchtime. He said you were disappointed because the change was less marked.'

Jessie shrugged gaily. 'Yes! That's how it was at lunchtime. But . . . it's like Mr Danby explained to me. As the treatments advance, sometimes they're slower to take hold. Well! I had a little nap in my room. I drew my curtains, lay down on my bed and fell into a perfect, most relaxing sleep. And when I woke up, just in time for my shift . . . this was how I found myself.'

I looked at Effie, who was as astonished as I was – disturbed, too, as if she was witnessing something that couldn't be true.

'I'm in my twenties again! I look no older than twenty-three!' Jessie started to pour our coffee. 'God bless Mr Danby.' She sighed. 'Bless him and his magical contraption. He's been sent as a blessing to us. To make our lives perfect and complete! How much we owe him! He's a boon to all womankind!'

As Jessie dropped the sugar cubes into our cups and poured the cream, I couldn't help thinking, It's driven her crazy. The shock has sent her insane.

'But it can't be *right*, can it?' I said.

We were walking along the prom again. It was our usual route, down from the Christmas Hotel to home, though we usually followed it at tea-time, before night had fallen as drastically as this – the stars were gloating over the pulsing, endless sea.

Effie was steeped in thought. She shook her head to clear it and smiled grimly. 'No,' she said. 'Indeed. It can't be *right*.'

'There has to be a catch,' I said. 'I don't for a second

begrudge Jessie her good fortune – I'm delighted for her, in fact. But what's happened to her simply can't have happened. It isn't possible. There has to be some kind of drawback . . . or payback . . .'

'Quite,' said Effie. 'The world doesn't work like that, does it? She can't just divest herself of all those years. She can't just turn the clock back. It's like fiddling with the gas meter – you'll be found out. We only get one go on the merry-go-round. And she's kidding herself if she thinks she can keep on galloping.'

'Still,' I said, 'she *did* look marvellous.'

'A miracle, she calls it.' Effie sighed. I glanced at her as we trundled along. She was grimacing. Her face was hawklike, white as a sheet in the moonlight.

'She says Mr Danby was an angel,' I added. 'An angel sent to improve us all.'

I saw fury rise in Effie's face. 'He's nothing of the sort. That's blasphemy, Brenda. She'll see it in the end. She'll regret all of it . . . in the end.'

I wish I'd never mentioned the angel thing. That religious talk can get Effie really fired up. As I said earlier, I can do without the religiosity, thank you very much. My father was obsessed with the idea of God. With the idea of *being* God, mostly. 'Did you hear all the old women cooing over her?' I said. 'She even got a round of applause. She's a walking advertisement.'

'That's what worries me,' Effie said. 'They'll be flocking.'

Now we were at the bottom of the hill, right on the sea front. This was the quickest way back, but it took us through the roughest part of the town centre. Here, the amusement arcade was still open, pouring its gaudy golden light into the bay. The music was cheap and tinny, and we could hear the crash and tinkle of silver and copper, clunkily mocking the noise of the sea.

'We should have gone the longer way round,' Effie said, eyeing the young people clustered at the entrance. They were loud and loitering by the pinball machines and those things with grabby mechanical arms and fluffy toys. Effie shrank from their boisterousness, but I was thinking, Oughtn't they to be loud? When else *could* they be loud, other than when they were young? And where else, in our tiny backwater town, were the youngsters able to make some noise, kick up some fuss? Good luck to them, I thought, as Effie and I took tight hold of our handbags to march firmly and bravely past Aladdin's Cave.

I didn't say any of these things to Effie, of course. She thinks I'm much too liberal in my outlook. She says she believes in Victorian values.

I don't. I didn't like them much the first time round.

'It's all right,' I told Effie. 'The kids can't even see us. We're invisible to them, two old dames. Anyway, what would they want with us?'

Effie pursed her lips. She was about to reply – sardonically, if I knew anything – when suddenly she stopped dead in her tracks. We were directly opposite the arcade entrance and she was staring intently at it across the road. 'Look!'

I saw immediately who she was pointing at and instinctively – with the well-honed instincts of now-seasoned investigators – we drew into the shadows.

Emerging from the shabby razzmatazz of the penny arcades was a dapper, fair-haired little man. He was accompanied by five extremely short women. They were a familiar but unprepossess-ing bunch, all still wearing their pristine coveralls. All six were gabbling excitedly in their weird language. Effie and I watched, astounded, as they linked arms and made off down the road, towards Cod Almighty, the chip shop at the end of the prom.

We stood there, frozen.

Until the moment – as Mr Danby and his harem slipped into the chip shop – when he turned and, very deliberately, waved at us. From all that distance away, he fixed us with a twinkling, ironic grin, and gave us a jaunty wave. And his simian assistants, giggling, did likewise.

For the next couple of days or so I tried to put the Deadly Boutique out of my head. As I was going about my daily business, though, I'd get flashbacks to the smug, simpering faces of the awful Mr Danby and his primate women on Wednesday night. It was plain they were ne'er-do-wells – and flaunting it. Only Effie and I could see the truth of this. But what could we do?

The *Gazette* carried an interview with the slimy owner of the boutique. That idiot of a journalist, Rosy Twist, was fawning all over him. 'Women have a duty to stay young and beautiful,' he was quoted as saying. 'I am their humble servant. I have been sent to help them.'

But why here? Why this small town?

As the weekend approached I kept my eyes and ears open as I moved about the town, buying groceries and scouting about. I saw a number of changed women, all looking pleased with themselves. It was quite alarming, all those clear complexions and newly fresh faces. I don't want to exaggerate – there weren't hundreds of rejuvenated women – but there were enough for it to be remarkable. For it to be obvious that the Deadly Boutique was doing a roaring trade.

On Saturday morning I bumped into Robert in Woolworths. I was helping myself to the pick-'n'-mix. A small vice of mine. Every Saturday morning I'll fill a large paper bag at the pick-'n'-mix counter, grabbing handfuls of chocolate limes, mint supremes, sherbet fizzers and anything else I fancy. My hands are rather large and I end up with quite a collection of sweets, usually.

'Hello,' he said politely. At first I didn't recognise him without his elf costume. He was in a rather battered flying jacket trimmed with sheepskin. He looked rather fetching. Turns out he's an aficionado of the pick-'n'-mix counter, too. Liquorice allsorts are his thing. 'I'm looking for something to take Jessie,' he admitted, as we queued to pay. 'She's in the doldrums today.'

'How come?' I said. 'She should be on cloud nine! She was the belle of the ball at the pie-and-peas.'

Robert's face darkened. 'She's holed up in her room. She reckons . . .' He looked incredulous. 'She says it's backfiring. She says she's . . . shrinking. Withering up.'

'*What?*'

'It'll be all in her head, though,' he added, more hopeful than convinced. 'She's always been paranoid about her looks.'

'She's shrinking?'

'I haven't seen her. She won't let anyone in. But it can't be true, can it? It's impossible!'

The girl at the counter put my sweets on the scale. I'd pick-'n'-mixed even more than usual. 'But what happened to her at the boutique was impossible, too,' I said.

'You think she might be right? That it is backfiring?' Robert seemed appalled.

I nodded, thinking, How nice to have a nephew who really cares about what happens to you.

We parted at the main doors of Woolies. 'Do you think she'll see visitors?' I asked.

He shook his head. 'But I'll ask her. She's very fond of you and Effie.'

'We're going to get to the bottom of this awful business. We're going to sort this Mr Danby out,' I said.

For a moment Robert looked at me searchingly. 'Yes,' he said. 'I believe you will.'

I realised that I'd come out that morning without applying my makeup as thickly and as comprehensively as usual. As he gazed into my face in the harsh light of the morning, I flinched. He would see the full extent of the scarring on my neck and temples under the thinnish foundation. What would he think? Car accident? Botched face-lift?

But he was discreet and said nothing, just turned away to carry his sweets and newspapers back up the road.

At home, I sat in my favourite bobbly green armchair in the attic and wolfed my pick-'n'-mix absently, stewing it all over.

I took a call about a booking for next week. Guests! A whole family, coming up from Norfolk. Sounded rather nice. Quiet. They've got two youngish children, which I'm not too keen on. But so long as they behave themselves . . . They arrive on Tuesday.

I let things wash back and forth in my head, munching sherbet fizzers, deciding on my next move. Then I was sitting bolt upright. I'd decided what to do.

*

'This time I'm going there,' I told Effie.

She scowled. 'Where? What are you talking about?' She was sitting in the gloomiest recess of her junk shop, at the cluttered old desk at the back. It was hard to get to through the tottering stacks of rubbish, especially if you're my size. Now she was rolling her eyes and seemed less than pleased to clap eyes on me.

'To the boutique,' I hissed, through clenched teeth, although there was only one other customer present to hear me.

Effie sighed. 'I do wish you'd stop bursting in here, Brenda, and telling me what you're going to do. Why do you have to go gallumphing about so dramatically all the time?'

Effie can be quite short-tempered and sour-faced when she's working in the junk shop. It's like she's a different person, operating under the weight of all that accumulated bric-à-brac. She didn't choose this life. She feels she inherited it, yet she's done nothing to alter it. Instead she's grown rather bitter and she's best avoided during opening hours.

But today I knew I had to tell her.

'I've phoned up. I talked to that awful man and I've made an appointment for myself.'

Effie looked me up and down. 'For a make-over?' I knew what she was insinuating – that I could do with one. I blushed. She was being cruel. That was Effie all over. She would never say it outright, but she could imply it with a raised eyebrow.

'That's the pretext and the excuse,' I said. 'I'm just going so I can get inside the place. I'm *infiltrating* it. Tonight.'

Effie was twiddling a propelling pencil. 'I see. What about me?'

My turn to raise an eyebrow. Not as elegantly as Effie, perhaps.

'What part do I play in this little escapade, hm?' She had lowered her voice so that the only other customer – the Reverend Mr Small, poking about in the crockery – couldn't hear.

'I didn't think you'd want to go back there!'

'I don't.' She sighed impatiently. 'But we're a team, aren't we?'

That was good to hear. I smiled.

'Oh, don't come over all mawkish, Brenda. Just tell me what time and what the plan is.'

'But they'll recognise you! After all, you were the woman the machine didn't work on.'

'So?' she said. 'I'll just say I got claustrophobic and went doo-lally. I'll say I'm with you to hold your hand because you're a bit nervy. They won't suspect a thing.'

'Hmm,' I mused. Mr Danby sounded a wily one to me. But Effie was right. We were better off going together.

When I told her what Robert reckoned was happening to Jessie, Effie became even more determined. 'Shrinking?' she gasped. 'Withering up?' She shook her head sadly. 'No good will ever come of this. Jessie's overreached herself.' She stood up and straightened her smart woollen jacket. 'I'm going to shut the shop. We've got to prepare ourselves. We've work to do.'

'I knew it! I told my helpers this morning. I said this would happen. I knew you'd return to our establishment. May I take your coat?'

Effie looked the wheedling little man up and down. Utter disdain. 'No, you may not.' She clutched it tighter and glanced in my direction. 'This time it is my friend who requires . . . your attentions.'

'Aaaah,' said Mr Danby. He licked this thin wet lips and

feasted his piggy eyes on me. I stared back at him, all the while taking in the details of the boutique. Everything was as Effie had described: the weird shaggy walls and the rubber plants. 'And your name is . . . ?'

'Brenda,' I said. 'I don't have a surname.'

Effie looked at me sharply, as if to say, 'What subterfuge is this? No surname?'

But it was quite true. I don't.

'Quite so,' said Mr Danby. 'And will Brenda be requiring a full make-over?'

I snorted. 'What do you think?' I said, with more bravado than I felt. 'Look at me! You've got your work cut out for you here, Mr Danby.'

'Quite so,' he said again. He was making notes in a tiny book and tapping his pencil against his teeth. 'You are a magnificent specimen, my dear.'

Effie looked shocked, both at his forwardness and his verdict. I blushed, of course, and thanked him.

'You are very well built,' Mr Danby added, catching my eye. I turned away.

'Look here,' Effie butted in. 'Will I be able to sit with my friend when you put her inside that nightmarish contraption in the back room?'

Mr Danby grimaced. 'That "nightmarish contraption" is nothing of the sort, Ms Jacobs. It is a highly sophisticated and unique device. There is nothing nightmarish or truly deadly about it whatsoever. Oh, yes, I know of your suspicions and your strange ideas regarding me. But, sincerely, all I wish is to bring a little light, life and youthfulness into the lives of you ladies. There is no wicked masterplan. No nefarious scheme.' He chuckled.

I must say, standing there listening to him in the plush, luxurious reception area of the Deadly Boutique, I was inclined to believe him. He was very smart in his pinstripe suit, with his hair smarmed down just so. He was very convincing.

I was being lulled, drawn in. I was starting to imagine what it would be like to be slimmed and primped, smoothed and ironed. To feel new again . . .

Effie wasn't having any of it. 'I've heard your silver tongue before,' she snapped.

'Indeed,' he said.

'I think you're up to no good. What about Jessie, eh?'

'Jessie is a triumph,' he said flatly. 'Any fool can see that.'

'But her nephew claims she's shrinking! She's withering up!'

'Nonsense,' said Mr Danby, sternly. 'Have you seen her with your own eyes?'

'Well, no. But her nephew has no reason to lie . . .'

'Jessie Sturgeon is a work of art,' he said. 'And if she continues her treatments here at my boutique she will be a work of art for a good many years.'

'It's unnatural,' spat Effie. She was getting very worked up. Probably the memory of thrashing about inside the Deadly Machine was coming back to her, full force.

'Listen to yourself!' Mr Danby laughed. 'You sound like a superstitious fool. A torch-waving peasant crying, "Kill the beast! Burn it! Get it away from our town!"'

My ears pricked up. What did he mean?

'I'm not superstitious,' said Effie, haughtily. 'And I'm by no means a peasant.'

Mr Danby gave a very Gallic shrug. 'No matter. You have

already spurned our treatments and I see no further reason to discourse on these matters. We will, of course, send you our bill for the few moments you stole inside our "contraption".'

'Your bill!' spluttered Effie.

Smoothly, the little man took hold of my elbow and led me towards an interior door. 'My assistants will help you to prepare for stepping into the machine, Madam Brenda . . .'

Madam Brenda! I liked that! It sounded impressive. I felt like a grand, imperious brothel-owner.

I was feeling quite woozy and complaisant. I let him draw me away from Effie's side. I was focusing on his cultivated, melodious voice.

'Wait!' cried Effie. 'You've got to let me come in with her! I'm her friend. I'm here to see that no harm comes to her!'

'My helpers are all she needs,' said Mr Danby.

'No!' Effie cried. 'I must come in with her. Brenda! Tell him!'

My voice came out softer and more dreamy than I'd intended. 'Could she, Mr Danby? Could she just sit and wait? She'll be no bother.'

'No bother?' Mr Danby said. 'No bother, you say?'

And then I was rocking gently on my heels, swaying back and forth. My ears were filled with reverberating voices: 'No bother?' yelled Mr Danby. 'Brenda!' howled Effie. 'Tell him!' Everything was chiming and echoing, as if I was in some ancient Jules Verne diving-suit and their voices were being piped to the bottom of the sea. My vision narrowed into two tiny points of light . . . then nothing

I was under.

And ready to be made-over.

*

At first it was like being in one of those sensory-deprivation tanks. I lifted my hands in front of my face and couldn't see a thing. It was silent, too, and I felt as if I was floating, bobbing about in amniotic fluid.

I should have known this was a mistake. I should never have come.

But something had compelled me. Was I really under Mr Danby's influence? Or was I being driven by my own subconscious desires to be born again? I mulled all of this over in a shambolic, bemused fashion.

I was naked, that much was certain. I blushed with shame, thinking of it. I had divested myself of all my layers of cardies and foundation garments in full view of Effie and those horrid simian assistants. The little women had picked up my clothes, item by item, as I dropped them on to the pristine white tiles. They had folded them neatly and piled them up, like nightmarish shop assistants. I had tried not to look at Effie, who sat there, looking horrified. I wondered what she'd thought when she saw the scarred and mangled hotch-potch of my naked form, which I was usually dead set on hiding from the world.

What had got into me tonight? Why didn't I care?

Effie had made worried noises as I stepped inside the gleaming chrome coffin-shaped machine. Inside, it was like a vast bread-maker. I ignored her protests and let the little women close the door.

The silence and dark lasted a few moments, and then the treatment began.

This was what Jessie had gone through. This was what all the women of the town were signing up to undergo. This was what had panicked Effie and made her push her way out. It didn't seem so bad to me. A few pulsing, flashing, multicoloured lights. Weird, ululating noises. A curious vibration, as if every molecule of my body was being set free to bounce about in the enclosed space. And, as Effie had said, the sensation of tiny hands pummelling and pulling at each portion of my body, stretching and moulding me like dough . . .

The Deadly Machine was supposed to roll back the years. It was supposed to smooth your furrowed brow and ease the tensions from your clapped-out body. You were meant to step out of it rejuvenated. All those years, and the evidence they had left, were supposed to be leached out of you. Effie had described it as being bled, or having life drained out of you by a vampire's kiss.

To me, it felt even more cataclysmic. Whatever the machine did reacted strongly with my – shall we say unique? – biology. Lightning flashed inside the enclosed space. I was jerked about like a puppet and an awful smell of burning filled my nose.

I was running across the moors, ragged and bleeding, pursued by hounds . . . I was begging in an underpass, frozen with rain . . . I was living in a tower in a grand mansion . . . I was being shown the door, disgraced . . . I was standing on my father's doorstep and he stared at me in horror. His smart visitors and his wife were calling from the drawing room, 'But who *is* it?' . . . I was walking through the zoo and children were screaming . . . I was lying on an operating table . . . I was opening my eyes. The first thing I saw was the face of my husband, leering down at me from a window high up in a stone wall, his face twisted in a mixture of rage and desire . . .

How far back was this machine taking me? How much further back was there to go?

Flashbacks! I was glimpsing moments from my past. And not the best ones. Just the most hair-raising, the most stressful. What was the machine doing? It was taking me back through my long, phantasmagorical existence, through the series of snapshots I had tried so hard to block from my mind . . .

My hands were playing the yellowish keys of a concert piano.

My breasts were suckling infants.

In some squalid alleyway, my throat was being slit.

Too many memories. Each part of my body has its own memory, its own favourite moments. Each part relived its past so that the different lifetimes overlapped, whizzing around inside my head. They reached a frenzied pitch and I screamed. My voice seemed like a compound of a hundred different women's voices. I was a crowd. I was Legion, howling in dismay at a ghastly sense of loss inside the machine.

Everything I'd deliberately forgotten, and everything I'd only half known, came flooding back in those moments.

It was too much for the machine.

There was an almighty crack. It was the sound of Excalibur coming free of its stone. Or Robin of Loxley's oak tree crashing down to the ground after a thousand years in Sherwood Forest. It was the sound of Prometheus being freed from his rock. And of lightning striking the conductors on the ramparts of Herr Doktor's castle . . .

It was a huge noise, which robbed me of my hearing for several minutes.

When I was pitched back into the immaculate laboratory, acrid smoke was billowing everywhere. I fell into Effie's arms – though, of course, she wasn't strong enough to hold me. The assistants were squealing, but I couldn't hear a thing. I couldn't even hear the Deadly Machine's final wail of despair. I felt the reverberations, though, as it shuddered, died and eventually was still.

'My God, woman,' Effie spluttered, crouching beside me on the floor. 'What did you do to it?'

She brought me my clothes and draped them over me. I felt like a huge baby, swaddled, understanding nothing. When my hearing started to come back, Effie was saying, 'We need to get out of here. We need to leave right now.' She was speaking in a low, urgent voice.

I was suddenly more aware of what was going on around me, having suppressed the lurid images in my mind.

Mr Danby had lost his composure. No longer the purring, composed little man, he was standing before his smashed, still smoking machine and screeching. He beat his fists against his temples and gnashed his teeth. He stamped his feet and swung round to face us. Unfortunate, as Effie was helping me to dress. It wasn't the most elegant confrontation of my life.

'You have ruined us!' Mr Danby shrieked. 'You have destroyed everything.'

Effie kept her voice calm and low. 'Ignore him. Let's just get you sorted and out of here.'

'The machine will never work again! You've spoiled it for everyone!'

At this, the overalled monkey women started to moan and pound their own temples with their tiny fists.

'You could have killed her,' Effie shouted back at him. 'I thought my ordeal was bad enough. But look at her! You could have murdered her!'

'There was nothing wrong with my machine,' he protested.

'Whatever happened is down to her. She sabotaged it somehow!'

'It couldn't . . . cope with me . . .' I stammered. 'Couldn't regress me . . .' I had a shocking headache and my extremities were numb. Other than that, I wasn't feeling too bad.

'She's a freak!' Mr Danby yelled. 'A monster!'

'Hi!' Effie cried. 'Don't you say things like that about my friend.' She left me to finish dressing and stormed over to confront him. His assistants leaped to protect him. They seemed wary of Effie. She was wiry and determined: she could have given them all a good thrashing and, after last time, they looked as if they knew it.

'You don't understand what you've done.' Mr Danby sighed. His whole body sagged. 'This machine . . . the treatments . . . they didn't hurt anyone. They couldn't. What we did here was for the benefit of all womankind.'

The monkey women chattered excitedly, agreeing with him.

'And these women?' Effie said. 'Are they indebted to your machine, too?'

'Hm?' he asked. 'Well, yes. They are. Not every patient regressed as far as my assistants. Not everyone would choose to go that far . . .'

'My God,' Effie exclaimed. 'You're insane! Who'd want to be like that? Is this what's happening to Jessie? Shrinking and withering up? You've turned her into a Neanderthal woman?'

'Australopithecus, actually,' he said. 'It sometimes happens. It isn't supposed to.'

I was fit, and decent enough now, to join in with their conversation. 'But why?' I demanded. 'Why bother? What do you get out of it? What makes you want to go round regressing women?'

'Time,' he said sadly. 'What my machine drew out of them was time itself. I was siphoning the distillation of their remaining years out of their cells and their veins. Oh, not in a way that would harm them. Indeed, mostly, it improved them. And I got to *bottle* time itself. The gorgeous, viscous juice of time.'

At that point we noticed the glass jars on the shelves on the far wall. Thick red and blue liquids.

'He's crazy,' Effie gasped. 'You can't *bottle* time.'

'Oh, I could,' Mr Danby said. 'That's precisely what I did. And now you've spoiled it all – you've spoiled everything.'

'But what did you want it for? What are you doing with it?' I asked.

'My mother is lying upstairs in this house,' he said sadly. 'She is very, very old, older even than you, Brenda. But her time now is short. She is a very special, very great person, you see, and I have been trying to buy her a little longer—'

'By stealing years and months from innocent women,' Effie accused him. 'You're like Jack the Ripper!'

'Hardly,' he said. 'Nobody lost out. Not really. Those women have only decrepitude waiting for them. Who really wants to be old, worn out and burdensome? My machine squeezes and pulverises the cells of their exhausted bodies, wringing out the last vestiges of energy and transforming it into that wonderful syrupy elixir. All my ladies have lost is but the cumbersome years of their decline. Now they are regressed and they enjoy a last, glorious burst of rejuvenation. And so, yes . . . I stole their time, technically . . . but wasn't it just wasted time? Time when they would be past it?'

Effie and I exchanged a horrified glance.

The madman ranted on: 'Now you see the glory of my plan!

You *do* see, don't you? I steal their liquid essence, bottle and stopper it up for my dear old mother and, in return, I give them one last golden swansong . . . but only because they ask. And they keep asking. They all want a make-over. It's a very neat arrangement.'

'It's vile,' Effie said, through gritted teeth. 'And all for some . . . vampire hag in your attic.'

'Mother will be so very disappointed. She will have to be told who caused this disaster. Someone will have to pay.' He clicked his fingers. 'Seize them, would you?'

In his mild way, he had commanded his simian assistants to attack us.

They weren't as mild and polite as their master. He ducked away and left them to snarl and bare their pointed teeth at us. They advanced with shuffling steps. Effie and I drew away from them, back to back, as if preparing for fisticuffs in a brawl.

'This is ridiculous!' Effie cried. 'Saturday night and we're having a fight in a mad scientist's laboratory!' She sounded almost gleeful. One of the monkey women launched herself at Effie, and was knocked back by a quick slap in the chops. As I'd suspected, Effie was useful in a punch-up.

Soon, all fifteen, twenty, thirty of the Australopithecine women were hurling themselves at us. Tiny arms and legs flashed out and we were pummelled and punched from all angles.

'Where's Danby gone?' grunted Effie, as she whirled into action with her recently acquired ju-jitsu. The women shrank back, horrified at this sexuagenarian dervish.

'He's fled!' I cried. 'Probably gone to explain himself to dear old Mamma.'

Effie grunted as she flung one woman at a huddle of her companions. 'Then I suggest we get out of here, the back way, and make good our escape.'

I waded through the attacking bodies, using every iota of my not inconsiderable strength. Those women were indefatigable, though, and determined to keep us captive. But we were determined too: we weren't staying in the Deadly Boutique a moment longer.

'Shouldn't we go upstairs and sort his mother out?' I asked Effie, as we reached the metal outer door.

'Sort her out?'

'Stake her through the heart, or whatever,' I suggested, 'so they don't start up again.'

'Stake her through the heart?' With one hand Effie was struggling with locks and bolts. With the other she was helping me hold the little women back. 'My God, Brenda, this is Whitby! We don't stake people through the heart!'

At that moment the metal door sprang open to reveal the chill mist of the backyard and alleyways.

'Will they follow us?'

But we didn't turn to look. Effie and I grasped each other's hands, pelted out into the freezing night and the narrow alleys, twisting, turning and heading for home.

We had to stop for a moment to catch our breath. We clutched our knees, breathing raggedly, outside Woolworths. 'Have we lost them?'

There came no slap-slap-slap of tiny feet in pursuit. There was nothing. Silence.

Town was eerily silent tonight. We were back in the centre outside ordinary shops. It felt weird, even to think about being chased by regressed monkey women – or about a man who bottled time to feed it to his ailing mother upstairs.

'What have we been involved in?' Effie asked hollowly. 'What kind of madness was that?'

'An adventure!' I grinned. Suddenly I had to ask her the thing that had been bugging me ever since the Deadly Machine had had its nervous breakdown and exploded with me still inside it. 'So, did it work on me? Did it transform me?'

'Hm?'

'The machine!' I said, as we set off again; not running this time but walking at quite a clip through the warren of streets towards home. 'Has it made me younger? Will I knock 'em dead?'

'Oh, erm,' said Effie, 'I can't really tell in this light. The street-lamps are too harsh. Maybe it has, maybe it hasn't. I'm not sure.'

I chuckled at her evasiveness as we set off up the hill towards our houses.

'Do you feel any different?' Effie asked me.

'Oh, yes,' I said, breathing deeply, and realising it was true. 'Do you know? For the first time in ages . . . I feel *alive.*'

Chapter Two:
The Green Family

A seaside holiday was just what they needed. You could tell that at first glance. The whole family was peaky. All four – Mum, Dad and the two kiddies – looked exhausted and jaded. They needed sea air, fun and some good home cooking.

It was Tuesday lunchtime when they arrived in a taxi from the station, laden with all their bags and cases, beach-balls and shrimping-nets. I rolled up my sleeves, got my pinny on and swept into welcome mode.

My B-and-B was immaculate and ready for them. I'd had a couple of days to prepare and everything was perfect. I'd also had a couple of days to get over Effie's and my Saturday night adventure. As yet there had been no reprisals – no sign of Mr Danby or his monkey women. That suited me: I was happy to put the affair of the Deadly Boutique right out of my mind.

'Welcome! Welcome to my home!'

For some reason I was behaving extra gregariously. I'm not usually so effusive with new guests. I think I know why I was like this. I was keen to get back to some kind of normality. I wanted to look after people and work at ordinary tasks. I wanted an ordinary family to share my space for a few days – and I didn't even mind there being children. I wanted all the recent weirdness to be assuaged by their ordinariness.

Hm. Fat chance!

All four were subdued, if polite. They had brought a lot of luggage with them for a mere four days, so as we struggled to bring it all in from the street our conversation was already hampered. Even so, they seemed shy and stilted, as if they weren't used to being sociable. It made me feel like some awful holiday rep.

'Is this your first time in Whitby?' I huffed, carrying cases, full of false jollity.

The young husband smiled and nodded, coming up the passage behind me. He had a fair, open face, a war-time haircut. He looked like a doomed fighter pilot. All four were the same: they looked *pure* somehow, almost glowing, standing politely in my hallway. They made its lilac-patterned wallpaper seem dingy and oppressive.

'Yes,' the husband said, trying to sound more enthusiastic than he could manage. 'I'm afraid we haven't travelled far out of our own county before.' He set his bags down and surveyed the hallway. 'This is quite an adventure.'

His wife was in a headscarf and a prettily patterned short-sleeved dress. 'Oh, indeed,' she added. 'I feel like we've reached foreign parts. How wonderful!'

She had a touch of Doris Day about her. In fact, there was something very old-fashioned about all of them. The only touch of modernity that I could see was the baseball cap worn by their younger child. The little boy had it pulled down over most of his face. What I could see of the rest was scowling at me. He, like his sister and parents, seemed very well scrubbed. He was even wearing a school blazer on the first day of his holidays.

The girl was older – fifteen, perhaps. She was in a long black cardigan with floppy sleeves pulled down right over her hands. She was a tall, skinny thing with long, lank hair. From her appearance you might have expected hormone-fuelled surliness and teenage rancour, but when she spoke she was as polite as her parents: 'This seems like a lovely place, Mummy. You certainly made the right choice of bed-and-breakfast!'

I blushed then, and again when her mother said, 'I felt drawn to the place in the brochure. I don't know why. I just knew this establishment would welcome us properly, with open arms.'

'That's what we need,' smiled the husband, ruefully, 'a nice break. We need to get away from it all.'

At this, his wife gave him an odd, sidelong glance – I wasn't supposed to notice but I did. 'Indeed,' she said. 'Come on, then, Ted. Let's go and inspect our rooms. I'm sure they're lovely.'

Katherine and Ted were the couple's names. The children were Susan and Gerald. Only Gerald stayed silent and unappreciative as I showed them their rooms. The others cooed and cried out in delight as I installed them in their sumptuous home-from-home with everything laid out just so. Gerald had the back room, facing out on to the trees and the little gardens of all the houses down my way. I tried pointing out to him the network of branches where the squirrels run about and chase each other. 'They're very funny,' I told him. 'You'll have to look out for them, Gerald. I could watch those silly squirrels for hours.'

I'm not very good with children. I don't have much experience. I hated that shrill, excitable tone I put on when I told him about the squirrels.

Gerald leaned his chin on the windowsill. 'Vermin,' I heard him say.

Still. I shouldn't judge any of them on first appearances, I told myself. They were so fatigued and wan! They really did look a bit green about the gills.

'Bless them,' I said. 'I feel a bit sorry for them. They paid me for the four days' stay in advance. In cash. I said, "No, no, that's not how it works." But the father, Ted, insisted. Just before they went out this morning, to explore the beaches, he pressed on me this wad of crumpled notes and coins, all counted out to the last penny.'

Effie made a *moue* of disapproval. 'How awful,' she said. 'Some people just don't know how things are done.'

'I said a cheque would have been fine, but he just stared at me blankly.' Actually – though I didn't say this to Effie – I prefer being paid in cash. I don't enjoy going to my bank. You can be pestered with questions in banks.

Effie glanced out of the café window. 'They're exploring the beaches today, you say?' She tutted and the little feather on her hat bobbed. 'Oh dear. I imagine they'll be having a miserable time of it.'

The heavens were slate grey and the rain had been constant since early that morning. It rolled down ceaselessly, miserably – but that hadn't deterred my young family on their first day. They had been full of energy this morning, restored and all wrapped up in chunky sweaters, rubber boots and waterproofs. They were undaunted by the weather and keen to explore. My heart went out to them as I waved them off, my hand full of crinkled notes and warm change. I felt bad that they were spending their cash on such a poor week, weatherwise, in our town. The year has turned, I think. Now we're truly in autumn, ready for the rapid slide into the stark depths of winter.

'Did you give them a list of all the indoor attractions?' Effie asked me.

'Of course,' I said. I know my job. Sometimes Effie treats me like an idiot. She reminds me that she was very great friends with the Jenkinses, the couple who ran my B-and-B for twenty years before my arrival in Whitby. It seems that Effie knows all there is to know about running such a place.

We were sitting in our favourite café across the bay, the Walrus and the Carpenter. It was a tiny, low-ceilinged place with many gingham-clothed tables crammed in. It was evidently designed for midgets and I always have some bother sitting in it, even on the more spacious corner banquettes. But Effie loves to go there and order a pot of tea or soup of the day after an hour or so perusing the smarter shops on that side of town.

We had been steeping ourselves in a very ordinary Wednesday, examining knick-knacks, old books, junk jewellery and paintings. I was looking for a picture to hang in the dining room. I hadn't yet come across quite the thing to brighten up that dowdy room. It was the place my guests ate their breakfast and I needed something grand and vivacious to go on the biggest wall.

Neither Effie nor I had said much about Saturday night and our narrow escape from the boutique up Frances's Passage. What was there to say? Obscurely, I felt as though I had made a fool of myself. I had gone barging in there, determined to sort out the mystery, and what had I achieved? Destroyed things. Given myself the screaming ab-dabs. Paraded around in the nuddy, caused an almighty fist-fight and, ultimately, put the Deadly Boutique out of business.

Oh dear. It sounded worse when I put it like that to myself.

I watched Effie spooning up vegetable soup and blowing on it. How easily she slips back into ordinary life, I thought. 'Perhaps we should have gone to the Christmas Hotel and checked on Jessie,' I said. 'We didn't go yesterday afternoon. She'll think we don't care.'

Effie sighed. 'I've seen quite enough of that place for a while, thank you. I was a bit gyppy after that pie-and-peas, actually. And, besides, didn't Robert phone you to say that Jessie was all right?'

It wasn't quite what he'd said. I was relieved to hear that she hadn't turned into a Neanderthal, or an Australopithecine woman, but neither was she the perfect Jessie in her mid-twenties any more. It had been a short rejuvenation. Her wrinkles had crept back. She had indeed shrunk somewhat. She had fallen into a depression. But she was lucky to have Robert taking care of her. I wished I had a nephew like that.

'So this family's come from Norfolk?' Effie broke in, clunking her spoon down and smacking her lips. 'Did they say whereabouts? I've family who live there, near Hunstanton.'

'They were a bit vague about the geography,' I said, 'but my geography's a bit vague, too. Katherine, the young woman, told me at breakfast time that they live in a small village right out in the sticks. Only about a hundred people. No tellies, no electricity, no nothing.'

'What?' Effie raised that eyebrow of hers. 'Surely that's impossible in this day and age.'

'"We're very cut off,"' I said. 'Those were her exact words. She said sometimes it infuriates her. They get snowed in. They never see anyone new. She said I must be able to see what an adventurous thing this holiday is for them.'

'How strange,' said Effie, searching the menu for cakes.

'I get the impression that those kiddies hadn't been out of that village of theirs at all – this is their first trip into the big wide world.'

'Imagine!' said Effie, running her finger down the price list.

'That's why they look so pale and worried,' I said, 'bless them. Little Gerald sat there at breakfast with his cap still pulled right over his face. I think he's a bit shy of me. I asked if he'd been watching the squirrels and he nodded once, very curtly. The daughter sat there eating nothing, saying nothing, with her cardigan sleeves still hanging down over her hands.'

'Well,' said Effie, 'I think I'll settle for a couple of boudoir fingers.' She motioned to the waitress. 'Go on, Brenda. I'm still listening.'

'The others ate with gusto, though. It was quite gratifying, actually. They had sausages and bacon and black pudding . . . They were wolfing it down – asking for seconds, even. It must be the sea air, invigorating them and giving them an appetite.'

Effie sighed. 'Or maybe they just want to get their money's worth.'

She can be so cynical. I wanted her to meet my visiting family so she could see for herself how nice and well brought-up they were. 'There's nothing wrong with them,' I said defensively. I smiled, thinking about them traipsing out in their wet-weather gear after breakfast. 'Except . . .' I frowned, remembering how the husband, Ted, had nudged his wife's arm when she spoke to me: 'I don't think Brenda wants to hear all about our boring homelife, darling. She's extremely busy.' The message had been clear: Don't tell her too much. Don't spill the beans.

But why? What was there to spill?

'What is it?' Effie asked sharply, seeing the abstraction in my face.

'Oh . . .' I said. 'There's something evasive about them. A feeling like . . . they're not telling me the whole truth . . .'

'Well,' said Effie, 'you're the expert at that, aren't you?'

I don't do this for everyone, but I thought I'd lay on a nice dinner for my new guests. When they returned that evening, it was to the delicious aroma of my steak and kidney pudding wafting down the hall.

Drenched, bedraggled, and worn out from walking, they were delighted.

'That smells heavenly!' Ted burst out. They were all beaming as I came out of the kitchen, drying my hands on a tea-towel. Very gratifying, that. There's nothing like making people happy. My heart was aglow in my chest.

Katherine urged the kids upstairs, to wash and brush up before dinner.

'It's nothing special,' I demurred – but I was glad when, twenty minutes later, they all trooped down into the dining room and they had obviously put on their smartest clothes. They settled at their table and, before I could dish up, insisted I join them. As if I was part of the family. Usually I keep a professional distance from my guests and I never eat with them. But that night I thought, Who cares about professional distance? There was something about them that I found touching.

Then the young husband asked if he could say grace.

I pulled a face. I don't like all that stuff, chanting and mumbling to unseen deities, letting dinner get cold. But I nodded brusquely and they all bowed their heads.

> 'The Elders will provide for us,
> If we do not stray too far.
> The Elders will tell us how to behave,
> If we do not stray too far.
> The Elders will take the sting out of our existence,
> And make everything easier,
> If we don't ask too many questions,
> If we are good and reasonable,
> If we do not leave home,
> And we do not stray too far.'

They blinked and smiled and waited for me to serve the dinner. I must say, it was a grace I'd never heard before. I thought it most peculiar. But, then, what do I know about family life? Or worship, for that matter.

They grinned encouragingly as I brought in the vegetables and the golden steak and kidney pudding.

'You're very good to us, Brenda,' said the young wife. 'I wish we could stay here for ever.'

Her husband shot her one of his looks.

The rest of that evening was pleasant, very peaceful. I don't know if they felt they had to sing for their supper, but that was what they did. After I had cleared up, they drew back their chairs, stood up together, like a barbershop quartet, and told me they were going to give me a medley of their favourite songs.

I sat bemused as they launched into the weirdest singing I have ever heard. Their voices were high-pitched and fluting: they rose and twined together in the most extraordinary harmonies. The words were unintelligible, but there was something compelling about the piece. It seemed avant-garde, futuristic, even – like nothing I'd ever heard before.

They were delighted by my enthusiastic applause. 'A whole concert! Just for me!' I cried.

They blushed and said it was time they retired for the night. It was only nine o'clock, but all four shuffled out – even the kids, not a word of complaint. Those kids were too well behaved to be true – him in his baseball cap, her in her cardie – trotting off early to bed, just as they were told.

Now, if I had a nature like Effie's, that would have made me suspicious. She has a cynical turn of mind. I do not. At least, I hope not. I refuse to be suspicious of folk who are well brought-up, polite and a little out-of-kilter in their behaviour, who chant strange graces before dinner and sing weird, unearthly songs afterwards.

The next morning it was a little brighter and dryer. A golden light was slanting in from the east, bathing the damp town gently and raising a light mist. My visiting family were keen to wolf down their fried breakfast and wrap up again. They wanted to go tramping about once more. They had miles and miles to explore, they said.

I surveyed the wreckage on the table: they'd had every sausage, egg and rasher of bacon – devoured the lot. 'Good,' I said. 'I'll have to get some more shopping in. You lot like your food, don't you?'

I hadn't meant to hurt anyone's feelings but the wife grasped my forearm as I cleared the plates. 'Are we taking too much? Are we being greedy?' She was genuinely concerned.

I tried to put her mind at rest: 'Of course not, no. I like to see healthy appetites. It's the sea air. It makes you ravenous and helps you sleep better at night. I wasn't complaining. Honestly.'

'Yes,' she said. 'Sorry. Ravenous, that's what we are.' She nodded abstractedly, and went to gather her tribe. They were milling in the hallway with folded waterproofs, the shrimping-nets, buckets and spades. Weren't those children too old for buckets and spades?

I decided not to ask. How sensitive they were. For some reason it seemed easy to upset them. I wanted to tell them, 'It doesn't do to be touchy.'

They seemed too thin-skinned, somehow, for this world.

That Thursday afternoon Effie and I had a little walk along the front. The wind was down, the sun stayed out, and it was quite pleasant to walk as far past habitation as we could. We were high above the great expanse of beaches, stretching off along the coast, and I wondered if we'd see my little family on their day out, little dots in the distance, playing on the dingy-looking sands. When I said so to Effie, she sighed. 'I think you're obsessed with them.'

'Obsessed?' I laughed it off.

'It would make sense. A poor, lonely old spinster latching on to them. You'd better watch yourself. They'll get sick of you, make you back off.'

I knew Effie had my interests at heart, but just then I resented her sticking her beaky nose in.

'Anyway,' she went on, sounding more urgent, 'I haven't told you yet, have I? I think there's something funny about that lot you've got staying with you.'

'Funny?'

'Oh,' she said, mock-casually, 'just *things*. People. Asking questions.'

'What people? Who?'

'I don't know,' she said. 'Just people.' At times Effie can be infuriating.

'Asking about my guests?' I felt protective of them and their secrets. I just knew, with every fibre of my being, that they were hiding something. I didn't care what it was, not really, but I knew other people would. I felt as if I stood between my family of guests and the rest of the prying, suspicious world. 'You'd better tell me, Effie.'

'Well,' she said, 'I had a man come into my shop this morning, first thing. He didn't seem very interested in its contents . . .'

No surprise there, I thought uncharitably. I think I've said before: Effie displays the most awful old rubbish in her shop. The place is called Who Would Want This? To me, the name always sounds like a sweeping, dismayed complaint.

Effie went on: 'He looked like a detective. You could see a mile off what he was, in his long brown coat with his hat pulled down over his eyes. Really, he could have gone to a fancy-dress party as someone's clichéd idea of a detective. I think he was meant to be incognito. Anyway, he sidled over to my desk at the back, where I was pricing up a box of vintage film magazines.'

I rolled my eyes. Effie goes in for too much detail sometimes.
'And he asked about your little family.'

'What?'

'Well,' she said. 'Sort of. He wanted to know whether I'd
noticed any . . . unusual people in town lately. A newly arrived
family. He said I looked like the type of woman who kept my ear
close to the ground . . .'

Evidently Effie had taken this as a compliment. I thought it
made her sound like a nosy parker. Which she is, of course.
'They aren't unusual,' I protested. 'They're just a bit naïve and
old-fashioned . . .'

'I said I didn't know. I hadn't seen anyone unusual for days. I
said that in a town like this people come and go quite often. The
plain and ordinary, and the completely outlandish. It was hard to
keep tabs on all the comings and goings. And, do you know, he
offered me cash? He brought out a wodge of ten-pound notes
and put them on my desk. That was for keeping my eyes peeled,
he said. I was mortified.'

'Did you give it back to him?'

'Of course I did. I'm nobody's spy. I asked him to leave my
premises at once. But he gave me his card and told me he was
staying at the Miramar.'

I shuddered. 'That's all we need to know about *him*, if he's
staying *there.*'

'Quite,' said Effie, still piqued to have been offered cash by
the wretched man. We both disapproved heartily of the Miramar.
It was a pink-painted, vulgar establishment a few streets away
from us. As it was further from the sea and the centre of the
town, it had to be a bit flash and glitzy to draw attention to itself.
It had a beer garden, a nightclub in the basement and various

other, even less salubrious features that its owner, Sheila Manchu, had taken pleasure in dreaming up. The most lurid tales filtered down into the town about goings-on at the Hotel Miramar.

'He asked me to be on my guard. He said, "Watch out for a strange husband with a strange wife and two strange children, a boy and a girl." He said, "They aren't what they seem. Not by any means." He said, "They have escaped. They have run away." And – get this! – the kiddies weren't the couple's to take. They've stolen them. They've *kidnapped* them!'

I decided we had walked far enough along the coast. The wind was whipping up and the light was beginning to fade. It was time to turn back. I swivelled on the heels of my court shoes and fixed Effie with a determined look. 'I don't know who this dreadful man is, Effie, or why he's impressed you so much with his silly, suspicious ideas . . .'

'Hang on,' she said, fishing in her shiny leather purse. 'Here's his card. "Frank". That's all it says. He's scribbled the hotel number on it. But that's all. How odd.'

'Exactly,' I said. 'He's the weird one. And I don't believe, anyway, that it's my guests he's looking for. There's nothing suspicious about them. You only have to look at them to see they all belong to the same family. Kidnapped the children, indeed! And, anyway, if a crime like that's been committed, why aren't the regular police going round asking questions? Hm? All he's got to qualify him is a long coat and a hat like a detective's.'

At this Effie fell quiet, and we ambled along in companionable silence. I was quite impressed with my own logic. Of course there was nothing in what this dubious Frank had to say. But, still, something – several things – was nagging at me. My paying guests were indeed out of the ordinary but not horrible, not weird or disturbing. I liked them. Suddenly I knew I would do anything I could to stick up for them. They were far too vulnerable.

'What surname did they give you?' Effie asked suddenly.

'What does it matter?'

'I don't know,' she said, 'but you've never told me. You haven't said their name once.'

I had to think. The truth was, I referred to them in my own mind by their first names and thought of them in their roles as father, mother, son, daughter, like archetypes, like Happy Families. 'Green,' I said.

'Well, that sounds made up for a start.' Effie snorted. 'Green, indeed.'

'No, it doesn't,' I contradicted. 'People are called Green. It's a name. They're as entitled to be called Green as anyone else . . .'

'I suppose you'd say the same if they were called Smith, wouldn't you?' Effie jeered.

She can be very sharp-tongued when she wants to be.

We wandered back to our houses and, really, I wasn't that keen to spend the rest of the evening with her, but we had made plans to eat together at Cod Almighty. I might not want a further grilling from Effie, but I fancied some battered whitebait.

We went our separate ways for an hour or so to freshen up and change.

'If he comes back,' she said, as we parted, 'if Frank comes back to my shop, I shan't know what to tell him for the best.'

'You'll say nothing.' I frowned, untying my headscarf irritably. 'There's nothing to tell him.'

'I think it's them,' she said. 'The people he's after. I think it's your Greens.'

With that she went off to her dowdy junk shop. Really, Effie can be heartless at times. These are people's lives! She likes to dabble too much. She enjoys stirring up trouble.

Anyway, I hauled myself up the passage to the side door, let myself in and knew at once that the family had returned. They weren't noisy but I could hear them moving about and calling to each other between rooms. I was pleased that they felt more at home, able to be themselves. For the first day or so they had been like church mice. I like it when people relax and unwind a little. So long as they don't go too far, of course.

I smiled at their carefree chit-chat and tried not to eavesdrop. I hurried up to my attic, made myself some hot masala tea and decided to catch the last few lazy rays of the sun by sitting out in my tiny patch of garden. So there I went, gallumphing down the stairs with my mug of spicy tea.

Outside, I cleared a few dead leaves off my deck-chair, which was still out from the summer. I sat under the interlacing branches of the beeches and sighed deeply, complacently. I'd been right to come outside. It might be the last of the sun till next year. I felt its warmth ease into me and I sipped my tea.

Sometimes, I thought, I wish Effie could be a nicer person. Sometimes, in fact, she was. This mug I was drinking from, with its sentimental message about friendship, caring and counting blessings, had been a gift from her. Just a few weeks ago she had presented it to me, like a prize. How proud I'd been. Like I had earned or won somebody's friendship, which seemed no mean feat. Effie had been embarrassed, making her feelings known like that. She isn't one for exposing herself.

I peered into my mug to fish out the teabag on its string. No harm in flinging it on to the flower-bed, I supposed. My teabag, my garden – it wasn't really littering, was it? I did a kind of lasso thing with the string and flung it a little way. That was when I saw the squirrels.

I'm not ashamed to say that I gave out a loud, squawking scream at the sight of them.

My squirrels! My ludicrous, over-excited, madcap squirrels! They had kept me entertained for months with their rivalries and endless games of tag.

Three were curled up dead in the flower-bed. Another was lying – brazenly, tragically – in the middle of the lawn.

I screeched again, dropping Effie's sentimental friendship mug.

I could hardly believe what I was seeing.

Each of my lithe, lovely, wholly domesticated squirrels had had its throat ripped out. Each lay with an expression of anguish and amazement on its bloodied, frozen face.

I didn't tell Effie about the squirrels. I buried their poor, dear little bodies and tried to put their fate out of my mind. Who could do such a thing? Who would want to?

A dreadful suspicion was lurking at the back of my mind. I waved it away and refused to give it credence. Instead, I got ready to trot down to the prom with Effie so that we could enjoy supper together at Cod Almighty. Effie always dresses up to the nines when she goes out in the evenings, even there when there's a good chance you'll come home smelling of chip fat and batter. As I say, this is a small town and you'll always see someone you know. Effie likes to keep up appearances, so I have to be smart to accompany her. She's never said as much: I just know that's what I have to do.

We took a table at the front of the restaurant so we could watch who was going up and down the prom in the lowering gloom. I ordered the whitebait I had been looking forward to all afternoon, then seized up the tiny fish one at a time and crunched them whole with great satisfaction. Effie picked delicately at her plaice, nibbling at thin triangles of bread and butter. She has very dainty manners.

Her eyes widened when she noticed someone over my shoulder.

'What is it?'

'Don't look now,' she whispered. 'Someone's come in.'

Of course, when she said that the first thing I did was crane round to see. I always get a nasty crick in my neck doing that. I heard Effie sigh with impatience at my obviousness, but what I saw took my breath away. Jessie was being ushered in by her nephew, who was as solicitous and careful with her as if she was an invalid. As Jessie made her cautious way into the lino-floored room she presented a stark contrast with the Jessie we had seen flaunting herself with her trolley at the Christmas Hotel.

'Her rejuvenation really *has* undone itself,' Effie gasped.

Not wholly, though. She still looked younger than she had a fortnight ago, before all the unfortunate business with the boutique had begun. But something extraordinary had happened to her. She was shorter and hunched. Her hair was coarse and shaggy and, if I wasn't mistaken, it was poking out of her sleeves, though she had tried hard to cover it up. Her face was decidedly simian, with a heavier brow and jutting jaw. 'What has she done to herself?' I murmured.

Effie's lips were as pursed as I had ever seen them. 'I think we both know the answer to that. And who and what was to blame.'

Jessie's nephew, Robert, was pretending breezily that nothing was wrong. He spotted us and asked whether he and his aunt might join us. He was aware, as we were, of other diners muttering as they observed this little scene. Obviously Robert felt he needed allies.

Effie beckoned them over.

Jessie was in a red anorak and Robert had to persuade her to take down the hood. She glowered at us and wouldn't join in with the conversation. She looked as if she wanted to get up and run home – and who could blame her?

'Isn't this nice?' Robert grinned. He was as well scrubbed as ever, and was wearing a black polo-neck sweater. He ordered, and their cod and chips arrived swiftly. I must say, Cod Almighty serves the best fish and chips I've had anywhere. Everything's so fresh and perfect: the fish arrives in a glistening cardigan of perfect batter; the chips are golden, fat and scrumptious. When I'm there, I'm swimming in a trance of vinegary pleasure.

But Jessie poked desultorily at hers. You could see she was utterly depressed. She picked up the occasional chip and chomped it, revealing alarming teeth.

Effie and I exchanged a worried glance.

'Brenda's got new house guests this week,' began Effie, brightly, to distract us all. Then she launched into an exaggerated description of the Green family, which amused Jessie not at all, Robert only mildly, and succeeded in irritating me. She made them sound like weirdos. She made them sound supremely suspect, and I was worried that other diners might overhear her ringing voice.

'I wish you wouldn't, Effie,' I said reasonably.

'What?' She tutted loudly. 'Brenda's grown rather close to

them, I fear, which is hardly professional. Where would we be if we all developed a close personal attachment to those we do business with?'

'Sometimes it can't be helped.' Robert piled chips into a sandwich. 'It happens all the time at the hotel. When you're looking after people, you can get fond of them.'

Bless him.

But Effie rolled her eyes at us. 'Well, I think Brenda's getting herself in too deep with some funny characters.' Then she went on to tell the tale of Frank, the supposed detective, and how he had come snooping round.

Now she had caught Robert's interest. His aunt merely stared at Effie and me across the table and spoke her first word that evening: 'Gloop.' It was a melancholic utterance.

Effie stared at her in surprise and dismay. 'Yes. Well,' she said, dabbing her thin lips with a paper napkin, 'I have formed the opinion that this too-nice-to-be-true Green family of Brenda's is, for some reason, on the run. They're fleeing from the authorities.'

'Oh, come now, Effie,' I said. 'You'll cause trouble for everyone with that tongue of yours.'

She shook her head steadfastly. 'I believe Frank was correct. That couple have kidnapped those children. I believe they're all trying to evade capture. And you, Brenda, are harbouring them.'

'Rubbish!' I said – rather savagely, I fear.

'Gloop,' said Jessie, in response to the antagonism hovering about our melamine table.

I hefted myself off our banquette. 'I'm going to powder myself.'

'Your *nose*, Brenda,' Effie corrected wearily.

I never have got the hang of that euphemism.

I went to the lav, anyway, and sat there thinking for a few minutes. Could there be any truth in what Effie was saying? I hated the thought of it. Could my instinct about people be so wrong? Surely not. Usually I was dead right. As with my other senses, I had almost supernaturally heightened intuition. I had warmed to the Greens immediately. Could they really be the opposite of what they seemed?

With a heavy heart I returned to the dining room, and cursed my extra-keen hearing, which allowed me to pick up Effie and Robert's conversation as I squeezed down the aisle: '. . . And I've never heard her mention any other friends, except the ones she's made here since the beginning of this summer, or any family. She's never even said where she hails from . . .'

Effie was rattling away, thinking aloud.

'Does it matter?' Robert said. 'She's just Brenda, isn't she?'

'Yes, but don't you see? She's very eager not to pry into the background of these Green people, and that might be for the simple reason that there's something in her own background she doesn't want looked into. She seems nervous about the whole idea of people's pasts . . . It's as if she has something to hide, as if she has reason to evade attention . . .'

'*Gloooop*,' said Jessie, firmly, as if to warn them that I had returned from the ladies'.

And, indeed, I had. I ambled those last few steps to our table, my face burning with confusion and shame. *How could you, Effie?* I wanted to shout in her face. How could you say those things about me to other friends of mine? How could she air her nasty suspicions like that? So casually. So blatantly and lubriciously. As if it were a game. As if people's feelings didn't matter to her one jot.

She, too, was blushing, I noticed, as I sat down. Did she know I'd overheard? Did she have a conscience after all?

I nibbled miserably at the last of my whitebait. They were cold and bitter now, and I wanted to go home. The evening was a rotten failure. My best friend thought I was strange and had suspicions about me. She was just tagging along with me because she thought there was some mystery in my background, getting a thrill out of the idea.

Well. I was damned if she'd ever find out what my secrets were.

I stood up heavily, made my excuses and pulled on my coat.

'You're going?' said Effie, brightly. 'But there's cake and custard and—'

'I'm tired,' I said.

'But—'

'Good night, all,' I said curtly.

'Gloooop.' Jessie nodded.

I left them in Cod Almighty. Now they could talk about me, behind my back, to their hearts' content.

That night I tossed and turned unhappily in my huge, rumpled bed under the eaves.

My bedroom is luxurious, like a Bedouin tent, all gauzy drapes, muslin and tapestried cushions, little mirrors sewn into the fabric, tassels, plush and velvet. It's my gorgeous retreat from the world. But even all that decadent voluptuousness couldn't tempt me into sleep that night.

I was dwelling on Effie's betrayal. Her sharp, whispered 'Shush, she's coming back from the lav.'

How nasty. I wouldn't have minded if she had been planning

a surprise party or a present. But no. She was gossiping, telling tales. She was speculating about why I don't fit in.

I turned my pillows over as each side grew hot, hard and annoying. I lay this way and that, and still those awful thoughts came tumbling through my head, like the coloured balls bouncing in the bingo machine at the Christmas Hotel. I couldn't shake them out.

I had been such a fool, these past few months, even to imagine for a second that I fitted in. Oh, I'd gone traipsing around, doing the things that ordinary people do, wearing the clothes they wear, saying the things they say. But somehow it was never a convincing performance. Not to myself. *You aren't an ordinary woman, Brenda. You aren't a natural being.* I'd taunt myself like that. *How can you hope to fool anyone? They can all see through your disguise, you know. Of course they can.*

They can see the pallor of my skin. They can see my scars – I know they can.

They can see where the joins are.

But I would hope – I'd fool myself, sometimes for days at a time – that I was fitting in, that I was getting away with it, that I was living a life like everyone else. My evidence was in things like . . . having a best friend. Effie had accepted me. She understood me, I'd thought. And she had respected my reticence about my past, about all my life leading up to the moment of my arrival in Whitby. She never trod over the line in the sand. She was unquestioningly my friend.

I'd thought I had Effie's unconditional love.

I decided there was no point thrashing around in my bed, bullying myself into sleep. I'd get up and sit at the kitchen table. Hot milk and walnut cake. That was the only thing for it.

Love! I pulled on my dressing-gown. Effie didn't know the meaning of the word. I felt foolish now. Friendship to her meant having someone to gad about the town with. A companion. Not someone you need to be loyal to. Someone you could bitch about as soon as their back was turned. Love!

I wondered if I needed to put my wig on just to sit in the kitchen. I glanced at the clock. Three forty. None of the Greens would be up, surely. I'd do without. Who cares? My head already felt too hot. My brains were already cudgelled. I'd sit there bald. Let them all come and see, if they wanted to.

What love have I *ever* had?

I trod across the landing, down the stairs, along the dark passageway, trying not to make any noise. I clicked on the lights in the kitchen, my flat feet slapping on the chilled stone floor. I pulled down the milk pan, threw open the fridge.

No, really. Think about it, Brenda. What love have you ever had in your life? Real love. Reasonless, loyal, unconditional love?

None.

Was that true?

Absolutely none.

I put a match to the gas. Watched the blue flames roar. Glugged the milk into the pan.

My father didn't care for me. He looked at me with curious, scientific interest. That was all.

He recoiled when I first came to consciousness. While I was raggedly breathing my first he lurched backwards with a cry. I smelt formaldehyde, burning hair and fresh blood. I smelt brimstone. The first sounds I remember hearing were his strangled gasps of horror and dismay. He knew at once that he

had made a mistake in bringing me to life. There was no com-
passion, no feeling in him for me. He wanted to have nothing to
do with me, his child. But child is the wrong word, is it not? For
I was never a child. That was something I never got to be.

I was born a mature woman. There was no mother, just my
father and me, alone in the ruined castle where he had brought
his equipment, all ready to continue his filthy work.

By then he claimed to hate what he had done. His first
creation had been a ghastly mistake. A monstrous man-thing, he
had escaped from his laboratory to wreak havoc in the surrounding countryside. He had warned that he would murder all
those my father loved, unless my father gave him what he wanted.

A mate. That was all the monster wanted. A better half.
A bride.

Me.

Herr Doktor had to be threatened and cajoled. He wanted to
turn his back on what he had made. In desperation he fled
abroad. The monster caught up with him. They chased each
other round the isles of Britain and finished up in Scotland,
where my father was forced to give in. He gathered together the
gory contraband of his science – the materials that would bring
me into the world . . .

I should never have existed. He brought me into the world
only to settle a bargain. I was the result of blackmail. I had my
husband to thank for my existence, my father told me. I was
created to appease that wicked creature's demands.

And my intended? What about him? What about our
marriage? Well, the whole shebang never took off. I can still see
him, the day that I was born. He watched the whole process
from a safe distance, staring down at me through the high

window in the stone wall as lightning lashed around him. He had clambered up there to watch the operation, to see that Herr Doktor was doing his bidding. His face was twisted and intent – one of the first faces I ever saw. His eyes were all monstrous greed. Desire mixed with horror.

I wanted them to want me for myself. Both of them. And they didn't, not really. I was just another failed experiment. They didn't want *me* at all. No one ever has.

My father looked upon his creation and saw that it was bad.

He imagined the horrible wedding to come. The honeymoon. The possible hideous children. And then he saw that he had blasphemed against nature. In those first moments of my life, as I blinked and struggled to sit up, as the storm raged about the castle, my father was picturing the army of monsters that might issue from me.

He couldn't stand the thought. He had gone too far. He quailed at the howling triumph of my husband, and felt despair at my touching, trusting confusion, as I gazed up at the two men.

Then my father made a decision.

To put a stop to me. Before I went any further.

He took up his surgical tools once more – swiftly, savagely – and set about undoing his work.

He tried to destroy me as I lay there, scant moments after my birth.

But I survived, didn't I? I fought back.

I was strong, even then.

The milk was bubbling, beginning to froth. I watched it boil over the lip of the pan, heard the satisfying sizzle as it put out the flames. I swore, and shook myself out of my miserable stupor.

'Oh!' The soft, surprised voice at the kitchen doorway jerked my attention from the milk. I dropped the pan almost guiltily, with a clatter, an intruder in my own kitchen.

There in the doorway stood Katherine Green. Her hair was pinned up and she was in a pair of striped pyjamas. 'Brenda, I'm sorry to have startled you,' she said, looking abashed.

'It's all right,' I said. My voice sounded harsh, compared with hers. It sounded deathly and hollow. I had clapped a hand to my bare head. How pathetic – as if I could cover my baldness. As if she couldn't see the gleaming scalp, its criss-crossing scars and old stitches. As if she couldn't see me in all my nocturnal glory.

'I was going to make some peppermint tea,' said Katherine. 'I didn't mean to disturb you.'

I tossed the milk into the Belfast sink and left the dirty pan for the morning. 'That's all right,' I said. Then I turned to her, monitoring her expression for any sign of a flinch. Would she recoil when I looked her in the eye? Was I so grotesque?

Nothing. She looked back at me evenly, with a pleasant, open smile.

'Katherine,' I said, 'forgive me, but I must ask this.'

She blinked. 'Yes?'

'There's nothing . . . about your family . . . that I should know, is there? Nothing important that you'd like to tell me?'

She swallowed hard and hesitated. Then she smiled broadly, meeting my eye almost defiantly. 'Why, of course not. What could there be? You know us, Brenda. We're as average as can be. As average as you are. There's nothing more to tell.'

I nodded. 'Yes. Of course. I'm sorry for asking. I'm not even sure why I did. I've been having silly dreams.' I turned to leave the kitchen. 'Well. Good night, then, my dear.'

'Good night, Brenda,' she said, as the kettle started to boil.

Bit fed up, the next day. Not at my best. Decided to keep myself to myself.

Not very professional, really. I left a note for the Greens, asking them to sort out their own breakfast. I lay in my bed, burrowed right down, and listened to them cheerfully seeing to themselves. They didn't mind that I wasn't very professional today.

I was disappointed in myself, though. We're all meant to be professional, these days, aren't we? Being happy when we don't feel it. Being efficient when inside we feel reckless and hopeless. We're all meant to put on a good show for the sake of others. Or what's the point? And usually I perform well. I'm faultless. Just some days, things aren't right.

The Greens fed themselves and then I heard them washing up and putting things away. I could hear the boiler running and the hot water thrumming through the old pipes of this house. They were treating it all like a big adventure. They were treating my house as if it was their own.

I listened to them go out. There was no rain on the roof. I peeked out to see the sun slanting through the skylights. It was a better day for them and their holiday. I was glad.

Perhaps later today I should pull myself together. I should go next door and make up with Effie. I had stormed out of Cod Almighty a bit melodramatically. It wasn't the kind of thing that impressed Effie. She'd have thought it exceedingly bad manners. She wouldn't see that it had been justified. I've heard her say, 'Brenda, there's never any need to cause a scene.' I'd embarrassed her in front of young Robert and poor Jessie.

It was after midday, though, when I felt fit enough to get up and throw on some reasonably tidy clothes. I put on a headscarf over my least glamorous wig and tugged on my housecoat: the one that declared to the world, 'I'm busy as anything today, and I haven't got time to stop.'

I stared at myself in the mirror, piling on foundation and heavy concealer. The Greens would be gone soon. I'd miss them. I'd cook something special this evening to make up for my absence at breakfast.

Minutes later I was outside the greengrocer's downstairs, at the bottom of our building. I hefted up a basket, and inspected the fruit and veg. Everything was oversized, vibrant with colour: courgettes, aubergines and fat tomatoes. Rafiq tried to interest me in mangoes, four to a box, fleshy and yellow. I couldn't see the Greens liking them: they wouldn't want anything too exotic. I smiled at him, and waved him away, and he could see that Mrs Brenda from upstairs was in one of her taciturn moods so he left me alone. I picked up bunches of thyme, coriander and mint, all cool and dewy in my fingers. I weighed down my basket with plump fresh lemons and oranges and eventually I struggled inside.

Leena was at the till, as per, busy with a tall man in a hat and coat. I ducked down the aisle where they kept the biscuits and cakes to look for my favourite masala tea, but all the while I was listening to Leena. She was trying to get rid of the man but he was persistent, asking questions, not buying anything. She was too polite to ask him to leave, I realised. All of a sudden I knew who he was and what he was doing. Anyone else, I would have strode up to that counter and rescued her from his questions. But the sound of his voice made me shiver.

'I'm going to leave you my card,' the man was saying, 'and my number at the Hotel Miramar. I want you to phone me if you see anyone fitting the descriptions I've given you. It's very, very important.'

'Lots of people come through my shop,' Leena protested. 'How would I know? I don't keep tabs on everyone.'

'These people might stand out . . . as unusual,' he said. 'And, as I say, you'd be doing a good thing if you let me know. They need to be brought to light. They have done something very, very wrong.'

He's talking to her like she's simple, I thought. His voice was cool and calm. But there was urgency underneath, which discomfited me. I braved myself, picked up my box of tea and my basket and marched towards the counter. I'd take a look at this Frank.

'Well, I'll see,' said Leena, braver now that I was there. She could dismiss the man now. 'Do you mind? I need to serve this lady.'

I perched my basket on the counter, pretending to find it even heavier than it was. I felt the man's eyes on me. I returned his stare. Under his wide-brimmed hat he was pale and unhealthy-looking. His skin was damp. He seemed . . . green about the gills. His appearance struck me, like the Greens' had on their arrival, as sickly and unearthly.

'And this lady is . . . ?' he said. 'I don't believe I've had the pleasure.'

Leena was starting to weigh my fruit and vegetables, ringing them into the till. She rolled her eyes at me.

'I live upstairs,' I said. 'What's it to you?'

'I'm looking for some people,' he said. 'I've knocked at your door a couple of times and missed you.'

He went on to describe the Greens. My heart thudded and I kept glancing at Leena, who carried on working, catching my eye. She knew I had the Greens staying. I knew she'd seen them, met them. I knew she had covered up for me with this man, and what we both didn't know was why the Greens needed protecting.

'What are they meant to have done, these people?' I frowned.

'That's between them, me and their people,' he said curtly.

'Their people?'

'The ones they ran out on,' he said. 'That's all I'm prepared to say.' He looked me up and down again. 'Does that mean you've seen them?'

He knew, I thought. I could see it in his thin, pasty face. He knew precisely where the Greens had been staying. He was just playing with me.

I paid for my groceries and shook my head at him. I knew I made myself seem even more suspicious, but I didn't care. I hurried from the shop, banging my hip on a stack of boxes as I left.

'Brenda?' Rafiq called. 'Is something the matter?'

What am I doing? I thought, as I nipped up the alley and let myself into my own place. I'm falling apart. Why am I getting so involved? Having fights and acting suspicious! Do I really want to spoil everything I've built up here?

I dashed upstairs, and put on some spicy tea to brew. The heady fumes helped me to think.

'We don't want to go, Brenda.' He gave me a weak, self-deprecating smile. 'We're having such a wonderful time. We feel so . . . gathered in under your wing. We should have booked for more than four days. It isn't enough. We've been talking this afternoon, and we all wish we could stay a little longer.'

Ted had taken me aside in the early evening. We were in the dining room, where I was laying the table for dinner. He was in a striped blazer – rather dapper – and he was petitioning me, almost wringing his hands.

That afternoon the family had walked up to the abbey. They had made the long journey up the many winding steps, and spent the rest of the day up there, among the ruins, at the highest point of the town. They had surveyed all the rooftops and picked out mine. They had realised how fond they had become of this place and they felt at home here. They had decided that they wanted to stay on.

'We're supposed to go home,' he said, somewhat shiftily. 'We're expected back in our village. People will be surprised if we don't turn up at the right time. That's the done thing, you see. It's unusual for any of us to leave at all.'

'That sounds a bit strange.' I frowned, setting out the condiments and thinking of the sinister Frank.

Ted Green shrugged. 'It's the way things are. We don't like it much, but our village has traditions and ways of doing things that no one outside would understand. When you live there, you just sort of put up with it.'

'Well,' I said, 'I've no other bookings till the end of next week.'

'Really?' His face brightened.

'Next Thursday,' I said. My heart sank. That was when the TV people were arriving. They were coming for that silly show, ghost-hunting and manifestations. And it was all down to Effie. I still hadn't confronted her about it. Effie, it was beginning to seem, was behind everything.

'We're running out of money,' Ted said, 'but we can manage a couple more days with what we have.'

Talk of money embarrasses me. He was gazing at me earnestly. 'I can drop my rates a little,' I said. 'You've been good guests. No bother. I'll do some sums,' I said. 'Stay till after the weekend, hm?'

Ted grinned, and I ushered him away so that I could finish cooking dinner. He dashed out, full of boyish energy, to tell Katherine. I shook my head, smiling, then heard someone yell outside. A sharp cry of triumph.

I hurried to the window and looked down into my garden. There was Gerald in a blazer like his father's. He was dashing about and jumping, grabbing at something, tying to seize it. He let out another cry as whatever it was got away from him. Then I realised what he was up to, just at the instant he succeeded in doing something I would have thought completely impossible: catching a squirrel by its bushy tail.

Gerald held the poor, dangling creature and watched its legs scrabbling at the air.

I was about to wrench myself away and hurl myself downstairs, but then I saw his mother. She dashed into the garden, heading towards him determinedly, as if this was a regular occurrence. Gerald gave a sharp yelp as she seized him and smacked his legs. He dropped the squirrel, which dashed off at tremendous speed into the trees. His sister, Susan, had come out to watch, looking amused. Gerald was twisting in his mother's grasp, complaining, and – to my astonishment – Katherine smacked him again, rather hard. At this point his beloved baseball cap fell on to the grass.

That was when I saw he had a third eye, burning bright

red in the middle of his forehead. It was large, wild and inhuman.

I dropped the corner of the net curtain.

By the time I'd raised it again, Katherine had picked up the cap and plopped it back on her younger child's head. She was still shaking and threatening him, but now she was leading him back indoors.

I knew I hadn't imagined it. I knew precisely what I had seen.

The child was special. A mutation. That was why they kept him hidden away. That's why someone was after them. Surely that was what this peculiar business was about.

I was happy to have them in my home. I liked them. I'd say that to anyone. I was drawn to the Greens as a family. They were decent and sweet. I felt included in their tight little band. I would subsidise them, too, help them. That much I had promised. I was going to give them extra days in my establishment at less than the going rate. I was happy to cover my costs. Just to have a bit of life and laughter in my house . . . That was enough.

But . . . if I had to lie, if I had to fall out with Effie, my best friend, if I had to avoid detective-like men in the shop and the streets, if I had to evade and conceal for this family, well, what then? Was it too much? I had enough evasions, enough lies to keep up already. I was juggling too many balls.

The Greens would have to come clean. They would have to tell me more.

But I am, as you must know by now, a discreet woman by nature. I like to keep myself to myself. That good old working-class dictum. Myself to myself. I belong, of course, to no particular class. How can I? Or, if I do, it is to a very rarefied underclass. Or perhaps I belong to them all. Everywoman.

As I worked in my kitchen, on the final stages of that evening's meal, I could hear the little boy, Gerald, crying out, protesting against his punishment. 'I want to go home! I want to go home now! You have to take me home!' And his parents were hushing him, shushing him. They didn't want anyone to hear this. Suddenly they sounded shifty. 'I want us to go home!' Gerald shrieked, as if they were torturing him. I imagined him thrashing around, kicking and lashing out with his fists. I imagined his eyes squinched up, reddened, wet with tears. All three of his eyes. Would the third eye cry? Or would it be impassive and baleful through all the hysterics?

I was straining new potatoes and green beans over the sink when Katherine crept up behind me. I jumped when she spoke. 'I'm so sorry about Gerald,' she said. She looked drawn and upset.

'Never mind,' I said mock-heartily. 'Boys can be a handful.' I reminded myself that he had been catching and killing my squirrels. That wasn't normal, was it? And the thought formed itself and amazed me: What kind of monster is this child?

'I saw you,' Katherine said, 'watching from the window when we were in the garden and Gerald was throwing his tantrum.' Katherine gazed into my face steadily. 'You saw, didn't you, Brenda?'

'Hm?' I said. What was the use in pretending? 'Yes, I did, I'm afraid. I wasn't quite sure what was going on. I was alerted by the noise. I'm sure he deserved a little smack, whatever he was up to . . .' I gave a fake laugh.

'I mean,' she said, 'you saw his eye. Under his cap. His third eye.'

'Well,' I said, popping the potatoes into an earthenware bowl, 'I did, really. Yes.'

Katherine sighed. 'We'll explain everything. You deserve to know. You've been good to us.'

'No, really,' I said. 'You needn't explain anything to me . . .'

Katherine held up her hands. She was looking at me as if she knew they could trust me. She knew there were secrets on all sides. Now she seemed older: much older than her years. 'You deserve to know what we're running from.'

Up the street a little way, Susan Green was enjoying her freedom. She was dizzy with it. She traipsed down to the sea front, with no money, no desire to do anything in particular. She could do anything, she realised. She didn't have to ask anyone. She hugged herself with excitement and moved along, past the chip shops and the arcades. She was a pretty girl and drew glances. Susan was oblivious to them, a broad grin plastered across her face, her hair streaming out behind her. But where to go? What to do?

I laid the table with the best tureens and serving dishes, with silver for the first time in a while. I was making it into a proper occasion. Salmon poached in wine and dill. All set for their revelations.

I wondered if they would say grace again. When I asked, Ted looked more serious and careworn than usual. He screwed up his face. 'I don't think so. I don't think any of us believes in it. Not any more.'

'Sssh,' Katherine said. 'Let's just eat.'

'Where's Susan?' he asked sharply.

'She was in her room,' said Katherine. 'I called to her on my way up. She said she would follow . . .'

Gerald was hunched in his chair, sulking under his baseball cap. 'She said she was sick of all the shouting and the paranoia. That's what she said. She went out.'

'Out?' said Katherine, hollowly. 'By herself?'

Ted bit his lip. 'She'll be all right. She's old enough. She won't get into any trouble.'

Katherine looked as if she didn't believe that for a second. 'She promised. She said she'd not leave our sight without telling us,' she sobbed, a despairing note in her voice. 'What's the use? We try to do things . . . to get away. But they both act up. Gerald, and now Susan. They won't listen. They'll never listen to us. They don't understand what's at stake . . .'

'They're only children,' Ted said gently.

'She'll be fine,' I put in. 'Susan's almost a grown woman. I'm sure she only went out to get some air.'

'She's no right to,' Katherine sighed, 'and it's very rude, too. After you've cooked dinner for us again.'

I started to serve. 'Hers will keep till she comes back.'

We ate in silence. I wondered when their revelations would begin.

Ted was thoughtful, solemn, as he ate. He and his family might have been worried about Susan, and everything else that was playing on their minds, but none of it affected their appetites. The three Greens present ate concentratedly until nearly everything I'd provided was gone.

Ted took a deep swig of wine and said, 'Brenda, we can't

thank you enough for everything you've done this week. Your care and your discretion.'

I spread my hands. 'My pleasure.'

They seemed so anxious. They seemed to want to get up and dash out into the streets now and start searching for Susan. They resisted the impulse, though.

'You need to know at least some of our secrets,' Ted announced. 'We've decided that much.'

I nodded. Now I didn't want them to tell me. I felt as if I was being pulled somewhere I didn't want to go . . .

'We're never going back to our village,' he said. He said it with gravity and resolve, his wife smiling sadly at him. Gerald was no longer sulking: he seemed rather cowed by his father's tone. 'We will never return to Norfolk. We will do everything in our power to stay away from that place, and make a decent life for ourselves elsewhere.'

He paused then to let me absorb this.

'It might seem like nothing to you, Brenda. People move about, change towns and alter their lives all the time. It happens every day. Or so we have recently learned. Here, in the outside world, people think nothing of changing their lives, homes, jobs and even partners. Imagine! Out here, in the wide world, things change all the time.'

I nodded, listening.

'To us, Brenda, this is heresy. It's shocking and new. Nothing in our own lives has changed. Ever. Everything was laid down for us, the rules and parameters of our ideas and future. Everything was dictated to us by the Elders.'

'Who . . . are these people?' I asked. 'You mentioned them in your grace the other evening . . .' I didn't like the sound of this.

I was imagining all sorts, I can tell you. Villages so remote and untouched by modernity that ancient rites and barbaric practices survived.

'The Elders are simply the oldest, most venerable and, as they would have it, the *purest* people in the village,' Ted said. 'Our great-grandparents. Now that the Old Man is dead and gone, his children are in charge of us. They care for all our needs, monitor our well-being . . . and they see to it that the Old Man's will is done, down to the last letter. We have always been under his thumb.'

That night Ted told me the whole story. He obviously felt I was owed complete candour, and I appreciated that. Of course, the story was pretty hard to swallow.

'In our village, on the green, there's a sort of monument, a twisted metal three-legged statue. Odd-looking thing. It's no statue, though. And it ain't no climbing frame for the kiddies. That used to belong to our great-great-granddad. The Old Man. It was his walking frame, those rusted struts, all buckled, bent and scabbed with fatigue.'

'You see, he had three legs, our great-great-granddad. Each was twenty feet long. When he died his walking frame was left out as a monument, among the grass and daisies, to remind the village of how he ruled round there, throughout the twentieth century.

'The invasion, all that effort . . . and all they ended up owning was that tiny little place, an obscure corner of our world.

'England's been invaded many times. Strangers come and strangers go. Warriors and village girls fall in love. Easy sometimes. People stay behind in the tidal to and fro. They become part of the flat, endless landscape.

'You see, it's always been a very small, close-knit, quite remote village, and that's why no one ever said anything about the affair. That's why word never got out into the wider world and none of the scientists, photographers or newspeople ever came sweeping in by helicopter and motor-car to scoop an exclusive. For a century and more the village has been quiet and life went on – as is its wont – and the last survivor of the invading force found himself part of things. He married a nice girl who worked in the local pub and they had children – strange-looking children, perhaps, but the villagers were kindly and accepted them. Tolerant, insular, sufficient unto themselves – and, what's more, they were terrified of my great-great grandfather. So the village ambled and idled through the twentieth century and, meanwhile, the great cities of the rest of the world were rebuilding themselves, rumbling, groaning, picking up the pieces after the invasion.

'As the decades went by he felt like he'd always been there. The villagers had built a barn at the back of the village pub and that was where he lived. Under extra tall ceilings. He kept himself out of sight, mostly.

'The villagers were kind to him. They acted on his every whim. Scared, I suppose.'

'It's an obscure part of England. He was safe from prying eyes. He considered it a miracle to have survived the invasion and to continue living on what was, essentially, enemy soil. He had acclimatised. He was safe. He was a very old man by the end, a century or so.

'All of his comrades, the ones he still remembered, had fallen for the fatal bacteria and somehow he had made it. They paraded through his nightmares and he thanked his lucky stars for his kinder fate. Sneezing warriors, phlegmy invaders, death-rattling, rheumy soldiers from afar marched in his dreams. Sniffles had taken them off in the end, and left him stuck behind, to live a sedentary, rural afterlife in Norfolk.

'Those who'd travelled so far to trample their horrid spiky legs all over this world, all they had left behind, besides a few monuments, was my great-great grandfather.

'Maybe some of us younger ones think it's time the tale was told. We are the great-grandsons and great-granddaughters of the stranger in our village. It's a hundred years later or more, a different century again. Enough time has gone by. Enough seclusion and enough secrets.

'The Old Man and his wife are dead. The old paterfamilias is long gone into the ground. He shouldn't exercise a tentacular hold on the sons of his sons now. But he did, while he was here. He was a stern task-master – he made them all learn his native tongue and gave them the sharp end of it when he was riled. He made us all know a little of our history, though it seemed to us like fantasy.

'Of all of his family, perhaps I was the closest. I don't know why. I was the quietest, the runt of the litter. He knew, perhaps, that I'd be the one eventually to tell the tale – he knew someone would have to. So he described his dreams to me. Only there could he gambol and kick about in his natural atmosphere, and I was privy to his fantasies. My grandfather told me how he would hover in the thin atmosphere and float weightlessly above the scarlet crags and dunes. He felt unencumbered – no family, no ties, a young warlord once more. He felt delicate and free, flicking his gorgeously suckered and bejewelled tentacles in the spicy, dusky atmosphere he remembered from home. Honestly, this is what my grandfather told me of his dreams. And I – wide-eyed – listened to it all.

'At first my granddad wondered why he'd been spared. There was no God where he came from, so he couldn't claim anything divine. All of his comrades in arms – comrades in multiple arms – sneezed, trembled, were racked with spasms and finally died of the common cold, but he was untouched by it all, remaining hale and hearty. In the end he put it down to his dalliance with the landlord's daughter, Gloria. She had made sure that the tender-hearted invader in the villagers' midst had a good time. In doing so, she'd passed on some of her earthbound immunities. Glo – my great-great-grandmother – gave him the gift of life. A life on earth. Along with her peaches-and-cream complexion, the not-so-delicate sweat of her brow, and the startling ampleness of her charms.

'Gloria's father wouldn't stand for it at first. She was mixing – collaborating. She was a disgrace to the family, to the whole human race.

'What you must remember is that at the end of the nineteenth century this was a place that never had heard much from the wider world. Amazing to think it. Not even a wireless then. Not many whispers of the global calamity penetrated its gloom. This rank, dank, hard-bitten, incestuous old place. Not a rustle in the long grass, not a hint of singed metropolis carried on the evening breezes . . .

'Until this lone Martian turned up, striding across the low horizon on attenuated metal legs. The villagers were flabbergasted. He stalked on to the village green and they all came out to greet him. They were assembled there, naive, insouciant, and oblivious to the danger that tripod creature represented. He glared down at them from his snug little cockpit . . .

'. . . and decided he liked the look of the place. Elected not to raze it to the ground, as per instructions. Finally he realised – incredibly – that he liked the look of the landlord's daughter, Gloria.

'Don't ask me how it happened. It was just love, I suppose. Amazing, really. And I should be glad. Without it I wouldn't be here.

'The landlord had his daughter horsewhipped in front of everyone on the village green. No one dared to intercede. But then the invader waded in to put a stop to it. And they all held their breath.

'He told me the story many times. My grandmother died twenty years before he did, and he always wept when he remembered how her father had whipped her, bringing beads of blood to her back, everyone watching. He wept and I knew that this terrifying person – his single great eye all salty and wet – was soft-hearted under the carapace. Jelly-soft. Why else the armour?

'That afternoon he declared his love for the landlord's daughter in front of everyone. He strode into the public display.

'They drew back.

'A single laser blast sizzled loudly on the air. They stared in appalled silence. Gloria's father lay blackened on the dead grass. A shadow of his former self.

'And still no one knew that that had been the fate of all authority figures – the world over – who had stood in the way of the invaders. Priests, generals, heads of states. All lay like the landlord of the Bluebird Inn. The villagers knew only that they had a new patriarch in town.

'The Martian loomed over the smouldering ashes of my great-grandfather in his battle-scarred silver armour. He was steady on his telescopic legs. The muzzle of his laser cannon smoked and his flashing red eye dimmed only slightly with remorse.

'Gloria stared at him in disbelief – he had murdered her rancorous, side-whiskered dad. She gathered up her dignity. Staunched her wounds. And the Martian offered her his hand.

'That is how the centuries turn. The blasting of the old and the ushering in of the new. With that dazzling cyborg, that devilish creature in his space armour with twenty-foot-long legs, lording it over the village.

'After that no one dared oppose him.

'Gloria continued to pull pints that glistened and frothed, a home-brewed ale with a green tinge. And she gave him children. Some said she would clamber up one of those silver legs, hand over hand, and a hatch would pop open on his shining dome. She would fling herself into his tight little carapace and there they would go about their conjugals. Obviously, my elderly grandfather never went into precise detail about it with me. But it was one rather large step for womankind anyway – into the close confines of the invader's clasp.

'She must have seen something in him that the rest of the world didn't.

'At their union the men of the village quailed, while the women blushed and speculated. Not many dared voice their thoughts. They decided that the mismatched couple must be in love, so they would live and let live.

'Over the decades, we greenish children started to appear, went to the village school and learned our lessons with the ordinary kids from thereabouts. No one mentioned our oddity – several limbs. Or – in some notable cases – the single crimson eye in the centre of the forehead.

'My grandfather never stopped watching the skies. Every night he'd peer up through the skylight in the tall barn at the back of the Bluebird and scrutinise the darkness, knowing where Home was. He would watch with a curious mixture of longing and fear. And I watched him do so until his dying day.

'He looked for those sinister solar flares from Mars and the soft phosphorescence of their saucers. He knew that one day they would set off again. Earth was too rich, too green, and they'd have its spoils, one way or another.

'Deep down my grandfather expected them to come back. One day they would dose themselves up with enough new drugs and have another stab at genocide.

'They would come to look at their descendants. And we had to be ready for them. The family has to be there, united, ready to greet them.'

Effie received another visit from Frank the detective. Her junk shop was closed, but he was persistent. She went down to answer the door, and this time there was no messing about. 'You know, don't you?' he said. There was something weird about his eyes, Effie said afterwards, about his whole demeanour. 'You know where they are?' And she nodded. She felt compelled to leave her home with him, just as she was. She didn't even lock up.

They came directly to my house, where Ted was just finishing his tale.

His wife and son were staring at him, and Katherine reached

across the table to grasp his hand. His son had removed the baseball cap. He didn't have to hide his third, gleaming eye now.

Then the knock came downstairs.

'Susan?' Ted asked.

As I went down to answer it, I knew it wouldn't be.

Effie was shamefaced, but I could see she'd no choice. Frank the detective stood at her back, on the doorstep, pressing a stubby silver gun into her side. 'Show me in,' he said.

I let him into my home.

Upstairs, Ted rocketed out of his seat and Katherine cried out. They stared at me accusingly. 'You've betrayed us.' I could hardly meet her eye. 'Brenda! How could you?'

'He'll take us back,' Ted said. 'He'll make us go back with him.'

I stood, helpless, as Frank advanced into the room. He was triumphant, sniggering horribly under his breath. He levelled the silver pistol at them, evidently relishing the moment. 'You can't leave our village,' he said quietly. 'Whatever made you think you could?'

Ted stiffened. With some dignity, he said, 'We want what's best for our kids. That village has blighted our lives. Can't you see how narrow and futile life is there, just waiting and living in suspense? Our children deserve more than that.'

Frank shook his head. 'That village is your only world. You're coming back with me. Tonight.' He glanced from side to side, puzzled. 'Where's the girl? Where's Susan?'

Ted and Katherine exchanged a glance. 'We don't know,' said Ted, truthfully. 'She went out without permission.'

'What kind of father are you? You can't control any of them,' Frank said, disgusted.

'I don't want to *control* my family,' Ted said.

Hurray for him, I thought.

'That girl is necessary,' said Frank. 'Her name is down for the breeding programme. That girl,' he laughed nastily, 'is promised to me.'

Katherine shrugged. 'Well, she's not here just now. There's nothing we can do about that.'

All this while Effie had been standing beside me. She nudged my arm, caught my attention, and raised her eyebrows in mute apology. Effie wasn't proud or stupid. She knew when she was wrong. And now, suddenly, she had realised I'd been right all along, especially in protecting the Greens' secrecy. This man chasing them was a nightmare.

Now Effie was edging closer to the table. Her hands, trembling but sure of their purpose, were reaching out for the heavy tureen that held the last of the potatoes. She was standing behind Frank. He had let her out of his sights. Suddenly I knew what she was proposing to do.

Just in time I darted forward.

Effie had grasped the tureen and hurled it into the air, hoping to brain Frank. But her aim wasn't so hot. Instantly on the alert, Frank twisted round, gun at the ready, and fired off a livid green laser charge. In my dining room! I flung myself in front of Effie and caught the beam full blast.

I've been hit by worse. It knocked me down and gave me a raging headache for a few hours, but I'm a pretty tough old bird. Of course, it would have sizzled Effie on the spot.

Ted took this as his cue: as soon as Frank fired his gun, he flung himself bodily at the man. They fell heavily to the floor, grappling and grunting. Effie, Katherine and Gerald surrounded them as they rolled around.

I was phasing in and out of consciousness, still absorbing the green laser fire, feeling nauseous.

Effie and the Greens soon had Frank flattened and exhausted, pinned to the carpet. Katherine's hair was awry and her voice shrill, as she told him, 'You'll leave us alone. You won't come after us any more. You'll let us live our lives in peace.'

Frank was bleeding from his nose and panting raggedly. He laughed up at her. 'I'll never let you go free. Why should I? What's so special about you four? Why should you be allowed to leave the village? Why should the rest of us have to stay?'

'We could *all* leave,' Katherine suggested. 'Why should any of us stay? What *for?*'

'They will come back,' Frank said, hushed, reverent, 'one day. And we must be waiting for them.'

'No,' said Katherine, 'they won't. And – even if they did, what would they want with us? We're human, Frank. Earthlings. We don't belong to them. We never did.'

Frank's face twisted in confusion and hatred. 'You will not be free – not ever. Even if you kill me now. The Elders will send others after you. You will be hunted down. You will come back in the end.'

Later, Susan tried to explain what had made her return to my establishment when she did.

'It was pure instinct,' she said. 'Intuition, I suppose. A hangover from when we were all of one mind. Back in the old days. But . . . I was just going round the little fairground, starting to enjoy myself, when I knew my family was in danger. I had to come back here immediately.

'Oh, I thought of resisting the impulse – I was fed up with

them. I was sick of being a fugitive, all smiles, pretending we were having a lovely holiday when actually we were as jumpy as hell. I was tempted to ignore the alarm bells that were ringing like mad inside me and just stay down at the fair . . . where the lights had come on, all lurid and gaudy now it was dark, and the cheap music was pumping out. And other teenagers were hanging around. Ordinary boys and girls, eyeing each other up, eating chips out of cartons, smoking fags and being dead cool. I wanted in. I wanted to belong to them. That was the world I wanted to live in.

'I went swishing through the fair in my old-fashioned dress and I knew they were staring at me. I stood out a mile, even though I tried not to. All our family does. We're conspicuous and out of step. I hugged my arms to me, hidden inside my cardigan, and tried to ignore the warnings in my head.

'But how could I? I had to give in. They're my flesh and blood. I know when they're in danger. So I walked away from the fair and back through the town. The streets were thronging with locals and visitors, everyone coming out for a good time. I wove through the crowd. It was the first time I'd ever been out alone in the world. What an adventure! I felt so sophisticated, so grand.

'And then I came here. To that disastrous scene. Everything was more or less as I knew I'd find it. You lot frozen in dramatic postures, stuck in some kind of impasse, with Frank on the floor, helpless yet still ranting, still making his threats.

'He still had the power, and you all knew it. We would never be free of him. Through him, our hateful family was speaking – and will continue to speak. Through him we could hear the Old Man cursing us. Condemning us to a lifetime of waiting.

'You all looked at me when I let myself into the dining room, quietly so as not to disturb you. Your heads whipped round. You weren't expecting me to come back. Perhaps you thought – maybe you even hoped – that I'd already made good my escape. But no, I came back.

'Frank looked up from the floor. Dirty old Uncle Frank, playing detective. He had the nerve to call me "dear" and "darling". He welcomed me back into the fold. My beloved. My betrothed. Did he tell you that, Brenda? That I was promised to him? I was meant to breed with him.

'And that was why I strangled him. Better that than bear his vile babies. Your faces! You were all so horrified, but what else could I do? I whipped off my cardigan. And that was a shock to you, too, wasn't it, Brenda? To you and Effie, your friend. You'd been used to me covering my arms with my cardie. You weren't expecting to see tentacles.

'I made you all back away from Frank. I even told my dad what to do and he complied, which was a first. I must have looked very determined – or mad. Well, I was. And I was furious. I advanced on Frank, flexing my spectacular limbs.

'We all watched the colour drain out of his face, didn't we? That was a sight to see. It was revenge enough, really, to watch him realise I had no compunction, no fear. That I would do anything to protect my family.

'Dear Brenda, I'm sorry for the bother, the upheaval. My parents are sorry, too. We're sorry to leave you with the mess. Are you sure you don't mind disposing of the body? You know, you've gone above and beyond the duties of a bed-and-breakfast lady this week. You have been a marvel. And so have you, Effie. I heard you had a real go with the tureen. Thank you, ladies, on behalf of my family.

'But we can't stick around here, I'm afraid. We really have to go.

'Soon the people at home will realise Frank isn't sending messages and they'll know something's wrong. Maybe they'll send others after us. More determined, more deadly. I don't know. But I do know that we can't stay still. Not yet.

'Where will we go? I don't know.

'Thank you, Brenda. Without you this would have been the end of our escape. We would be going back now to the village at the back of beyond. You've set us free on the world.'

Susan Green said some of this at the time, as the family were preparing to leave. The parents were subdued – shell-shocked, almost. Susan had taken over: she was the responsible adult now. The rest came in the form of a letter, a few days later; the postmark was smudged, but we thought it read Scotland. That letter arrived at my house after Effie and I had disposed of Frank's body, deep under my rockery, after everything had died down and I'd had a chance to clean my B-and-B once more, in preparation for the next visitors.

Chapter Three:
Manifest Yourself!

That night – the night before the TV people arrived on my doorstep and encouraged all hell to break loose – I dreamed that my husband came back to me. I still call him that, though we fell short of consummation. Sometimes when I pull my gorgeous silk and satin bedclothes over my head I get too hot and have the most lurid dreams. Of course he isn't coming back to me: after all this time it simply isn't possible. He has to be dead.

Anyway, he would scarcely recognise me now.

In my dream, he sailed back into my life across the sea from the extreme north. In Whitby it was the depths of a blue winter. He came frozen in the most beautifully clear iceberg, which had detached itself neatly – so neatly – from the mother berg somewhere in the Arctic. Prostrate, beseeching, suspended within, like Prometheus, he floated back to my shore, as if seeking me out.

I found him on a shingle beach, washed up and melting slowly in the weak November sunshine. Just a man. A well-built man. He was nothing to fear, surely. He wasn't the monster that everyone had made him out to be. At least, in my dream I didn't think so. His skin wasn't green. And his joints weren't bolted. He was no kind of primitive creature. Although I had barely seen him before, had spent hardly any time in his company, I would have recognised him anywhere. We were meant for each other. Were *made* for each other.

That was my dream.

As I gave the place a last tidy, and prepared myself to allow new people – strangers – into my home, my mind was filled with thoughts of the husband I was meant to have. He was supposed to share eternity with me.

Fat chance.

Perhaps, even after all this time, he is still out there somewhere, testing his limits in the ice and tundra. That was the last place anyone saw him. He found it necessary to go everywhere and do everything. Explore the world. He wanted to – whatchacallit? – *carpe diem:* seize the day. Well, I never saw the point in that. 'Live within your resources,' I say. 'I am an imperfect woman. The only woman on earth not made by God. He was an imperfect man. Don't rock the boat.'

I was born in the Orkneys.

My father lived for a little while in a castle there. He was obsessed with his work. His successes drove him – it is fair to say that he was in the unshakeable grip of past success.

I had no mother.

What a terrible thing.

I can remember the moment my eyes first opened. I had language immediately. I had the gift of tongues. I saw Herr Doktor looming above me and knew he was my father.

Curiously, my organs and limbs felt natural and lived-in. I saw my husband grinning in at me through that high window and was ashamed of my nakedness.

My father, Herr Doktor, balked at his creation. He saw that I was an abomination. I was nothing spectacular to look at, it's true, but did I deserve what happened next? My father attempted to murder me, only minutes after he had completed delivering – that's not the correct word. Only minutes after he had completed *orchestrating* me.

Already mad, he left me for dead, to fend for myself, while he was pursued by demons of his own, actual or otherwise. My father and husband ran off to chase each other, leaving me to do what any woman has to do at one time or another. I picked myself up, pulled myself together and decided I would have to look after myself.

I travelled through Scotland. I explored a little of this half familiar, sometimes hostile world. It was a vagabond existence that I followed for many years, knowing that I didn't belong to this race of men, women and children. Even the animals I encountered – and killed to eat – were more at home on this earth than I. I've never been one for fitting in.

But I did try. I moved around. I tried to keep a low profile. I settled here and there, in villages and towns. I explored hills and valleys, set myself up in big cities. Sometimes I was hounded out. Folk would cotton on to my oddity, especially in the early years. Later I would discover how not to unnerve them. I didn't want them chasing me into the night with blazing torches. I did moonlight flits, changed my disguise and started again somewhere else, far away.

Decades passed and I realised I wasn't growing any older. At least, not at the rate that humans do. My strength was unsapped; I was untouched by disease and decay. At first I revelled in my longevity. I marvelled at my unnaturalness. I lived a dozen lifetimes, one after another. I was a pauper, a princess and many things between. At one stage I loved pretending to be all the things I wasn't. And I drew fascinated stares. I drew intrigue. I cloaked myself in mystery and found that adventure was my forte. I could tell you some tales about those years! They were my wilderness years and my glory years. Through the nineteenth and twentieth centuries . . . Well, I barely stopped.

But even super-humans grow weary.

I started to hanker for somewhere quiet, somewhere to rest my old bones and settle to ordinary, everyday tasks.

I made my way here, towards the fresh air. Something like a siren voice called me. I knew this was the town for me.

And at last I settled by the sea.

Effie was carrying on as if nothing had happened. I was amazed. The woman has hidden depths, I'm sure. We had buried a man in my back garden, under cover of night and Effie was behaving as if nothing was out of the ordinary.

I met her in the shop on Monday morning and we chatted with Leena, who asked after the nice little family staying with me. I told her they had gone, that they stayed a little longer than they had planned but now they were back on the road, destination unknown. Yes, they were pleasant, weren't they? Effie was standing there with her basket of rolls, apples and porridge oats, nodding and agreeing over how nice the Greens had seemed, how quiet and ordinary. She didn't nudge me with her bony elbow, or turn to raise an eyebrow

ironically. Perhaps she wasn't even lying awake at night, thinking about those tentacles, like glossy, deadly eels, coiling and
tightening round Frank the detective's throat. Perhaps she wasn't
thinking about Susan throttling him right in front of us on my
Axminster carpet.

So, a new week was starting. All of last week's excitements
were over. Like Effie, I was stocking up on a few essentials. That
afternoon my new people were arriving.

'Though really, they're *your* people, aren't they, Effie?' I asked
her. We dawdled out of the shop into the sharp, spangling
sunlight.

'My people?' She frowned, doing her absent-minded act.

'You invited them.' I hadn't asked her about this yet. There
hadn't been many quiet moments recently. 'The cable-television
people.'

She looked genuinely surprised. 'Oh, my Lord,' she gasped.
'I'll never get a hair appointment in time. I shall have to dash
round Rini's. I'd completely forgotten about it, Brenda. When
do they turn up? When does it all start?'

She was gabbling, all in a flap. She went back to her house,
still muttering to herself. It served her right, I thought. Fancy
inviting people round to hunt ghosts and contact the dead in
your home. Letting them film and broadcast all your business. It
was asking for trouble. Effie was usually so careful about how she
presented herself to the world. I had a feeling she had consented
now to let chaos and randomness into her house. Well, it was all
her own doing.

I wasn't certain yet whether I had quite forgiven her for all the
goings-on of the past week. She had gossiped and speculated
about me with Robert and Jessie in Cod Almighty. And there was

the matter of her mistrust and what amounted to her betrayal of the Greens. She had come through in the end, of course, and done the right thing: she had put her life on the line to save them. At the last moment Effie had seen what a mistake she had made and attempted clumsily to redeem herself. But as yet I wasn't fully mollified. She hadn't liked the Greens at first, and had suspected them of all sorts of things. She hadn't trusted my judgement that they were – are – good, decent people.

The conclusion I drew was that Effie didn't trust me, either. Not deep down. She thought that I, too, was shady, duplicitous, freakish.

Effie has a small-town mentality.

So, that Monday morning I didn't leap into action – as I normally would – to offer to help tidy Effie's place and get everything in readiness for the advent of the TV-show people.

No. I had work of my own to do.

They brought so much equipment with them that I was afraid there wouldn't be room for it all in my little house. They weren't even the technical people, with their cameras and lights – they were up at the Miramar, and they were already setting up their machinery, laying miles of cables, in Effie's house next door.

The stars of the show were staying with me. They had brought enough of their own paraphernalia with them, even without cameras. The presenter, Eunice, and her entourage dragged in case after case of outfits, makeup and hairstyling gear. I wondered, as I watched them, what all the glamour stuff had to do with ghost-hunting, but I didn't say anything. I simply welcomed them, introduced them to the rules of my establishment and let them get on with it.

Eunice had my best room. Rather, she took it. She was a tall blonde with huge, unnaturally shaped breasts and pumped-up lips, condescending – and nervous, I thought. She was followed in by her hairdresser, a plump girl called Lisa Turmoil, who was a bit more friendly. She joined me in the kitchen for a pot of spicy tea, while Eunice settled in upstairs.

'Who is the third room for, then?' I asked. Lisa was pursing her lips and examining my wig from where she sat at the breakfast bar. I was wearing the smartest, the one with the gorgeous streaks. I thought it very sophisticated.

'Ah,' she smiled, 'that's for Brian. He always arrives after the others, every location we go to. He's the psychic and – besides the spirits – the real star of the show.' She beamed at me. There was something immediately engaging about Lisa, I thought. She didn't take any of this stuff, or herself, too seriously. 'I could reshape that wig for you, if you liked. Give it a more contemporary feel.'

I blushed, pouring the dark tea.

'I hope I haven't embarrassed you.' It was her turn to blush.

'How could you tell?'

'Professional.' She tapped her snub nose and produced a business card: *Lisa Turmoil: Hairstylist to the Stars.*

I wondered what her rates were like, compared to Rini's.

'And I'm not just the hair person on this show.' She grinned. 'They've put me in front of the cameras, too – only because I'm already on the payroll and I'm a good screamer.'

'A screamer!' I laughed. 'Oh dear. Is the show very frightening?'

'Don't you watch it?' She seemed surprised. 'I thought every-one did. We're a cult hit.' She looked very proud.

'Oh,' I said. 'I don't watch much television, as a rule. And I don't like anything spooky.'

She nodded, sipping her tea. 'It doesn't bother you, then, all of this stuff going on next door, raising the dead, and so on?'

'I didn't get much choice,' I told her.

It was years ago, now, that I went to see spiritualists, a fad that didn't last long. I don't know what I was trying to prove or what I wanted to find out. Something drew me, though. I went to those amateurish little services and sat quietly at the back, mumbling along with the not-hymns and the not-prayers. I sat among those friendly, well-meaning people and I wondered, But what if something comes through for you, Brenda? Something startling and true? What will that do to you?

The other people at those events were wrapped up in their private determination to prove that spirits existed and visited us in our world. They were still grieving for lost loved ones. They wanted to be haunted by them because they were proof that another world existed beyond some mystic veil. Did I want that proof? Is that why I skulked out on Sunday nights to sit at the back, listen, mumble and observe apparent visitations?

No. I wanted to learn that it was all fakery, which would have reassured me. I wanted to discover that those psychics were charlatans, that their beliefs were laughable. I wanted to be a materialist and discover that this world was all. For ever and ever, and that's your lot. Amen.

I hoped against hope.

I didn't want anything beyond this vale of tears.

I wanted to return to the dust.

In the end I stopped going. I could see that my search would end in disappointment – for me. When I stepped into those places a shiver went right through me. Dread. Conviction. They were saying to me, those spirits, Here we are. Taunting you. Waiting for you. We'll get you one day, Brenda. What right have you to walk upon the earth when we can't?

I wanted no truck with them.

Effie, now – I know Effie is very interested in all this business. She's drawn to spooky things. You just have to look at the books in her house, hidden among all the layers of junk. There are shelves and shelves of arcane, leatherbound volumes about witchcraft and demons. Those nasty tomes had belonged to her female forebears. I could picture them, generations of Effie-like hags, stretching back and back into the past, all stirring, spelling and writing down their recipes for disaster.

Effie doesn't seem to know half of what's contained in that house of hers. Or what it has contained and experienced. Which, as she explained to me, later that afternoon, was what compelled her to contact the production team. 'In any case, I'm a huge fan,' she said. 'It's one of the few television programmes I regularly tune in to.'

She was beside herself with excitement. Her hair was frosted and teased, and she was all dolled up to look her best for the cast and crew of *Manifest Yourself!*. When I had explained who was staying at my establishment she could barely contain herself. Eunice! Lisa Turmoil! And . . . Brian the psychic was gracing my B-and-B with his divine presence!

She perched herself carefully on my settee. I could tell she was light-headed – from peroxide fumes as much as anything.

Brian was installed now in my smallest room, at the back. I

hadn't seen much of him. He'd been reserved and hunched in an anorak, face and demeanour like a bloodhound's. He had arrived alone from the station and had wanted to go straight to his room for a lie-down to 'replenish' himself, as he put it.

'Didn't he say anything else?' Effie asked. 'Has he started picking up vibrations yet? Has anything flashed across his consciousness?'

I shook my head. Effie hadn't said a word about my hair. She hadn't even noticed that Lisa Turmoil – bless her – had given it a shaping, a setting and a going-over with her miraculous hot tongs. I was very proud of my do. I was in my new lime-green frock, too, with all the ruffles at the front. It's a bit bosomy and daring and I don't know why I was going to all the effort, but there was something in the air. A touch of excitement and celebrity, I suppose. A sense that great things were about to unfold.

'You look very, very nice, Brenda,' Effie said.

Sometimes she's not such a bad best friend.

I was beaming at the compliment when Brian the psychic walked into my front parlour. And what a transformation from earlier! Now he was definitely 'on'. He was in a long black leather coat – everything he wore was black and purple. His golden hair was teased up into a bouffant and he was rattling with jewellery. He was heavily tanned and lined – as if he had taken the sunbed a bit too far, I thought. There was a sofa-ish, Italian-leather look about him. But, still, it was an impressive entrance into my front parlour.

He paused before me and Effie, then raised his jewelled hands before his face. 'Ladies . . .' he said. 'I wanted to apprehend this opportunity with you, so to speak, before the evening's events, to allay your fears, such as they might be.' He smiled at us. Dazzling. He'd had a lot of dentistry.

'Fears?' I said. Effie was staring at him, as if he himself were an apparition.

'There is no necessity for fearfulness,' he said. 'None whatsoever. The beings that will manifest themselves literally from the ether and elsewhere are benign. I sense that. Yes, I can sense that now. My spirit guide, Rolf, is telling me that we will encounter nothing, so to speak, that will give us pause for alarm tonight.'

He was speaking a curious form of English that I was having some difficulty in following, and his accent was broad Geordie, which I've always found hard to understand.

'Are you . . . are you *reading* anything right now?' Effie asked hesitantly.

Brian's expression went vague and he looked as if he was listening to a distant noise. 'Various things,' he said. 'Nothing palpable yet. Nothing concrete. I'm still acclimating myself to the environs. You're Effie, aren't you?'

She shook his hand, flushed with pleasure. I sloped off to make tea for them, and when I came back Lisa had joined them, worn out after Eunice's beauty regime.

Shortly afterwards Eunice made her spectacular entrance. Effie was even more star-struck at meeting her. I had assumed she'd think Eunice a vulgar sort of person, especially in the tight-fitting jumpsuit with the zip pulled artfully half-way down. But Effie behaved as if she was meeting royalty.

I wheeled in the tea and coffee, biscuits and sticky buns. I answered a series of knocks at the back door, and let in the production team with more bits of equipment. Everyone had a clipboard and everyone was frowning in concentration. Only Brian sat serene, smiling vaguely and listening, presumably, to his spirit guide.

The producer – a slick young man called Trevor – asked Effie to sign a sheaf of forms, something to do with injury or disaster. She was signing away her right to comeback, I realised, should anything go wrong this evening. I raised my hand, tried to say something, to stop her, but Effie had signed with a flourish. Well, I thought, if she's not bothered, then I'm not.

I was holding a china plate of French fancies under Brian's beaky nose when I heard him say, quite clearly, 'You still think about him, don't you, Brenda?'

I jerked back. 'You what?' My eyes narrowed. 'What did you say?'

'He was your . . . intended.' Brian's eyes looked into mine. 'He had every intention . . . but it all went to the bad, didn't it? Ah, now . . . the signal's faltering . . . weakening . . . Wait! I feel now that you . . . were prevented from having the kind of consummation you both wanted . . . It was all tumult and confusion, wasn't it? And . . . he ran away into the night, and you were separated for ever . . . But you wonder sometimes . . . Sometimes you have nightmares – and your leg! Your poor leg! Will you ever dance on the stage again? Oh – that must be wrong . . . But you wonder whether anything will come right . . . and whether you will be happy . . . even so long after. Even now.' He stopped and frowned, as if whatever jumbled voices he was listening to had faded again.

'No,' I said stiffly. 'None of that is true.' I jabbed the plate at him and, bewildered, he took a squashy yellow cake. 'I don't know what you're talking about.'

*

In the end I had no choice. Effie cajoled and persuaded me to go next door with them and be part of the show. It wasn't until the moment that they all stood up with their clipboards, brushing off the cake crumbs and setting down their tea cups, that she asked me. She dragged me to one side and practically begged me to come for the filming. They were starting at ten and going right through the night.

Effie didn't want to be alone with them: 'Heaven knows what they'll call up.'

'But you should have thought of that earlier!' I had pictured an early night for myself. I wanted to dispel all thought of ghosts and apparitions.

'Please, Brenda. Now that they're here I'm rather nervous . . .'

Odd to hear her sound discomfited. We'd faced a few unusual events in recent weeks, and I'd heard her terrified, perplexed, furious and horrified, but never spooked like this. But I was feeling spooked too. 'All right,' I said. 'I don't want to be on camera, though.'

'Oh,' she said. 'Just stand in the background, then. No one will see you. They film in the dark with infrared or whatever they call it. Everyone just comes out as a green blob anyway, so you needn't worry.'

When we were in Effie's house, and Eunice was doing a few factual, linking pieces to camera – breasts pushed up, voice all breathy and mysterious – I was more interested in having a good look round. I'd never been in the upper storeys before and I hadn't realised how extensive the place was. Effie must have had twenty rooms at her disposal, all book-lined, stuffed with antiques, dust sheets and the ineradicable scent of must. I hung back with her as the crew went from room to room, deciding on locations and making plans. They kept ticking things off on their clipboards.

Poor Effie, I thought. What a gloomy place for her to live. No wonder she can be so snappish and unfriendly. Why didn't she get it sorted out? She couldn't be short of a bob or two. It was hard to credit that next door, through that brick and plaster wall, my B-and-B was so light, comfortable and warm. Effie had hardly any mod cons and the house was freezing: we were all huddled in our coats as we stood on Effie's landing.

'Now, you're Effie, aren't you, and you're the current owner of this eighteenth-century townhouse near the centre of this ancient fishing town?' Eunice was interviewing her earnestly, pushing the microphone into her face.

'That is correct,' said Effie. 'I've lived here all my life. My family has been here since the house was built.'

'Wow,' said Eunice. 'That's just so amazing. So there's a lot of, like, history here for you, yeah?' She glanced at her clipboard. 'And a long history of sightings and paranormal activity on the site.'

'Almost from the beginning,' Effie said. 'Among all the books here, there are various journals left behind by my relatives – my great-great-aunt Lucy, for example – and some describe hairraising phenomena, visitations, you might call them, down through the years to the present.'

I was pleased that Effie was more fluent than Eunice, who stammered and kept looking at her notes. Perhaps she was nervous.

'I must say,' Eunice said, with a glance at Phil, the

cameraman, who was peering into his lenses, 'there's a very strange atmosphere here that I felt almost as soon as we stepped inside. All these old things, all this junk lying about, adds to it.'

'It's the books I'm curious about,' Effie piped up. 'One of the mysteries I hoped we might look into tonight.'

Eunice frowned. 'Why are they mysterious?' She picked up a battered volume from a nearby stack. 'This is all in foreign . . .'

Effie nodded. 'Some are in very strange languages. And many seem to be filled with magical lore. Somebody, at some time, was heavily involved with witchcraft and magic. Maybe they all were.'

Eunice drew a long, over-dramatic breath. 'And . . . are you a witch, Effie?'

'Certainly not,' she said. '*That* tradition has not been continued in this house. But I would like to know more about some of the secrets it must hold.'

'Cut there.' Eunice beamed. 'That's marvellous! Just the right note of intrigue and menace. You're a natural, Effie. A star.'

Effie patted her hair. 'Really?'

'Can we take the lights right down now,' Eunice called, 'and bring in Brian? We might as well see if he can pick anything up.'

Suddenly I saw that Eunice was calling all the shots. She was behind every decision. She was much more than a bosom and a husky voice. As all the men rushed to do her bidding, and Lisa applied fresh hairspray to all of our dos, I touched Effie's elbow and drew her aside. 'What was all that? You've never told me that you come from a long line of witches. Were you making it up for the cameras?'

'What?' She was scandalised. 'Of course not! Haven't you looked at any of the books in my shop?'

I couldn't say that I had. When I read I like spanking new volumes. Old books make me think of dust mites, mould-chomping worms and my father working late in his cellar. He had lots of ancient texts. Old books give me the willies.

'This house is full of magic,' Effie said, as someone turned down the lights. 'The air is thick with sorcery . . .'

Now the only light coming into her upper rooms was from the lamps in the sloping street outside. We could hardly see each other, but the cameras were still trained on us, ready to record every flinch, twinge and shriek . . .

'. . . as we prepare to spend a whole night in the haunted house of the Whitby Witches!'

'Oh dear,' Effie moaned, as Eunice finished. 'It does sound a little cheapening, doesn't it? I wonder what poor dear Aunt Agatha would have to say about all of this.'

'You might find out,' I told her.

Brian the psychic had joined us. Apparently they had made him wait outside until they were set up and ready for him. Eunice liked him to arrive cold, as it were, so they could record his first impressions of a place. I must say, they were keen to keep everything on the level. They didn't seem to be fakers.

Brian smelt of fish and chips and best bitter. Lucky beggar! With all the excitement I'd forgotten to eat anything.

He moved into the room stealthily, holding up both hands, his face pale and vague in the weak light. 'Ah, yes . . .' he murmured gently.

'Is Rolf, your spirit guide, telling you anything?' Eunice asked.

'Not as such, Eunice. Nothing from Rolf just . . . Ah, yes. Hello? Oh. Hello?' He sounded like an old-fashioned switchboard operator. But then, I reflected, to the spirit world, that was probably what he was.

But there I went again, believing in it all. Unquestioning. I'm supposed to be a rationalist, materialist. That was what my father intended. 'Spirit? Pah! Religious twaddle!' was what he would shout. 'Show me where the spirit resides!' *Thwack!* would go his hand on the anatomy charts. I would gaze at those gorgeously colourful maps of the human interior. 'Where?' he would demand. 'Where is there room inside us for something so ineffable and vague? Twaddle! It's all twaddle!'

But you would have had a hard job convincing any of the group in Effie's house that there was no such thing as the spirit. They had their microphones, their infrared cameras, light meters and heat sensors turned up to maximum sensitivity so that they would pick up the tiniest footfall, cough or spill of dusty particles. They said they were looking for evidence, but they were already convinced. They had worked on the series for three years, I had been told, and had seen things to make my hair stand on end – they had stared at my newly brushed-up wig.

We listened. We waited. We crept from room to room, *en masse*, thirteen of us, shuffling and dragging electrical leads with us, like the Ghost of Christmas Past with his chains. Our faces glowed green on the monitors as we tensed, jumped and cried out at the slightest sound: boats honking in the harbour, calling to each other, seagulls screaming and wheeling over the chimney-pots. Effie and I heard those noises every day and night, but now every one was determined to be sinister.

'Sinister,' Eunice said, echoing my thoughts. 'That's the word for this house. It has a sinister atmosphere. Sorry, Effie. That's not nice, given that it's your home . . .'

Effie was at my elbow. 'That's all right, Eunice. I know what you mean. But, as I say, I've never lived anywhere else, so I wouldn't know what a . . . normal place feels like.'

'It feels like someone . . . brooding,' said Eunice. 'Making horrible plans and stewing over them. Plotting revenge . . .'

'My female relatives – the ones I knew – were never a happy bunch,' Eunice said, and bit her lip. I think she was starting to regret this night: maybe she felt she was letting them down, airing their woes on national television.

But nothing had happened. Not yet.

The next thing was the vigils. We were given walkie-talkies and told to sit and wait in the dark for unusual events. Effie and I were packed off to one of the book-lined rooms at the top of the house. Downstairs, the stars of the show were doing the same.

'Is that one of those orbs of floating light?' I asked. We were both perched on a saggy *chaise-longue* and I was squinting at what I thought might be a manifestation.

'You're just seeing stuff floating on your eye,' said Effie.

We seemed to sit there for hours, all tense. After what seemed like a lifetime we started a conversation in whispers. I wondered what was happening to the Green family, and where they had travelled to.

'Don't you think they should have gone home?' Effie said. I'd been given a little pen torch and swung it round to light her. She looked quite serious. 'Are you crazy?' I said. 'You saw what Frank the detective was like. The Elders of their village must be horrible. Anyone would want to run away.'

Effie did her sucked-lemon face. 'Don't you think they're better off with their own kind?'

'No,' I said. 'They were coerced into staying there. What could be good about that?'

'But they were . . . different. That girl had tentacles!'

'So what? Should we lock them up? Hide them away?'

'Perhaps,' whispered Effie.

I made a loud noise of disgust, not trusting myself to use words. Eventually I said, 'All the Greens want is an inconspicuous life in the real world. That's all anyone wants, isn't it?'

Effie shrugged and we fell quiet again. The tall old house creaked and settled around us. We'd both lost sight of what we were meant to be doing. My heart was pounding – with anger, rather than fear. 'The Greens were held back by their Elders, who thought that people outside of their village would never accept them. But . . . in the hundred years or so since the invasion, the world has become a better, more tolerant place, hasn't it? And the Greens think it will accept them for who they are.'

'Do you think so?' Effie asked. 'A girl with tentacles? A boy with a third eye?'

I remembered my conversation with Katherine Green, just before the family left. It had been along just these lines, and she had caught me unawares when she asked, 'This outside world accepts you, Brenda, does it not?'

I looked at her in shock. 'Pardon?'

She apologised swiftly. 'Forgive me,' she said. 'Forgive me for noticing . . . but you aren't quite a natural woman, are you?'

During that week the Greens and I had lived in close proximity. Katherine had seen me without my wig, glorious in all my scars. I was dumbfounded and scared by her quiet voice, but

I met her eye. She looked shocked, still, by what had transpired in my living room, and that her daughter had turned murderess to keep the family free. I believed I could trust her with one of my own secrets.

'You're right, Katherine. I'm not quite natural,' I'd said. 'I'm the only woman on earth who was not of woman born.'

She nodded, biting her lip, but didn't ask any more. Tact. I like that. It's a gracious attribute.

For some reason I didn't feel I could tell Effie as much as I had confided to that woman, the young mother of a fugitive family. I just don't trust her enough.

Now Effie was saying, 'Don't you think people should stay in the place they come from?' She gestured at the darkness. I had an impression of her hand flailing, but it was fiercely dark. Her movements reminded me that we were marooned up there, in the still of the night, waiting for horrible things to happen. 'This is where my people belong. All the women in my family, going back all those years. So . . . shouldn't I stay here to honour them?'

I shook my head. 'You don't understand anything – you haven't been anywhere or done anything—'

'Oh!' she broke in. 'And I suppose you've done and seen it all, Brenda. You're a regular international woman of mystery.'

'Perhaps,' I said. 'And, as far as you're concerned, that's how I'm going to stay. Who knows? Maybe you'd turn me in to the authorities or anyone who gave two hoots, given half a chance.'

'I don't want to know anything about you,' she spat back. 'I don't care who you really are or what horrible things you've done in your past. But I know there was something. Something you feel guilty about and ashamed of. You've got some kind of sordid past!'

At that moment there was a load of noise from the floor below us. It was a combination of several things: furniture crashing and creaking, shrieks from the production team – notably Lisa Turmoil who, as she had explained to me, had been promoted because of her talent for screaming. Then, it sounded as though something terrible was happening. The mélange of noise carried on for several heart-stopping moments and Effie had seized my sleeve with both claw-like hands. She kept tight hold of me.

But I was up on my feet. 'Come on!' I urged. 'It's all going on downstairs.' I had to virtually drag her along with me.

'Down there? We can't! Stay here! It can't get us here! Let it have them!'

'Effie,' I growled. 'We have to go down. We can't leave them with it, whatever it is. And I'm not afraid of spooks, are you?'

Underneath all the shouting and screaming, there was this awful, rumbling voice, huge and raucous, making itself heard above the hullabaloo. I knew it didn't belong to any of the crew, and I couldn't hear what it was saying to them, but I had to know. I had to get closer. My heart was pounding and my blood was racing through my ancient veins. Was it something really, truly supernatural?

'You're coming downstairs with me, lady!' I barked at Effie. 'You brought all this on. You wanted them raising spirits round your house. You're the one with the witchy relations. Have some courage, woman!'

Effie was almost hysterical. Her skinny body had seized up and she was gibbering. 'It's him! He's come back to torture us for sticking him in a hole in your garden! It's Frank! He's going to get us, Brenda!'

'Rubbish,' I snapped, and hauled her along bodily to the top of the stairs. I wasn't having any more of her nonsense. Of course it wasn't Frank. He couldn't have come back already, could he? And besides, that voice . . . that rumbling, terrible voice . . . It sounded more like . . .

'Be careful,' I told Effie sharply. 'You can't go thrashing about like that on the stairs. Come on. We shouldn't leave your visitors to fend for themselves . . .' My nails were digging into her thin arms. She came reluctantly after me to the next floor down. There, we could listen more closely to the abandoned shrieks and the clattering furniture.

'They're in Great Aunt Maud's old room,' Effie whispered, calmer now. She resisted less as I drew her towards the door. She was starting to tremble and moan.

Inside the room we found a scene of chaos. Tables, chairs and nightstands, undisturbed for years, had been turned over and scattered. Crazy shadows were flashing all over the place as the production team waved their torches, seemingly searching for something. Even among all the noise and mess, the cameraman and the sound engineer were keeping a tight hold on their clunky equipment. Eunice was on the bed, as if she was on a ship in a storm at sea, yelling at the top of her voice, with Lisa crouched by her, whimpering. After a few moments I worked out the focus of their attention. And whence that huge, booming voice was emanating.

Brain the psychic was standing in the centre of the room with his head flung back and his arms spread wide. A fierce seething of energies came off him and buffeted us back, preventing anyone from reaching him. Even more odd, he was hovering several feet off the ground.

'Oh,' said Effie, mildly. 'Blimey.'

'Join us, please,' bellowed Brian, without a trace of his Geordie accent.

'He's possessed,' Effie muttered. 'I've seen it before.'

'Don't be shy,' he intoned. 'You need to hear what I'm going to tell you.'

'Are you real?' Eunice was yelling, the sheets whipping up round her, and her hair hanging in tatters. 'Can you achieve a physical manifestation for us?'

'I wish that awful woman would be quiet,' said the voice speaking through Brian. 'She's been shouting at me for ages. Does she never listen?'

One of the production team – a bald, burly man called Steve – was glaring into a particular piece of equipment and shouting, 'Brian's body is completely blue on the heat register! His temperature's dropping right down! It'll kill him if—'

'Your psychic is quite safe,' Brian told them. 'I will make sure he survives this. He has done well. He has acted as the link between us.'

'Who are you?' Eunice shouted.

'I wish to talk to those two.' His hand shot out, isolating Effie and me, seemingly bathing us in a murky light in the sudden stillness of the room.

'Are you Maud?' Effie asked bravely.

Brian laughed for some time. 'Naturally you expect your forebears to return to you. And it's true that that brood of wicked harpies did come crowding round me. They appeared in their finery, fully expecting to manifest themselves before you. When they heard what you were planning here, Effryggia, they were pleased. They were glad to learn that you have not forgotten them.'

Effie was holding her breath. She nodded.

'You mustn't abandon their work,' Brian said hollowly. 'They have left you the texts. You must learn from them. There are reasons why you are here, in possession of all this knowledge. Do not ask me what they are. You can't know yet. But you have been retained here, Effryggia, for a purpose. It is why Brenda has been drawn here to live by your side.'

'What?' I couldn't believe what I was hearing. 'What are you saying? *Drawn here*?' Suddenly I was furiously indignant. 'I came of my own free will, I'll have you know.'

'Oh, yes?' said Brian.

'It's true. I've roamed around everywhere. Nowhere seemed right . . . and then this place . . .' Suddenly I saw that the night-vision cameras were trained on me. Everything was being recorded. I had to shut up. But I couldn't. Something about this visitation had got my hackles up. 'I chose what to do with my life. Where to live. Who to be. What I was going to become. Nobody else had a hand in it. No Fate, no god, no father or destiny. No one apart from me!'

'No one?' asked the voice, quieter now. Almost mocking.

'I have made my own life,' I said.

The voice was silent for a moment. Then it said, 'You have been led here. You are here at the behest of higher powers.'

'Higher powers?' cried Effie.

'Rubbish,' I said. 'Look, who are you, anyway, to talk to me like this?'

The voice chuckled. 'Haven't you realised, Brenda? Do you really not know who I am?'

My heart lurched, as if it was dropping free of its moorings. I felt nauseous suddenly, as people are reputed to do, in the presence of powerful spirits. 'No,' I said. 'I have no idea who you might be. I have no relations. No family. I recall no one who has passed over to the other side . . .' I spoke fiercely, determined to deny him.

'Think, Brenda. Think right back. Think hard, Brenda. Don't pretend to forget. You know me. You've known so many people. Think, Brenda. Remember me.'

'No!' I yelled. 'No!'

'Can you give us a name?' Eunice yelled, still struggling to stand against the waves of power. She was remembering her duty and what she usually did during these moments of communion. 'Please, tell us your name. Or even just an initial—'

'Silence,' said the voice. 'It isn't you I'm here for. And time is short. I won't waste my breath on you. Why should I want to be on television? Which spirit *would*? You people, these days,can think of nothing more exciting than being on your precious television, and you suppose mistakenly that all the dead must feel the same. As if, having been born too soon to experience TV, we must be ushered into your future as swiftly as possible, and make our appearances, fret, strut and take our bows. Well, I have no interest in appearing on your . . . cable channel.'

Brian waved his hand again, jerkily, and the camera crew jerked likewise, some of them crying out. 'He's wiped it! Everything's gone!' It was a magnetic wave, was what they said afterwards. No recordings of the night were intact. Brian's visitor hadn't left a single trace of himself.

'None of the dead I know would ever come to you,' he told the quivering team. 'Why do you suppose they would want to be

131

recorded, taped, transcribed and broadcast? What you are doing is futile. The only reason I came here tonight was to warn Effryggia and Brenda.'

I licked my dry lips. 'Warn us about what?'

'Your purpose,' he said. 'To guard the entrance to the Bitch's Maw. To watch over those souls exiled from hell.'

I hadn't a clue what he was on about. I supposed he was talking figuratively. Brian shook his head. 'I mean it. You will be watching over the damned. Some have already appeared in this town. They need to be taken care of.'

'Who . . . ?' But already suspicions were forming in my mind. 'What is . . . the Bitch's Maw?'

'You will find out soon enough,' he said. 'Hell is too busy. It's bursting at the seams. You must be here to catch them when they come spilling out . . .'

'But why?' I shouted. 'Why me?'

'Because *you* have no soul, daughter. *You* have nothing to lose.'

And then, suddenly, he was gone.

I found myself sitting on the dusty, threadbare carpet. I tried to collect my wits as Effie fussed about me, and the television crew gathered round Brian, who had sagged to the floor when the spirit had left him.

'He called me daughter,' I said. 'Did you hear him, Effie? He called me his *daughter* . . .'

There was no need to continue with the filming. The whole night's work had been ruined and dawn wasn't far off. Eunice and her crew had no option but to declare the project a disaster.

'They're gutted,' Lisa Turmoil told us, as we made our way

downstairs. 'Those were the most spectacular results they've ever had. We've never seen Brian as possessed as that. If only the equipment hadn't failed!'

Effie and I shrugged. What could we say? Myself, I was relieved that no record existed of the night's events. I had no desire to be on telly, glowing green in the night-vision, yelling at Brian.

I shuddered as we went down all the staircases to Effie's ground floor. I couldn't stop. I felt like we'd had a near miss. I felt like we had brushed past the Angel of Death, almost touching its wing tips. That was how I felt and, from their faces, I could see that the others felt the same. We had escaped some dreadful fate. We had dabbled with something best left alone, something bigger and nastier than any of us, and it had let us go. We were safe again.

Down in Effie's dusty shop a pale light was coming through the smudgy windows. Dawn was breaking over the bay. Brian still hadn't said a word in his natural voice to reassure us that he hadn't lost his marbles. He was just murmuring in a troubled way, and the crew had to half carry him out of the shop, into the street and my place, where they could put him to bed. After that Eunice dismissed them for the night to their beds at the Hotel Miramar up the hill. You could see the relief in their faces when they departed.

Us girls decided to retire to my front parlour for an early-morning nightcap.

'Look at us,' Effie chuckled, accepting a glass, 'drinking brandy at this time in the morning.'

'I think we've deserved it, don't you?' said Lisa, next to her on the chintz.

Eunice had pulled a heavy jumper over her skimpy catsuit and glugged back her brandy in one go.

'Are you okay?' Lisa asked me. 'The spirit – whoever he was – seemed to seize on you in particular.'

'He did,' I said, staring into my glass. 'And at first I thought I knew who it was. But now I'm not so sure.'

'He called you "daughter".'

'I had no father,' I said. 'Well. Hardly. It couldn't have been him. It simply couldn't. No . . . it was something horrible and wicked speaking through Brian. Something I'd rather forget.' I knocked back my drink, relishing its heat.

'It was a warning,' Effie piped up. 'That's what it was.'

'About messing with spirits?' asked Lisa.

Effie was looking pinched and worried. 'No. It was a warning about what's still to come. For Brenda and me. All that strange talk about the damned, and hell bursting at the seams. The voice suggested we had a role to play. And I believed it. I believe we're here for a reason, and we'll find out what it is before long.'

'I don't like talk of hell,' said Lisa. 'I don't like to believe in it.'

'I think it's closer than we know,' said Effie – Effryggia, as the spirit voice had called her. Effryggia, with her witchlike forebears and her books of arcane knowledge.

'I still don't like the thought of . . . being drawn here. I don't like the idea of predestination,' I said. I picked up the brandy bottle. Now it was completely light outside. 'I want my free will back,' I said. 'I just want my life to be still my own.'

Effie looked me in the eye. 'I don't think it is, Brenda. It never really was, was it?'

Chapter Four:

Murder at the Christmas Hotel

Things had been pretty strange lately. They were about to get a good deal stranger, nastier and more dangerous. Hurray!

I really hadn't settled there in search of excitement and adventures. I've already explained that what I really wanted was a quiet life and to keep my head down. Just recently, though, as autumn set in, it seemed that strangeness and mystery-filled adventures were purposely seeking me out.

Effie and I were about to learn that there was a reason for that.

A few days after the cast and crew of *Manifest Yourself!* had left our town, a bit shell-shocked and worse for wear, it seemed that everything had gone quiet and returned to relative normality. In the shop downstairs Leena asked if anything had happened during our television recording. Had the dead come back? She laughed. I'm afraid I was rather frosty with her. I didn't want to talk about it. I wanted distractions. I wanted pulling out of myself before I got gloomy and depressed. It was as if something in the terrible voice that Brian had channelled had filled me with doomy thoughts . . .

'Come on,' I told Effie. 'We're going out tonight. Let's get our gladrags on.'

Even though I suggested the pie-and-peas night at the Christmas Hotel, Effie agreed. She hadn't thought much of it last time, but I could see that she, too, wanted to be among noise and laughter. And those pensioners' nights were the rowdiest to be had round here.

Robert was waiting by his tureen of mulled wine, dressed as an elf as per usual. Effie and I let him take our outdoor things and I asked after his aunt.

'She's better than she was,' he admitted. 'More human, at least.'

Effie tutted quietly, as if Robert had said something awful.

'But there's something else, isn't there?' I asked. I could tell by the look on his face.

'It's this place,' he said. 'There's something going on here. Bad stuff. Jessie won't stop talking about it—'

'Ladies!' We were interrupted by the proprietress bursting through the doors into the foyer. Resplendent in her wheelchair, she seemed more triumphantly festive than ever. The elves who pushed her looked even more slavish and ground down. 'I knew we'd soon have you as regulars.' Mrs Claus cackled. 'People get addicted, don't they? They can't resist the good cheer and excellent fayre we offer. Welcome! Welcome!'

She was wheeled through the swing doors into the main dining hall, where carols were ringing out and the excited hubbub of a hundred or so pensioners greeted her.

'Try as I might, I just can't stick that woman.' Effie sighed. She glared at Robert. 'How do you elves put up with her?'

'There isn't much choice, really. Who else would employ us?'

He came with us into the dining hall to show us to a table. It was only then that I realised the felt holly leaves and berries on his tight-fitting green pants were meant as a Christmassy fig leaf.

All around us, at the other tables, pensioners were munching heartily, gravy dribbling down their chins. Effie was disgusted. 'Have they lost their manners? Have they gone feral?' As they ate, some were mumbling along with a sickly version of 'Winter Wonderland' playing over the speakers.

Once we were settled on our usual table and glancing through the menu, which offered little more than pie-and-peas, Robert bent close to my ear and whispered, 'Can I meet you for a quick word later on?'

I saw Effie's ears prick up. 'Of course,' I said. 'Is it about your aunt?'

'Something else,' he said. 'About this place.' He looked very shifty now. 'Elves are disappearing.'

The pies were even more delicious than they had been last time. The hotel must have changed its supplier. They were thick and golden-crusted, suety and hot, devoid of the annoyingly cavernous pockets of air that ruin most modern pies. Even Effie was uncomplaining about the food that evening.

As ever, there was widespread geriatric jollity at the Christmas Hotel – the popping of crackers and rustling of party hats, the wheezing cackles and the tinkle of fork tines against false teeth. Holding court over all, Mrs Claus sat at High Table, tucking into what appeared to be four of her pies and a mound of mushy peas.

The woman was gargantuan. Her eyes gleamed with delight at all she surveyed.

'Gloop.' Jessie was at our side, bringing dessert wines and menus. She was standing a little straighter and had shaved. Her 'gloop' – right in my ear – was one of the most melancholy sounds I have ever heard.

'Did you? Did you eat? Did you eat everything?' she asked. I was pleased that she was getting the hang of human language again. Effie looked miffed that she was thrusting her face at us and asking questions, but she had never been fond of Jessie.

'We had the lovely pies,' I said.

'Oh. Oh dear. Oh dear me.' Jessie took our plates and loped off.

We watched her go. 'Maybe there's a spell in one of those old books of magic in your house,' I said thoughtfully, 'and you could turn her back to normal.'

Effie tutted. 'I very much doubt it.' She can look proper toffee-nosed when she wants to. 'Anyway, she's better like that. She could be very boastful before, when she was glamorous.'

'I think I'll pop out before the bingo begins,' I said, struggling up, 'and powder myself.'

'Your *nose*, Brenda,' sighed Effie. 'And hurry back. If they start without you I won't do your books. I can't keep up with them all. They call the numbers too fast.'

I ambled and shimmied my way back to the main entrance. Now I was being furtive and spylike in my new print frock. I'd put it on especially for my night out and I was afraid it made me look frumpy, matronly. But I had to meet an elf on secret business.

Robert waved me into the coffee lounge. It was gloomy and

neglected, compared with all the noise and life elsewhere. The room was filled mostly with chairs arranged in a circle round a tall fireplace. A hefty china pig sat on the mantelpiece with a curious expression. I had the oddest feeling it was listening in on us.

'She's giving us something to control us. Haven't you noticed how docile the elves are? We're like her slaves.' The words came bursting out of him. Evidently he had been bottling them up for days.

'What?' I gasped. 'Who? What's she giving you?'

He paced around on the threadbare monogrammed carpet, running a hand through his cropped hair. 'I don't know what it is. Some awful drug to make us submissive and biddable. She's slipping it into our cocoa or our booze. I don't know. No, it's the cocoa. Definitely.'

'Mrs Claus?' I said. I shivered. I wouldn't have put it past her. I thought of the elves who pushed her about in her wheelchair and attended to her every need. They were strapping lads, every one of them, but their expressions were placid and unnaturally cheerful.

'I've only just become aware of this in the past few days,' Robert said. 'Until then I was as drugged as the rest of them. I just couldn't see what she was up to.'

'How did you work it out?' I glanced at the pot pig on the mantelpiece, its face screwed up in concentration. Could it be bugged?

'I'd missed a few nights in a row,' he said. 'We're given our night-time cocoa in the kitchens – it's a ritual. Everyone has to have cocoa at eleven, even those of us who can't bear it.'

'I see,' I said. 'I suppose it helps you sleep.' I imagined Mrs

Claus pouring it into mugs held by a line of tired Christmas elves. 'I wonder what she puts in it.'

'Something to pacify us,' he said. 'Something to dull us to the rigours of being continuously filled with Christmas cheer.' He shuddered. 'Because I've managed to duck out of the cocoa ritual, I've become aware of what everyone's like. It's a nightmare here. It's like being mad. I've had this slowly dawning realisation that, among all the tinsel and streamers, everyone, but everyone, is completely bonkers . . .'

I put on my best figuring-it-all-out face. I was so pleased that Robert had thought to bring his problems to me. I was determined to do my best for him. 'So why did you miss out on the drugged cocoa, these past few nights?'

'Ah,' he said. 'I've been slipping out into the town in the hour before midnight.'

'Oh,' I said. 'Is that not allowed?'

He looked scandalised. 'There's a curfew on all of us at the hotel. We have to be in for the night, every night. No one out after eleven, by order of Mrs Claus. She tells us that Whitby is a weird town, teeming with demons, and that we wouldn't be safe out there. And we believe her! She drugs us and we believe every word she says!'

'But it's nonsense,' I said. 'True, there are some strange goings-on, especially recently, but it's nothing like she says. Why, me and Effie have been out late quite a lot – whenever we fancy it. Just the other night we were making a TV programme all the way through the night until dawn!' I was showing off for this bright young boy, and I knew it.

'I always thought she was lying,' he said. 'This curfew is just an extension of her determination to control everyone. Mrs

Claus wants to be in command of everything her staff get up to. She was furious when Auntie Jessie rejuvenated herself without permission. So, anyway, I started sneaking out in the night, and hoped that my absence in the cocoa line wouldn't be noticed.'

'Good for you,' I said. 'Sneaking out to do what?'

'Oh . . .' he said. 'Just running about the town, mostly.'

I chuckled. 'Do you mean running after fellas?'

Robert coloured. 'Okay. I do. I was getting up to naughty stuff. And it felt gloriously rebellious and liberating. Especially when I thought of all the other elves, tucked up in their beds before midnight. Sleeping deeply, ready to wake at dawn for yet another Christmas Eve, starting all over again . . . And, meanwhile, there was I, out on the sands where the sea had been, being rude in the dunes with complete strangers.' He looked like he expected me to be shocked.

'It sounds thrilling,' I said. 'Rude in the dunes, indeed.' I think he'd imagined me to be a good deal more prim, like the elderly B-and-B lady I apparently am. But I've seen far too much of life to be shocked by anything, let alone the various rudenesses of men.

Robert laughed at himself. 'Anyway. Maybe it was the stiff, salty air, the sleeplessness or just the shock of good sex, I didn't know at first . . . but I returned to the hotel refreshed and with all my senses sharpened. And I didn't like what I saw. The whole place is rotten and dirty, Brenda. The decorations have been up for years. Everything is fly-blown and mothbally. There's an air of corruption about the place . . .'

'What do you want me to do?' I asked.

Even through the walls we could hear the boom and crackle of the microphone. It was bingo time in the dining hall. Effie would be cursing me, spending so long powdering my nose, leaving her to check all the books.

Robert smiled, pleased that I wanted to help. 'You see, these suspicions and half-formed thoughts had been swirling about in my head for a number of days. I didn't know if I was imagining things or not. And I felt weird, too, with sleeping so little and having to work so hard for the pittance she pays us . . . But then one night, at the end of last week, I bumped into Martin in the dunes.'

'Martin?'

'Another elf. He'd sneaked out too. He wasn't surprised to see me there, among the scrubby grass. It's where all the fellas from town go lurking and cruising, looking for a bit of action.'

Action! Robert's story was certainly an eye-opener. Wait till Effie heard all this!

'It was odd, bumping into a fellow elf, in that night-time place of freedom, badness and revelry. I knew it was him straight away. And he said exactly what I've been telling you. About the cocoa and the drugs. And the way we're made to feel contin- uously cheery and Christmassy against our will. He'd formed the same suspicions as I had.'

I imagined them confessing their outlandish ideas to each other, under the moonlight, on the dunes, like creatures out of *A Midsummer Night's Dream*, frolicking about, limbs entangled, as they whispered their paranoid thoughts.

'The thing is,' he said, 'Martin's gone. He vanished at the weekend. At first he wasn't there at breakfast on Sunday morning. I went to check his dorm, up in the attic. None of his pals had seen him since the previous day. And he isn't the first elf to go missing in recent weeks. It's five altogether.'

'Five!'

'Mrs Claus won't call in the police. They haven't disappeared, she says. She shrugs those monstrous shoulders and grins. What can she do? Her elf workers are so flighty. They come and they go. Will-o'-the-wisps. She's been let down before by them. This is how it goes.' Robert was growing agitated. 'The truth is, she's got runaways here. Illegal immigrants. Kids who've left home and not told anyone where they are. Anything could happen to them. Anything, Brenda!'

I nodded resolutely. 'We'll help, Effie and I.'

'Good,' he said. 'I knew you would. You're just the person we need. Someone who can deal with this . . . strange kind of stuff.'

'Honestly, Brenda! And you actually sat there and listened to all of his nonsense? But I shouldn't be surprised. You're always being taken in by people. You're too soft, you are.'

Effie was just vexed because she'd come close to winning the big prize. Just one number left. Pipped at the post by someone called Big Sue, who was wearing a woollen hat indoors and whooped like crazy when her number came up. Effie had pursed her lips and slowly, calmly, ripped her bingo books into the tiniest pieces. Confetti all over our table. 'I never win anything,' she moaned. 'Even when I thought I was having a TV show made about me it had to go to the bad, didn't it?' She looked at me as if that had been my fault.

As we walked home along the dusky, windswept prom, I was in no mood for one of her nasty tempers. She'd be sniping all night if I didn't pull her out of it. 'Well, I believe him. Robert's a sincere young man.'

'Brenda, dear!' Effie crowed. 'Listen to what he was telling you. He was saying all kinds of unrepeatably disgusting things that you, nevertheless, saw fit to repeat to me. He was telling you that he habitually runs about the sand dunes in the evenings, looking for like-minded men to – to do terrible things with.'

I had to laugh at that. 'Terrible things? Really, Effie! You're so prim sometimes. He's young. Let him have his fun. He's only talking about sex—'

'Ssssh!' hissed Effie, though there was no one to hear us. 'I've never heard anything so disgusting. This is a family tourist destination, Brenda.' She clutched her handbag tighter under her bosom, as if even the mention of such things might summon up hordes of lawless, lascivious men, clambering up the cliff face and on to the prom. 'Anyway,' she went on, 'drugs, indeed! Yes, I imagine that drug-taking does go on among the younger staff members at the Christmas Hotel. But I don't for one moment imagine that narcotics are administered with their nightly cocoa. I've never heard the like.'

I sighed. 'You must admit, Effie, that Mrs Claus, as she calls herself, can't be quite right in the head.'

'Who am I to say? She's certainly eccentric. As I say, I personally can't stick her. But I'm sure she'd never harm anyone.'

But there was something in that woman's huge, jolly, red-veined face that unnerved me. She was like a ripe Christmas apple past its best: shiny on the outside, but all wormy and cankered within. I didn't share that thought with Effie.

We bade each other good night outside Effie's shop. I watched her lock herself indoors, imagining her shut up in there for the night with all her ancient junk and her arcane books. I wondered vaguely if, since the TV crew's visit, she had attempted to penetrate the mysterious texts left to her by her female forebears.

I assumed that was precisely what she was doing. I pictured her sitting up each night by candlelight, devouring Wiccan lore, dabbling with forces best left alone. Well, good luck to her. From the sound of it, we could do with some extra powers at our disposal.

I hauled myself wearily up the stairs to my luxurious attic. No guests this week. I could languish, spread out and ponder recent events.

In a way, Effie was right to resist being drawn into Robert the elf's concerns. It was too soon for us to plunge into another mystery. I was still dealing with the shock and repercussions of our last bizarre affair. I could still hear that voice booming out of Brian, the psychic Geordie. Talking about our destiny. Our duty. About hell bursting open and filling our town with . . . what? The damned? Demons we would have to deal with?

What fitted Effie and me for such a task?

But then I had the answer. Effie had magic and good sense at her fingertips. And I was unnatural. Soulless. Strong and good-hearted – I *am* good-hearted, even though I was made a monster. I wish the best for those I meet in this world.

Is that enough for dealing with the damned?

Before going to bed I had some hot milk and flipped through the lunchtime post, which I hadn't yet had a chance to examine. Among the junky flotsam there was a letter in a Jiffy-bag from Lisa Turmoil. It was chatty and sweet. She hoped to return to my B-and-B some time with her boyfriend for a weekend break, rather than on business. The crew of *Manifest Yourself!* were back at work, keeping awake at night and scrutinising the swarming darkness in chilly castles and old pubs, with small, unspectacular results. There had been nothing like what had made itself apparent in Effie's house. They couldn't hope for that kind of success again.

As all their recordings had been ruined, there wouldn't be a show about Effie's house. I would never be seen on TV, shouting like a madwoman. Except . . . one recording *did* exist. Lisa, she explained, in her tiny, neat writing, had recorded the weird encounter at the climax of that night on her mobile phone. For some reason it had survived.

She had sent it to me on the enclosed disk, which I fished out and took to my kitchen stereo. Bless Lisa. She could have gone straight to Eunice and the film crew with it. She could have exploited it. But she wanted me to have it. She wrote that she thought I needed to hear it. I should listen very carefully to what had been said, in the heat of the moment, during the still watches of that night last week.

I played the disk with the sound turned up. Those voices rang out. Mine, all crazy and distraught. And Father's. Welling up out of the distant past. Reverberating from the broad chest of Brian the psychic, filling his mind, blocking out all rational thought. Here came that voice again, coaxing me, cajoling me, telling me what was to come.

I listened to it several times.

Then I dashed to the sink. I was heaving and retching, and before I knew it I had thrown up everything I'd eaten that night. Pie, peas, the lot.

Strange thing was, Effie told me the next morning that she had done almost exactly the same. She put it more delicately than I did, of course, but she intimated to me, as we walked across town for morning coffee, that her stomach had given her gyp in the night. Like me, she had been hunched over the sink and the toilet. She had thrown up until nothing was left inside her, then lay about moaning, feeling wrung out and anguished, just as I had.

We crossed the river and made for the Walrus and the Carpenter, drawing in deep, calming lungfuls of clean sea air.

'Something disagreed with us,' she said, whey-faced and grim. An idea seized her. 'Those pies! We said we thought they were different. A new supplier!'

'Or the dessert wine,' I said. 'We put away a couple of bottles, you know.'

'Did we?' Effie frowned. 'I'm drinking more on these evenings with you, Brenda.'

I glanced at her sideways. I'm not a big drinker and I think she was using me as an excuse. Often I've smelt sherry on her breath in the afternoon. She could be getting through untold amounts in that house of hers.

Cling, cling, went the little bells on the door of our café, which we found almost empty. The tourist season was well and truly finished and you only ever saw regulars and locals about the place now. We settled into our corner seats and asked for mint tea.

'That's the last time we go to one of their bingo nights,' Effie said. 'Something poisoned our systems and we're not going back for more.'

'Robert was saying—'

'Oh, not him again.'

'He was saying how he'd suddenly realised it was dirty. Under all the decorations, it's all dust and decay. It struck him when he'd missed his drugged cocoa.'

Effie rolled her eyes, flipping through the morning paper.

I seized her wrist. 'Effie! Perhaps we were drugged, too, and it made us sick!'

'I think it was probably the filth.' She shuddered. 'I wish you hadn't told me that. Or that nasty gossip about elves rolling around in the sand dunes. *And* they have a monkey waitress.'

'Poor Jessie,' I said. 'Don't be nasty about her.'

'I wasn't,' said Effie, turning pages carefully. 'I was just pointing out. Her hygiene must have suffered as a result of her misfortunes.'

The door went *cling, cling* again, and a tall man in a dark suit came in. He was middle-aged and very handsome, I thought. There was something very proper and dignified about him. We only saw him from the back, but it was enough to form a pleasing impression, as he went up to the waitress and asked – in a deep, cultured voice – whether he was allowed to smoke in this establishment. The young waitress gazed up into his eyes and seemed to go weak, judging by her stammer as she told him he'd have to sit in the smoking parlour downstairs. 'Thank you,' purred the tall, dark man, and popped down the rickety wooden staircase.

I glanced at Effie and saw that she was drinking him in, too. 'I might have to visit the ladies',' she said, 'and take another look at him.'

I was surprised. It wasn't like Effie to be so forward.

But he was a fascinating man. Compelling.

Effie slurped the green mint tea. Her digestive complaint was forgotten. There was something avid about her expression.

*

The male of the species was a topic that Effie and I hadn't discussed a great deal. Effie once claimed that she had 'never quite got the hang of them'. She found them mostly brutal and dull-witted. She didn't like their company, she said. She found women more insightful and *simpatico*.

But Effie never really talks about love. She wasn't describing, in our scant conversations about men, passion, desire or being drawn into someone's romantic orbit. She was talking about minds, thoughts and words. She was talking about who she would rather talk to and spend her waking hours with. And, in that sense, her sympathies were with women. She liked women's intuition, their sometimes callous grasp of the real conditions of living. She liked the way that women can and will dissect everything. They claw at language till they make themselves and each other understand. They toy with nuances and shadings of meaning. No man had ever done that around Effie. Men, in Effie's book, were taciturn, plain-speaking.

But I wasn't really talking about the intellect. Or meaning. And I wasn't talking about who you spend your waking hours with.

I meant, rather, the darkest bits of the nights and who you spend that time with. And I still didn't feel close enough to Effie to broach that topic. Not at all, in fact. It seemed impertinent to ask whether she had any time for men then.

I have uses for them still. Though I doubt – I truly doubt – that anyone would look my way now.

In the past they had. Some of them good men, others wicked. A few were wicked in quite a good way . . .

I have my hankerings now and then, but I've had to give it all up. All that sexy, terrible business. I've taken myself out of the game. Declared myself null and void. I've torn up my dance card, shredded it into sugar-paper fragments, as Effie had our bingo books. I was missing that final number, too. I was never lucky in the end.

Given my unnatural longevity, it seems as though an army of lovers has paraded through my life. Usually I keep mum. I don't want to seem vulgar. And only a few of my paramours stand out. Only a few could make my tree-trunk leg quiver, or my second-hand heart skip a beat.

Enough. It doesn't do to dwell on my romantic past.

Sometimes, though . . . Sometimes I think about my moments of conquest, those nights when all that mattered was my lover and me and what we'd get up to together. I remember how I would crush those men beneath me. They loved that! As I rolled on to and squashed them with my pillowy vastness, I conquered them all. I took them into the huge fortress of myself and some of them came willingly to be imprisoned where they could learn my secrets for themselves.

Most were horrified when they knew the truth of me. It wasn't many who learned it all, and few of even that select group could cope with the facts. That disappointed me. I was a gargantuan slave mistress, and they felt I had locked them away in a castle of hideous secrets. They clawed the walls and tried to escape. They were caught in a nightmare with me: the nightmare of my life. I cooled their fevered brows as they tossed and turned, but they wanted to be free, I knew.

No mortal man was ever brave or strong enough for me.

All of them let me down.

And I am doomed to be alone. After all this time, I know that. It's taken me long enough to learn my lesson. But we go on hoping, don't we?

The trembling ghosts of my lovers are walled up inside me, plastered securely behind walls in hidden recesses in the deep, deep cellars of my mind. Cellars I try not to visit. There, though, I remember them. Each and every one. The tall ones, the noble ones, the midgets and freaks, the fat men and robbers, the heroes and saints, the dullards, the perverts, the mercenaries and kings. I've had my share, I really have.

But I try not to dwell on things like that. Getting myself all stirred up. I'm an old woman now, and my glory days are in the past.

What started me on all of this?

Ah, yes: Effie catching a glimpse of that gorgeous man.

She nipped downstairs to the damp smoking parlour in the Walrus and the Carpenter and went into the loo, even though the cubicle made her claustrophobic.

She came back all of a swoon. 'I got a good look at him, Brenda,' she said. 'He smiled at me. Can you believe it? He looked up, nodded and gave me this smile, as if . . .' she shivered '. . . as if he already knew me. Inside and out.'

I'd thought that evening was going to be quiet. Still feeling delicate, I ate a light supper and sat quietly, listening to the radio, mulling over the recent days. Effie had invited me round to help her go through some of her books of magic, but I hadn't fancied it. She was systematically examining and cataloguing them, which I thought was a good idea, but I couldn't face it that night. I think, for the first time in her life, she was feeling a bit nervous alone in her house.

I dozed in my armchair. The fruity voice that came on the radio between long, stately pieces of music laced through my dreams. At times it merged with the echo of that disembodied voice on the disk Lisa Turmoil had sent me and I thought spirits were speaking to me through Radio 3. I woke up suddenly, disturbed, and heard my phone ringing.

'Sorry about this at nearly midnight,' Robert said. 'I thought you needed to know. It's my aunt.'

'Jessie?' I was fuddled and woozy, but I knew immediately that something terrible had happened.

'She's gone,' he said. He sounded shattered.

'Dead?'

'No, no,' he said. I could hear the noise of the fairground behind him. Evidently he had slipped out of the hotel to make the call. 'Vanished. With all her belongings.'

We both knew that Jessie was in no fit state – mentally or physically – to dash off anywhere. And she certainly wouldn't have gone without telling Robert first. He was her minder.

'She was saying some very strange things,' Robert continued, 'before she . . . went. Making accusations.'

'Against whom?'

'I'd rather not say on the phone.' He was distraught now. 'Could you meet me, Brenda?'

'Now?' I glanced at the clock on the sideboard. It was almost dead on midnight.

'I'm sorry about this. I would never ask if—'

'It's quite all right.' We made a quick arrangement to meet on the prom and, next thing I knew, I was pulling on a thick sweater, heavy boots and a suitable hat. Then I rang Effie to let her know what was going on.

She surprised me. 'You're not traipsing around on your own with that boy,' she said. 'Give me a moment. I'm coming with you. I was never going to sleep tonight – not after the disturbing things I've glimpsed in those horrible books . . .'

I met her outside her darkened shop. She was wrapped up in her camel coat, a huge scarf looped about her neck. We walked together down to the sea. 'I wish I'd never even started looking into them,' she said. 'I'd have been quite happy in my ignorance, not knowing what nasty stuff I had tucked away on my shelves.'

I shivered in the sea mist. The cobbles underfoot were freezing over and we had to tread carefully. 'What kind of thing did you find?'

'I thought it would just be old spells. Herbology and all that. But there's all this disturbing stuff about ancient gods and monsters . . . and nasty drawings of them, lizardy things, creatures that look as if they come from the depths of the sea. And apparently they're behind the scenes of everything we do. They send misfortune and demons to us. They hate us and want to destroy us.'

'No wonder you're having sleepless nights.' I looked at her anxious face. 'Maybe you should leave it alone for a bit.'

She shook her head. 'There's information that I think we're going to need some day soon. We have to be prepared as best we can. Those books aren't just nonsense. I believe – I'm starting to believe that everything in them is based on the truth.'

Now we were on the prom where packs of boozers and late-night revellers were still drifting about, turning home for their beds. We spotted Robert standing alone by the railings, opposite Woolworths.

'I can't believe we're joining him on one of his nocturnal jaunts,' said Effie.

'Now then,' I said. 'Remember, he's lost his aunt. She's his only living relation.'

When we walked up to him he surprised me by clasping me in a bear-hug, then kissing my cheek. No one has done that for years. I was touched, feeling myself blush as he turned awkwardly to Effie, nodded and said good evening.

We walked along together slowly.

'What were the accusations she was making?' I asked.

'They were against Mrs Claus,' he said. 'Nobody's supposed to criticise her. She's perfect and beyond reproach. That's what all of her docile staff understand. But Jessie has been wayward recently. As you know, she's not been herself since all that business at the Deadly Boutique. The process she underwent there seemed to regress her to a more instinctual, impulsive personality . . .'

'Indeed,' said Effie. 'She—'

I nudged her, knowing that she was about to say something insulting.

Robert went on: 'Jessie no longer fitted in at the Christmas Hotel. She wasn't submissive and obedient. She didn't kowtow like the rest of them to our monstrous proprietress. She didn't toady round the guests either. She became temperamental, and flew into rages when she felt herself overworked and anyone asked her to do something extra. In the kitchens she threw tantrums – even Mr McFee, the chef, was alarmed. Then, when she was doing chambermaid duties, she trashed the room of some woman who'd spoken sharply to her at dinner the night before.'

'Oh dear,' I said. 'I thought Jessie enjoyed her work.'

'She used to,' he said. 'But whatever Mr Danby did to her in his Deadly Machine changed her irrevocably.'

Lovely vocabulary he had, that boy. I couldn't help admiring it as we strode along in the dark.

'Well,' he went on, 'all of this soon came to the attention of Mrs Claus. I was aware that my auntie had been summoned for private meetings in Mrs Claus's chambers several times in the past fortnight. This was serious. Everyone dreads the thought of being called to her boudoir. But Jessie didn't care. She had become fearless! She had been a bit nervy before, though you'd never see it if you didn't know her well. She put on a good front. But her recent transformation – disastrous for her looks – had improved her confidence no end. Funny, that.'

'Indeed,' said Effie. 'What about the accusations?'

Robert stopped. We were at the bottom of the steep hill that led up to the row of hotels that terminated in the Christmas Hotel, the grandest and oldest of them all. We stared up at its pale front, then across the bay to the rocks and the abbey. 'I've had just about enough of this town,' he said. 'First, my auntie gets made over at some dodgy boutique until she's almost dead! And now this! Vanished!' My heart went out to him. He seemed about to cry. I could sense that Effie was embarrassed and impatient. 'This is an evil town,' Robert said quietly. 'There's something wicked here. A brooding presence behind the scenes, watching over us and laughing at us all . . .'

I caught Effie's eye as Robert fell silent and, in that moment, we acknowledged that this boy – a humble elf from the Christmas Hotel – was right.

'And the accusations?' Effie prompted gently.

'Hm?' He turned back from staring at the stark abbey and the roiling clouds over the sea. 'She said she knew where the disappearing elves had gone, Martin and the others. She had proof, she said. She went round telling everyone. She came to me first with her suspicions. I was shocked and laughed. I thought it was too ridiculous. I told her to watch out, she'd get herself into hot bother, casting aspersions like that. I'm sure it was legally actionable, the stuff she went round saying about Mrs Claus. You know the way she talked, since her regression? She said: "They're dead. They're dead and disposed of. They're dead and hanging up in the cold meat lockers. Gloooop. I've seen them. I've seen them down there. I've seen Mrs Claus and that wicked Chef McFee. Glooop! Making them. Making them into. Making and baking them into pies!"'

Effie gave a little shriek of horror.

But I had already guessed what was coming. It had to be that. I struggled hard to keep my composure, to marshal my thoughts, to string a sentence together that would refute the possibility of cannibalism at the Christmas Hotel. But my mind had gone as blank as the cloud-obscured sky.

I heard Effie make some peculiar noises as she tried to bring herself under control. 'It's nonsense,' she said. 'It has to be.'

Robert shrugged solemnly. 'How can you be so sure? We don't want it to be true. Of course we'd rather it was impossible. But we don't know that, do we? It seems that anything is possible here. Any horrible, nasty thing . . .'

I plunged my hands into my pockets and took a deep breath to stop my insides quivering. Action: that's what was required. 'There's only one thing we can do,' I said.

Both of them stared at me. Suddenly I felt like the leader of our little gang. All my innards were doing somersaults. At one level I was being sensible and decisive, at another I was thinking about golden pastry, thick gravy and glistening meat . . .

'We have to break into the kitchens. We need to see those meat lockers for ourselves.'

Effie's mouth dropped open. 'Can't we just call the police?'

'They won't do anything,' Robert said. 'I reported my aunt's disappearance, but they weren't interested. I explained her curious condition and state of health, but they said she might have gone off on a little holiday. I think they're scared of Mrs Claus. Like everyone else in this town. That's how the old monster gets her own way. When I told the police where Jessie and I worked, the desk sergeant shivered. One thing was certain: he wasn't keen to go investigating things up at the Christmas Hotel.'

'I must say,' said Effie, 'I'm not terribly keen myself.' The poor thing was looking green. 'But we have to, don't we? No one else will. Poor old Jessie won't just have wandered off. Something must have happened. Something bad.'

I was glad she had decided to be practical and determined. I knew that both of us were teetering on the brink of the screaming ab-dabs.

Before we could change our minds, we set off up the hill to the hotel.

We walked into the close at the back of the row and the moon came out, glowing on the white buildings. They looked like they were made of bone. Every window was dark, sightless. It was strange to think of the hundreds sleeping there, in those hotels, that night, yet it was so incredibly quiet. Dutifully, all the guests had had an early night. The omnipresent will of Mrs Claus could be felt in that weighty silence. I wondered that I had never felt it before, under the false jollity and glee at the Christmas Hotel.

Robert had his own keys. I'm sure he shouldn't have had such a comprehensive bundle in his capacity as a lowly elf. But he was used to sneaking about at night without leave. Effie and I snuck down the stone stairs behind him into the small kitchen yard, which was stacked with crates, bins and empty bottles. Nothing out of the ordinary or very sinister. Not yet, anyway.

We listened to Robert jangle the keys, finding the right one, and held our breath.

I couldn't have asked for two braver, more stalwart companions. They kept absolutely quiet, Robert in front, Effie bringing up the rear, as we crept into Chef McFee's gleaming domain. Even with only a few pools of milky light to see by, I could tell that his kitchen was immaculate. Every stainless-steel surface was free of grease and crumbs; everything had been wiped and disinfected within an inch of its life. I was pleased to see that the slapdash, cheery mess above wasn't mirrored down here. Moonlight glinted off the pots and pans, and the evil-looking armoury of knives.

'Hadn't we better arm ourselves?' said Effie, thoughtfully, eyeing them.

I was shocked. 'I refuse to carry weapons,' I said, 'whatever the situation.' Now I sounded prim.

Ever the pragmatist, Effie picked up a carving knife, and slipped it into her handbag. 'We have to be prepared for any eventuality,' she mumbled.

I couldn't see her stabbing anyone. Nevertheless, I think she had reached the age when she felt that she could do anything: there was nothing she couldn't get away with – she'd say she was doo-lally and plead diminished responsibility. Or she'd look so respectable and proper in the dock that the judge would be sure to let her off.

That made her seem rather dangerous.

Robert waved us across the slippery tiled floor. 'We have to open it very carefully – I don't know how noisy it is.'

Before us was a tall, solid steel door with a wheel on the front. We might have been robbing a bank and this was the safe where the gold bullion was kept. Robert stepped up and grasped the wheel with both hands. We all braced ourselves, flinching, ready for a shrieking noise to rip through the air, or even an alarm to go off – something, at any rate, to bring our enemies running . . .

Robert winced, and inched the wheel round anti-clockwise. Luckily, it slid smoothly, soundlessly. Effie was gripping my upper arm, and she was starting to pinch.

'I've done it,' Robert whispered.

'You've unlocked it?'

In answer, he stood back and the heavy door swung open – just a couple of feet but we felt the chill immediately. It was as if all the warmth and living moisture in the air had been sucked instantaneously into that fearsomely dark maw. The cold was terrifying. It burned my nose and throat as I tried to breathe quietly and not to choke or panic.

We were going to have to climb inside that cave of ice. We knew how big these freezer lockers were. They went back and back and back. To know for sure, and to prove or disprove what we hoped to, here, tonight, we were going to have to clamber into that frosty blue cavern.

Robert had a pen torch, which he trained into the dark hole. We crowded in and glimpsed heavy forms hanging from savage hooks. They were pigs and sheep, surely, opened and gutted, dangling there submissively. They were like tree-trunks in a frozen forest of the dead. Robert stepped in and we followed him. The frost crunched underfoot: the loudest noise in the place.

'For Gawd's sake, Effie,' I said. 'Don't let that door slam shut on us.'

She made a disparaging pshaw noise in response, but I knew we were all imagining being locked inside it. Would we run out of oxygen before we froze? I wasn't sure. I knew that, with my singular biology, I would survive longer in the cold than my companions, which was of little consolation. Freakish to the last, I would have to watch them die, unable to save them.

Enough of these morbid thoughts, I told myself. I had to stay focused. It was like walking a tightrope, braced between my two best friends in Whitby, advancing deeper into the meat locker, dodging and slipping and veering between the pendulous bodies of pigs, sheep and who knew what else. Even I – resilient as I am – felt my lips turning blue and crystals of ice forming on my eyelashes. That journey, inch by inch in that hellish place, felt as if it would last for ever – until suddenly Robert, ahead, held up his hand. We stopped. We held our breath.

'What?' hissed Effie, wriggling round to peer over my shoulder. We were too confined and she could see hardly anything. I was pressed against a frozen body, which felt like stone against the side of my face.

'We've reached the back wall,' whispered Robert, sweeping the narrow beam of his torch about the place, seeking out the corners of the steel walls, fixing the parameters of our prison. 'There's nothing here,' he said, with relief in his hushed voice. 'Just dead animals.'

'Hmm,' said Effie, evidently relieved too.

'Let's get out,' Robert said. 'We've checked it. Jessie was wrong, thank God. Now we can go . . .' He turned round, twisting awkwardly in the confined space, and that was when his foot connected with the crates lined on the floor against the back wall. He had missed them with his torch just as, presumably, he – or any other interloper – was meant to. 'Oh,' he said, and I heard the dread in that single syllable. 'Boxes. Down here.' He crouched.

'Boxes?' said Effie. 'What size? Hm? Are we talking hatboxes? Shoeboxes?'

'Bigger,' said Robert. He reached forward to check if the lids were nailed down. I bustled to his side, still holding my breath.

'How many?' said Effie. 'What kind of boxes? You still haven't said.'

I turned to shush her: her voice was rising in pitch and volume.

'Don't you shush me, madam!' she said, even louder. Tell me, Robert! What have you found? What size boxes?'

'Coffin-sized,' he said dully. Then came the sudden rending noise of wood splintering and cracking. Frozen wood breaking apart in someone's hands as they struggled to lift a lid.

'What?' Effie cried, pummelling my back to be let through. She wanted to yank me aside, and Robert too, to find out what we could both see as he shone the torch at the box in front of us. 'What is it?' Effie almost shrieked in my ear.

I let her through. I didn't want to. I wanted to protect her. I wanted to save her the sight. She didn't have to see it. Robert's and my witness was enough. But Effie is always headstrong. She wanted to see for herself. And I was frozen there, in below-zero shock and awe, at the sight of poor Jessie's placid, simian face, gazing up at us, blue-whiskered, from inside that box at our feet.

Effie let out the most horrific, bloodcurdling scream. You would have thought it was enough to bring every stalactite of frozen meat crashing down from the ceiling of that nightmarish room.

Undignified haste. That's the only phrase for it. We knew we had just moments before Effie's distorted ululations brought everyone running. The three of us turned and pelted out of that meat locker – I hit every frozen carcass on my way. We left them swinging on their hooks as we tumbled back into the kitchen.

There we heard voices, footsteps, the sound of people being roused from their beds. Effie was still making terrified whimpers and I had to take hold of her to get her to move. I'd forgotten the layout of the large galley kitchen, and had to depend on Robert to show us the way out.

We had almost made it to the door when a great cry went up from the other end of the room. We had been discovered. The chef was there in his night-things, aggrieved and formidable, while the night porter was flashing a torch about, shouting at us.

'Run!' Effie wailed. 'Leave me. I'm puffed out. I can't move.' She was sagging in my arms, as if she wanted to lie on the floor.

'It's two old women.' The chef laughed. 'What are you doing down here? Were you after a midnight feast?' He had mistaken us for hotel guests. Maybe that was a good thing. We could talk ourselves out of this.

'He works here,' said the night porter, gesturing at Robert. 'He's one of the nancy-boy elves. What are you doing down here, then? What was all the noise about? What are you doing to these two old ladies?'

I saw that Robert's face was white with fury. He swore and launched himself across the room at them. It was as if he wanted to tear them limb from limb. The shock had turned him mad – his poor, dead auntie, his only relation in the world, lying in the freezer like so much mince. Effie and I could hardly move to stop him. He went by us in a flash, and the next thing we knew he had his hands round the chef's fat neck, attempting to choke him to death.

The night porter raised his heavy torch high above his head and I had only a second to cry out a warning, but it smashed on to Robert's head and he was out cold. He slipped to the tiles and Effie shrieked again. 'You've killed him!' she howled. 'You've killed him stone dead.'

The night porter checked that that wasn't the case and hoisted Robert up. 'He might wish I had when he has to explain himself to Mrs Claus.'

'You're going to kill us all!' Effie cried. 'Just like Jessie. You're going to put us in there!' She flung out a bony finger at the meat locker, its door still hanging open. 'You're going to put us in there dead, like Jessie.'

The night porter frowned at the chef. 'What's she on about? Jessie? Jessie the waitress?'

'They've killed her!' Effie said. 'She's . . . in there!'

The chef looked thoughtful. He knew, of course, that Effie was speaking the truth. Obviously the night porter wasn't party to the same schemes. I could see that the chef was having to box clever. He didn't want the porter poking about in the freezer. He had to play it cool. Dismiss Effie's rantings.

'It's true,' I said calmly. 'They're storing dead bodies in there. Employees of the hotel.'

'What?' The porter looked as if he was on the verge of laughter. But it was hysterical laughter, I thought, as if he knew, really, that evil things were going on in this establishment.

I said, 'The chef is . . . feeding the corpses to the guests.'

The chef gave a nasty laugh. 'They're unhinged. Look at the state of her. She's a madwoman. I've seen her around the town. She's crazy.'

'Feeding . . . corpses?' said the night porter.

'You should look in there,' I urged.

The chef stepped forward, blocking the way with his considerable bulk. 'He doesn't need to go looking at anything. There's nothing to see. She's just trying to wriggle out of it. She's an intruder here. All three of them are. They need dealing with. They need taking to Mrs Claus. She'll know what to do.'

'Yes,' said the porter. He was an oldish man. He'd worked there for years. He'd never known trouble like this and he was out of his depth. 'Yes, she'll know . . . She'll tell us what to do.'

I looked at Robert, lying like a dead weight on the floor, and at Effie, whose hands had flown up to her face. I supposed I could have taken on the two men – I might even have been able to batter them, get the three of us to freedom.

As the porter and the chef advanced on us, I was still making up my mind whether to fight or to give in. I felt Effie pressing against me, terrified out of her wits, poor thing.

The time to put up a fight wasn't then. We had to give in. Besides, I wanted to see Mrs Claus. I wanted to find out what she was up to. I had a few questions for her.

*

We were bundled into a lift like prisoners, and taken straight to the top of the hotel. The proprietress's suite was, like my own, in the attic but hers was even more elaborate and luxurious. Downstairs in the hotel, everything was worn and shabby, but up here no expense had been spared. We wandered into the lair of the gargantuan Mrs Claus, staring about us in awe at its gorgeousness.

She was wrapped in a silk kimono and perched on a velvet settee. Word had been sent ahead by the night porter that we were on our way. She seemed tired but alert, her complexion more florid than ever without makeup, and her hair crammed under a net. As we shuffled in, her eyes flashed with malice and amusement.

'These are the intruders, madam,' said the night porter, with a little bow. They were all so scared of her, and I still didn't know why. What power did she wield over them?

'They were in my kitchens,' growled the chef. 'They'd broken in through the back way and went inside the meat locker,' he added significantly.

Mrs Claus nodded. She glared at the three of us and I'm afraid we must have looked rather defeated and exhausted. She fixed on Robert first. 'I took you in when you had nowhere to go,' she said. Her voice was choked with sweetness, as if she had been eating Mars Bars half the night. 'Isn't that true? You had no family, no roots, no job that you were qualified for. I let you live here and work for your keep. I saw that you were trained in the hotel trade. Like all of my family of elves, you belonged nowhere and to no one. I took you in and gave you a purpose . . .'

Robert was staring back at her, incredulous. 'You made us into your private army of slaves.'

A throaty chuckle from Mrs Claus. 'Perhaps. But I was paying for the privilege, wasn't I?' There were other elves in the room, dressed in their green and scarlet finery. They were ready for action, I saw: ready to jump to their mistress's defence. They looked glazed, drugged: their eyes stared blankly at us.

'Now,' said Mrs Claus, 'you two ladies. I can't see what business it is of yours whatever goes on in my establishment. I do not poke my nose into your goings-on, do I?'

'We came here because—' Effie began.

'I haven't finished,' Mrs Claus cut her off brusquely. 'You see, I've been very interested in some of the things in which you two have involved yourselves over recent weeks. You, Brenda, harbouring that strange young family to keep them safe from the wicked world, hm? I could have tipped off those who were looking for them, made a pretty penny out of that, but I kept shtum, didn't I? Just like a good neighbour should. Wasn't it thoughtful of me?'

How did she know about any of that? I was clenching my fists, scared to hear what was coming next.

'So many things I could take an interest in. Your rockery, for example, and why it was that you two ladies suddenly decided to go digging in it one night. What was the urgency? A rather deep hole, I understand.'

Effie was nudging me bonily.

I didn't understand: where was this monstrous woman getting her information from?

'Oh, I'm discreet, though. I know many, many secrets. I even know what was said in your house, Effie, that night when you had the television people there. It was a seance, wasn't it, hm? I understood better than any of you what came through the ether

that night. Oh, and the Deadly Boutique. I learned all about
what the two of you got up to down there the other week. How
you ruined Mr Danby's thriving concern. You were the ghost in
his machine, Brenda. You doomed his mother. She's clinging on
for dear life, but she doesn't stand a chance after what you two
did, blundering about and smashing things up.'

I was aware that Robert was staring at us, as were the
porter, the chef and the other elves. What was he thinking?
It sounded as if we made a habit of breaking into people's places,
causing chaos and getting caught up in weird, supernatural
affairs.

'I don't see what any of this has to do with what's in your meat
locker,' I said, keeping my voice steady.

'Ah, Brenda,' chuckled Mrs Claus, 'and you're the biggest
mystery of all, aren't you?'

She looked me up and down and, all of a horrible sudden, I
felt exposed. All my innards and nerve endings felt as if they were
illuminated and tingling in the X-ray of her gaze. 'There's
nothing mysterious about me,' I said gruffly.

'I think there is,' she said. 'Have you told anyone? Your new
friends in your new town? Are they aware of your history? Your
provenance? Hm? How much have you told them, Brenda?'

'Shut up,' I said quietly. I was sweating. I could feel all their
eyes on me.

Mrs Claus tossed back her head. 'You've kept it all bottled up,
haven't you? Years and years and years of telling no one, of
skulking about from place to place, moving on again, never
getting too attached to anyone. Yes, I can understand that. I can
see how that might be the best thing for you. Being as you are.
A woman like you.'

'What do you know about any of it?' Even to myself my voice sounded low and dangerous.

'I know enough, Brenda. I know enough to make a few phone calls. Whisper a few dearly held secrets in the right ears. And then what would happen? What would become of you?'

'What's she on about?' Effie piped up. 'What phone calls, Brenda? What does she mean? The police?'

'You're so prosaic, Effie,' laughed Mrs Claus. 'But, yes, I imagine the police would be rather interested to hear about Brenda. As would Social Security and the Ministry of Defence. But so would MI5 and the Ministry for Incursions and Other Wonders.'

'MIAOW?' I gasped. 'You know about them?' I had encountered the ministry's agents a number of times over the decades. As had been explained to me by various operatives, they were supposed to be 'terribly, terribly' secret.

'Of course,' she said. 'How do you know I'm not an agent myself? I could be doing their work right now.'

I thought about this. Could she have been sent to nobble me?

'So many people would be interested to hear that you are alive and kicking, Brenda. They would love to know that you'd come to light here, in this sleepy little fishing port. The British Museum, the Natural History Museum – I imagine they would slap a compulsory purchase order on you immediately.'

'I am not a *thing*,' I said. 'I'm not available for a museum to *buy*.'

'You would have to convince them of that. I think you would find your human rights a matter of dispute. You would have to try very hard to convince the world of your right to a human identity. Especially when it became aware of the events you have been involved in, the atrocities in your wake. It looks rather as if death and disaster dog your footsteps, doesn't it? Just think. How much support would you find if the truth came out?'

I opened my mouth to speak, but nothing came out. She had robbed me of my anger, silenced me with her threats. All I could think about was being paraded in front of these authorities, the judges and experts, pundits, professors and officials. Doctors. *Surgeons.*

She was quite right, I was sure. I knew what would become of me, should I come to their attention.

'I don't understand, Brenda,' Effie broke in. She was astonished at my submission and my silence. 'What is she saying to you? What does it all mean? What have you *done*, Brenda?'

'It's just words,' said Robert. 'She's just weaselling and wriggling. She's threatening Brenda. Bullying and brow-beating her, like she does with everyone. She's a wicked old hag. An evil succubus.'

'Robert,' laughed Mrs Claus, 'you flatter me.'

'*What have you done to my aunt?*'

'Ah,' said Mrs Claus, slowly and gently. 'You found her, I hear. Now, that is very unfortunate. How terrible for you. What an awful shock. You must be brave, my dear. You must be a brave little boy. Your poor aunt, I am sorry to tell you, is dead.'

'We know that,' he spat. 'We saw her. Frozen blue in your meat locker. And, presumably, about to be hacked into pieces and baked into a pie.'

'What?' Mrs Claus gave a strangled cry of delight. 'A pie? Auntie Jessie baked in a pie? A waitress pie, hm? A chambermaid tart?' She chortled and wiggled her fat painted toes at the end of the kimono. 'Now, whatever gave you such an idea, my boy?'

He paused. 'Well,' he stammered, 'Jessie did. She kept telling me, and others, that that's what you and Chef were up to. The vanished elves. Baked in pies.'

'Delicious!' cried Mrs Claus. 'Ridiculous!' She clapped her hands with glee. 'Do you hear that, Chef McFee? We've turned cannibals here at the Christmas Hotel! It must be true, if dear old Jessie was saying so. Tell me, Chef McFee, do you have many recipes for human flesh, hm?'

The chef was laughing, too. A wheezing, discomfiting noise. Beside him the night porter seemed uneasy, as he tried to join in with the laughter.

'Pies, indeed.' Mrs Claus shook her head. 'My dear boy, your poor aunt's mind was gone. It had shrivelled to the size of a raisin. Her good sense had vanished. She had become a most peculiar person, in the last, late days of her life. Since her final visits to the Deadly Boutique, I believe she had lost her reason, along with her youthful looks. Pies, for goodness' sake! I love my little elves! Why on earth would I feed them to my clientele?'

Robert flinched. 'I don't know. But my aunt is still dead. Why is she dead? Why is she in your meat locker?'

The woman's face twisted into a sympathetic leer. 'We have been trying to get hold of you all evening. Since yesterday we have been trying to think of the best way to tell you. The gentlest way.'

'What?'

'Your aunt's body was exhausted. It had taken too much punishment in the Deadly Boutique. You know what Mr Danby was up to? He was draining the life force out of the women who visited it. He was using his bizarre machine to drain the excess years out of them, bottling all their unwanted time, then siphoning it into his old mother. Well, at least that's finished now. But the process was tricky and sometimes disastrous. Your poor auntie reverted, didn't she? Her body couldn't stand the strain. She was discovered in the morning room yesterday. She'd been dusting, bless her.'

'You didn't tell me.'

'As I said, we wanted to break it gently.'

'I thought she had vanished. Been murdered. Because she knew too much.'

Mrs Claus tutted. 'You've been hanging around with these two silly old women. They've filled your lovely head with their paranoid, lurid fantasies. They've made you believe outlandish things.'

'But Jessie's in the freezer . . .'

'Only until tomorrow. We could hardly have her lying about in the hotel, could we?'

'I – I don't know what to think . . .'

'Don't believe her,' snapped Effie. 'She twists everyone round her little finger.'

'You're tired, my boy,' said Mrs Claus. 'You need to rest. You need to absorb this terrible news about your aunt. You need to get over the shock.'

'Yes,' he said. 'That's right. I feel . . . numb with it.'

'That is to be expected.' Mrs Claus clicked her fingers. 'Colin, Timothy.' Two of the elves dancing attendance on her stepped forward. 'Take Robert back to the staff quarters. See that he rests. Give him anything he needs. Take him some cocoa. Comfort him as best you can.' The elves nodded and gave their mistress a queer, elvish salute.

'Robert . . .' I began, before they whisked him away, but the words died in my throat. It was hopeless, I knew. The anger had died in him. He had been reabsorbed into life at the Christmas Hotel.

Effie and I were left standing there, facing Mrs Claus. Effie jutted out her chin defiantly. 'What are you going to do with us?'

The proprietress rattled cerise nails against perfect teeth. 'I'm not sure yet, Effie dear. But I can't have the pair of you running about the countryside, broadcasting my secrets to all and sundry. I shall have to think carefully about how to proceed.'

She knew she had won this round. The fight had gone out of us. When she commanded her chef and her porter to drag us away and lock us up, we could barely summon the energy to resist.

They took us to a tiny box room, hidden at the top of the building, where we were roughly tied up and gagged.

Escapology turned out to be an amateur enthusiasm of Effie's. Which was handy, although she had mastered only half the skills necessary to free us. She had learned enough, though, to undo the most chafing and uncomfortable knots. Then she ungagged us.

With all the wriggling and writhing (where on earth, I wondered, had she *learned* escapology?), Effie wore herself out. We sat there, semi-liberated, in the attic gloom. Then: 'I've got a knife!' she remembered. She fished around in her bag and produced the glinting implement.

'Pity you didn't think of it sooner,' I said.

'What? Fight our way out?' She whistled through her false teeth. 'Stabbed them all and made a run for it? I think there's been enough violence, don't you?' My wrists were burning as she sawed at the thick rope. 'Keep still, woman.'

'I don't believe her for a second,' I said, 'about Jessie dropping dead. Do you?'

'I don't know what to believe,' she said tersely.

'Look how shifty they are. What sort of people hide bodies in meat lockers? So maybe they aren't making them into pies, but they're definitely hiding something. I think Jessie got too near the truth.'

Effie grunted with exertion, sawing through the last tough fibres of the bonds that held my wrists. She moved on to my ankles. 'They're all hellish creatures, as far as I'm concerned.'

'What?'

'All of them. Mrs Claus. Mr Danby. All these strange people we keep coming up against. What was it that voice told you the other night? Hell is bursting at the seams? Some of its inhabitants are already here among us? Well, I think we've met some already.'

'I believe you're right.' Now I was thinking about Robert, drawn back into the world of this macabre hotel, whisked away from us, drugs in his cocoa, hidden away with the elves.

'And you, Brenda,' Effie said. 'Are you one of the damned?'

I swallowed. 'I don't know what you mean.' But I knew she had had to ask, after everything Mrs Claus had insinuated. The owner of the Christmas Hotel knew so much about our recent activities, and seemed to know so much about me, and she had aired snippets of those secrets tantalisingly in front of Effie. It was as if she understood how little I had divulged about myself, even to my best friend in Whitby.

'I don't think I'm damned,' I said hesitantly. 'Not if that word means what I believe it means. There's no place reserved for me in hell or anywhere else. Nowhere in the hereafter will have any room for me. I have to stay on the earth. I'm made of clay. Nothing else.'

I felt Effie's hands withdraw. She had stopped sawing at the ropes. I felt her inch away from me. 'What are you?' she said, in a small voice.

I paused. 'You . . . have had certain ideas about me. You've had your suspicions. You knew I wasn't quite normal. I rather hoped, Effie, that we could leave it at that. You trusted me. You knew as much as you needed to know.'

'That was fine,' she said, 'for a time. I could live with not quite knowing who . . . or what you are. But things have changed, haven't they, Brenda? I feel like we're stepping into a situation . . . a whole world of new and terrible dangers. We . . . I need to be prepared for whatever we might face.'

'You're right,' I said. 'You deserve to know the truth.' I rubbed my sore ankles together. 'Would you mind continuing to free me? I'm not going to hurt you, am I?'

Effie shook her head dumbly, and set back to work. 'I've been going round in circles, trying to figure out what it was about you,' she whispered. 'I was beating my brains, trying to work it out. I've formed the most outlandish theories. I thought you were . . . Well, never mind.'

'You thought I was what?'

'I thought you'd been a man at one point. Sorry, I shouldn't have said. I thought you were a man trying to live as a woman. I thought, Don't pry. Live and let live. And then I thought . . . perhaps she's a criminal. A murderess who has paid her debt to society and wants to start afresh. Or perhaps you were on a witness-protection programme, living under an alias. I mean, it's all very strange, you having no family, no friends, no history to speak of. Just a few vague mentions of your travels, all the different places and people and homes you've known.'

Poor Effie. It didn't seem fair somehow, that I'd kept her in the dark. As a person, Effie is quite straightforward – prosaic, Mrs Claus had mockingly called her. She likes to know what's what. No ambiguities. No vagueness or coyness. I must have driven her crazy with all my evasions.

'Then,' she went on, still sawing away, 'I realised something odd. About your age. I thought you must be about the same as me. Remember that chat we had about bus passes? But you drop in references to things that even I'm too young to remember. The abdication. I remember you saying something about the newspapers then and I was brought up short. Could you really be as old as that? You mentioned the Martians' invasion. That was at the end of the nineteenth century – the very end! There seemed no way you could be that old. And I stared at you, trying to gauge how old you are. And it's very hard to tell, Brenda, because of how thick you wear your makeup. And – forgive me – the scars on your face made me wonder . . . whether something truly awful had happened to you. During the war, perhaps. Or some accident that had left you terribly damaged and traumatised. Things, at any rate, that you would never, ever talk about. And perhaps you were an amnesiac – you didn't even know what atrocious things had happened to you . . . to make you like this.'

Effie fell silent. Hot tears were going down my face and they itched. They made all that makeup feel sticky and claggy. 'Am I really so monstrous?' I asked. 'Am I really so strange to look at? I thought – I hoped – I was blending in?'

Effie got up and twisted round. Still kneeling, she came closer to me. We're both bad at proximity. We're neither of us touchy-feely people. But just then Effie overcame her natural reserve and hugged me. Hard and rather fiercely. 'You're not a monster,' she whispered.

By then I was sobbing loudly. Ashamed to think of it now. There we were. Locked up. Mortal danger. Me crying like a baby. 'You don't understand, Effie. I really am a monster. My father's second monster. He created my husband. And my husband demanded that a second creature was made. A female. A bride, Effie. *Me.*'

Not much more was said that evening.

There would be time, later, to talk further. Should we escape, that was.

Now we had to turn our attention to effecting that escape: to leaving this sinister hotel safely and getting home.

But I had let my mask drop. I had let my secret out. The worst thing I could imagine doing. I had told Effie the most frightening, unbelievable truth about myself.

I had watched her face as she swallowed it. As she understood. Her eyes had widened fractionally. She had nodded. Then she set to work again and soon we were free, rubbing life back into our limbs.

'The door's not terribly secure,' she said. 'This lock isn't up to much.'

I took my cue. She knew how strong I was. I had no need to hide it now. I took a few steps back and launched myself at the boxroom door. Its lock splintered easily from the wormy wood.

Effie and I advanced into the long corridor, she brandishing her stolen knife, me prepared to punch somebody's lights out. But on that top floor we saw no one. We found a staircase, smelling of lino and bleach, and hurried down several flights. Still we saw no one. Dawn was breaking over the headland. We peered out of a dirty window to see the pale, streaky pink light. 'Shall we try to find Robert?'

Effie shook her head. 'I think he'll be safe for now. And we don't want to end up in the same place as Jessie.'

I was in two minds. I didn't think Robert would be particularly safe, but he would have to take his chances. Effie and I had a duty to look after ourselves.

We emerged from our staircase on to an upper landing at the head of the stairs that led to Reception. In the gloom before dawn, all the tinsel and streamers were even more macabre. The fairylights on the tall artificial tree failed to instil any cheer: they were icy blue.

'Almost there, Effie,' I whispered.

'I can't believe we haven't been seen—'

Just at that moment the night porter spotted us. He was slumped in his alcove, dozing on the job. He jerked awake with a cry of outrage as we were hustling ourselves down the staircase and thundering past him across the monogrammed carpet. 'You two!' he yelled. 'You two again! Sneaking out! After we found a nice snug room for you!' He was on his feet, heading towards us.

I judged the distance to the main doors. Could we outrun him? They would be locked, perhaps. He was the night porter. That was what he was there for: to unlock the doors when strangers came knocking. The light slanting through them was chilly and bleak, but to me it was beautiful. It meant freedom.

A new day. Fresh air. Things that, at various points in that night, I hadn't expected to experience again.

'Let us out!' I shouted. 'How dare you lot keep us prisoner? Let us out of this madhouse!' If I woke some of the guests early, I didn't care. Let them come down. Let them see what all the fuss was about.

Effie produced her knife and waggled it at him menacingly. He shrank back, laughing uneasily. 'You may well laugh,' she said, seething with anger, 'but if you don't let us out I'm going to cut off your testicles. Your precious mistress can use them as baubles for her tree, for all I care.'

He laughed and, with a speed I couldn't believe in a man of his age, darted forward to bring down his hand on Effie's wrist in a stinging karate chop. The knife clattered to the floor and poor Effie was hoisted sideways, landing heavily on the carpet with a dreadful crunch. 'Ha!' cried the night porter, and I realised he must be just as crackers as the rest in that hotel. He rounded on me, preparing to do his worst.

Effie howled in pain. She was struggling feebly to stand up.

'You'd have stayed in your cell,' the night porter said, 'if you'd known what was good for you, until it was time for us to deal with you.' He was ranting, producing flecks of spittle. I think he'd been having the cocoa, too. He and I were dancing warily about each other, keeping back, darting forward, missing each other's swings. Once he came a mite too close, so I rewarded him with a slap. My shovel hand must have set his ears ablaze. They'd be ringing for days. Then he jabbed me hard in the gut and I doubled over. He'll get me now, I thought. I've had it. Effie was clambering gingerly to her feet, but she'd be no help, ju-jitsu lessons or no . . .

Someone was rattling at the front door, hammering hard on the outer windows, wanting in, calling for attention in a deep, commanding tone.

The night porter was distracted enough for me to help Effie up. She assured me that nothing was broken, but she was trembling with fright.

'We aren't open!' the night porter yelled through the door. 'I can't let you in!'

The muffled, booming voice rang out again. Was it the police? We couldn't quite see.

'Please!' Effie shrieked. 'Help us! You, out there! They're keeping us prisoner!'

The night porter hissed as we approached and waved us back. Effie bent painfully to retrieve her knife.

'I will not let you in!' he shouted. 'Now, go away! You'll disturb our guests!'

Then something odd happened. The porter hadn't unlocked the door. In fact, we'd watched him putting on extra chains to prevent the interloper getting in. But that made no difference: the door unlatched itself, seemingly of its own accord, and swung inwards, easily and smoothly.

The night porter stumbled backwards with a cry – he almost bumped into us. Effie and I let him fall to sprawl full length on the parquet floor. I'd have gladly kicked him as he lay there, had my attention not been taken by the man who was now stepping over the threshold into the hotel.

'You!' Effie cried. There was terror in her voice, but of a delicious kind. A delighted terror. She grasped my arm for support as the intruder stepped towards us.

It was Effie's handsome stranger from the café. In the

morning light he was more alluring than even the first time we had seen him, immaculate in his black suit, hair smarmed back just so. His eyes were emerald: dazzling.

'Is something untoward going on here? Are you two ladies in need of my assistance?' His voice was honeyed and warm.

'Oh, yes,' gasped Effie. 'Oh, yes, we are!'

He nodded, and glanced down at the night porter, who was trying to get up off the floor. 'This gentleman is refusing to let you leave the building?'

'Ha!' cried Effie. 'That's the least of it, believe me. But, yes, getting away from here is chief among our concerns.'

'Very well,' said the stranger. 'Possibly the good gentleman is just evincing a certain patronising caution for your well-being. Perhaps he believes that ladies shouldn't be out and about in the early hours, before the town has come properly to life. Could he, perhaps, be worrying needlessly?'

This was a cue for the night porter. He was gibbering and spitting, but he nodded quickly at the intruder. I couldn't tell what had got him so worked up, but it seemed he would have agreed to anything. He just wanted us away. He wanted that man out of there.

'Excellent,' said the man. 'Perhaps I should walk out with these two delightful ladies. Perhaps I should offer them my protection and lead them away from this place. There can be no possible objection to that, can there? No?'

The night porter shook his head, dribbling and drooling like an idiot.

There was a magnetism about the stranger. A powerfully intense force of personality. Was it something to fear?

Effie, too, was in a trance. But it wasn't a fearful one.

'Let us go, then, ladies,' said the stranger, 'and leave this place. I will walk you home and you can tell me what has transpired here this evening. I am sure it is quite a tale.'

The night porter stood by and let the three of us pass.

It was glorious, stepping out on to the prom in the early sunshine. I felt the tepid warmth on my face and breathed deeply. I watched the tall, dark man hook arms with Effie, and lend her his solid support. He flinched a little at the sun, but only for a moment.

'You haven't told us your name,' I heard Effie say, as we walked away from the Christmas Hotel. I followed them, shambling, exhausted. I was a physical and emotional disaster area. I didn't want any more adventures for a long, long time.

'Haven't I introduced myself?' The suave gent laughed. 'How remiss of me. My name is Mr Alucard. I'm new in town.'

Chapter Five:

A Fancy Man for Effie

I spent most of the next day asleep, catching up on all the hours I'd been involved in gruesome adventures. When I woke, something like a day and a half later, it was easy to believe that none of the business at the Christmas Hotel had been real.

I felt somewhat shame-faced about the escapade. What had we really accomplished? Effie and I had only just escaped with our lives. We hadn't been able to save Jessie. We had earned the enmity of Mrs Claus. Robert was still there, at the mercy of his employer.

And my secrets were out. Mrs Claus had revealed she knew a disconcerting amount about me. She had toyed with me. And then I had confessed just about all to Effie. Should I have fobbed her off? I wondered. I'd gone too far in telling her so much. She would wake up, like me, with a pounding head and a confused, horrible impression of our adventures, and would pause at the thought of who and what I claimed to be.

Really? No, surely not. That's impossible . . . isn't it?

I stirred myself. I got myself together. I made myself ready to face the world. I examined my post in the kitchen as I ate my breakfast and gathered my wits. A postcard from Lisa Turmoil, making a tentative booking for herself and her fiancé. And another, more cryptic one, with a Scottish postmark, from the Greens: doing well, still on the run, grateful for my help and understanding, the risks I had taken for them.

I tried to phone Robert at the Christmas Hotel, but they wouldn't connect me. I wasn't sure whether they knew who I was or not. I didn't even know if Robert was there. I'd slept all this time . . . They might have done away with him. I might be too late. But he could look after himself, couldn't he?

I didn't want to go back there. One escape from that place was enough.

Downstairs in the shop, I tossed a few provisions into a basket. I hadn't shaken off a persistent, buzzing headache. It was like being a radio, tuned slightly wrongly.

Leena was too bright and smily as she rang up my groceries. 'We haven't seen you for a few days,' she said. 'We thought you might have been away.'

I shook my head as I packed my shopping bag. 'I've had rather a lot of late nights recently,' I said.

Leena laughed. 'You pensioners! You live the life of Riley. Out every night, running about the place!'

I found this a bit irritating, to be honest. Leena is a nice girl, but inclined to be insensitively dim. I mean, it's not as if I've been painting the town red. I tried not to scowl across the counter at her.

'Look at Effie!' she said. 'She was dolled up last night in her finery. I've never seen her in an evening gown before. Jewellery. She even had earrings in, and I know she can't bear them.'

'Effie?' I said. 'Last night?'

'She came here to give us a twirl, said she was off on a posh night out. She went knocking at your door to give you a twirl, too, but there was no answer.'

I'd still been fast asleep. Trying to knit myself back together, after the terror and upheaval of our narrow escape. How on earth had Effie managed to get out and about last night? And why was she dressed up to the nines?

'She didn't tell you, did she?' said Leena, smugly. 'She never told you she's got a new beau.'

'What?'

Leena giggled. 'You needn't look shocked! She isn't that old. And Effie's quite a handsome woman. She's very smart.'

'She's got herself a boyfriend?'

'Well, I think that's pushing it. But she went out last night with . . . a gentleman caller, I suppose you might call him. Yes, that's the right phrase. I caught a glimpse of him when he was knocking at her door. He's very distinguished-looking. Dark and svelte.'

'Svelte?' I said. 'She's got svelte men taking her out?'

Leena was well and truly tickled by that. I was taking more umbrage than I should have done. I just couldn't believe that Effie was swanning about the place when I still felt – even now – like absolute hell. Where did the woman get her energy?

I took my shopping upstairs and unpacked it quickly, thumping the tins and packages down rather heavily. Of course I knew who was calling on Effie. I knew who was paying court to her. It had to be him, didn't it? She had turned his head. Lucky old Effie. She'd be cock-a-hoop, crowing about it for weeks. I thought about the way he had linked arms with her as we ambled down the prom after our escape the other morning. So! Effie had snared him, then. She was a proper siren!

I thought about the Effie I knew, having tea with me at the Walrus and the Carpenter. Explaining, in a hushed tone, how she had never really got the hang of men, never really given them a whirl. And how, now that she was so much older, she was sure that any temptation was behind her. She could see little use for them. It was a sweet, rueful confession she had made that day. Effie was an old-fashioned spinster. She supported herself. She needed no one else. She came from a long line of independent women.

But she had gone to the corner shop last night to give them a twirl. He was taking her dancing, she had told Leena. Effie, dancing about on the arm of a man!

A dark, dapper gent, impossibly handsome.

I was glad when the phone went, and I was glad it was Robert, speaking hastily and quietly, suggesting we meet in town for a coffee. Unfortunately he suggested a rather dingy, greasy place close to the prom – somewhere I would never normally go – then rang off abruptly. There was no time to suggest somewhere more salubrious.

I pulled on my coat, yanked on a headscarf against the November wind, and trotted down the hill into town. There was a biting edge to the air, a proper hint of winter. The seagulls sounded aggrieved as they hopped across the rooftops and soared into the hard enamel blue of the sky. The abbey was looking particularly fine in the sharp, cold light: a jagged silhouette. You could still trace the outlines of its tall windows, and where the missing bits should have been, even though it looked like a mouthful of broken teeth. I suddenly realised that, in all my months here, I hadn't yet made the pilgrimage up the hill across the bay to visit it, or the church. I hadn't toiled up the hundred and ninety-nine steps. I wasn't sure why. Maybe soon. There was something enticing about the place, and I could do with a good, exhausting walk. I imagined sitting up there, among the worn buttresses and graves, assailed by the winds and staring out to sea, having a lovely epiphany, all to myself.

In the meantime, I descended into the hurly-burly of the town. Everyone was already decorating their windows and shopfronts in readiness for Christmas, still more than a month away. The sight of tinsel and fairylights made me flinch. That hotel had given me an aversion to them that I hoped wasn't permanent. It was as if its spirit of yuletide tawdriness had crept down the hill like sea mist to infect the town.

Robert was waiting for me in the greasy spoon. It was a poky place and I had to cram myself between the tables, which were full of people smoking. Rough-looking types, Effie would have said.

But it was good to see Robert. He was in his flying jacket again, all windswept and pink-faced. He looked as tired as I felt, though, and smoked a series of cigarettes as we talked.

'They took Jessie's body away,' he told me. 'The funeral's next week. It'll be quiet. Maybe you and Effie . . . ?'

'We'll come.'

'Heart failure, they said. Stress from the machine, the make-overs.'

'You don't believe that, though?'

He seemed confused. 'I don't know any more. The other day I'd have believed anything, but . . . Mrs Claus is so plausible. She wants to protect us. She means well. We're her staff . . . and we're like her extended family. I don't believe she would really harm us . . .'

I was amazed by his *volte-face*. 'That's not what you were saying the other day, Robert.'

He looked me briefly in the eye. 'Mrs Claus has explained things to me. All that business about pies and cannibalism, it was ridiculous. How could I ever have believed such a thing?'

'So you're going to stay there? At the Christmas Hotel?'

He spread his hands helplessly. 'Where else can I go? Where else do I belong?'

'But what about the missing elves? The other day, you were convinced that—'

'That was the other day, Brenda. Mrs Claus has explained everything to me. These boys come and go. Some are here illegally. They stay for a bit, then drift off. They don't have any consideration for anyone. I was . . .' Now he couldn't catch my eye and stared into his glass cup of frothy coffee. 'I was quite wrong to suspect Mrs Claus of the worst. She does her best for everyone at the hotel. Those who submit to her care and love, take part in her festivities, they're safe. They will always have a home. Some people fling that back in her face. They're so ungrateful. And for a woman with a heart as big as hers, that's really hurtful.'

'Robert! I can't believe I'm hearing you say this.'

'It's true, Brenda. My auntie Jessie was an unsatisfied soul. She was never quite happy. I was just lashing out, blaming anyone to hand . . .'

'Robert,' I said, determinedly, 'you know as well as I do that that hotel proprietress is a wicked, conniving slug of a woman. She's a monster! She'd have done away with us all, if she could have got away with it. And I don't believe that we're safe from her, now. She's demonic, man!'

Robert stared at me levelly. 'No, Brenda.' He sighed, and lit another fag. 'She has explained to me about you, too.' He shook his head. 'Who are you to call other people monsters, to talk about who is demon-possessed?'

I was screwing up a paper napkin. I wanted to be out of there. His voice was too loud, even in the café's genial hullabaloo. 'What has she told you about me?'

His eyes were searching my face now, incredulous, appalled. It was the kind of unflinching glance I've always dreaded, hated and kept away from. I never thought Robert would look at me like that.

'You must be almost two hundred years old,' he said.

'Almost,' I said quietly.

'Your hands are so big. One larger than the other.'

I looked down at them, shredding a paper napkin. 'Two different donors, I suppose.'

'You walk with a slight limp. One leg is longer than the other?'

I nodded. The left is slender and elegant. A dancer's leg. The right isn't at all like that. If I tried to dance, I'd list in endless circles.

'What big ears you have,' he said. 'What big teeth.'

'Stop it, Robert,' I burst out. 'Stop it!'

This wasn't him speaking. It couldn't be. It wasn't like him at all. I hadn't known Robert long, but I could trust him. He wasn't cruel. It was her, speaking through him. Mrs Claus. She could control what her elves said and did – I grasped that suddenly, in that dingy caff. The thought was horrifying. I stood up abruptly. 'I'm going.'

He shrugged, puffing at his cigarette.

I went on: 'And you can tell your precious Mrs Claus, that I'll find a way to sort her out. She's not getting away with this. Ruining people's natures. Spoiling their lives. Sooner or later I'll get her.'

Robert rolled his eyes. 'She's safe. She's not scared of anything. Or anyone.'

I picked up my bag and tied on my headscarf. 'Just pass on the message, Robert. She doesn't know yet what I'm capable of.'

'Whatever,' he said carelessly.

'I hope . . .' I looked at him, but yet again he refused to meet my eye '. . . I hope that soon you'll feel a bit more like yourself.'

But as I left that café I felt that the old Robert must have gone. Vanished into the ether with his poor aunt. All that was left was this nasty-mouthed replacement, in thrall to the wicked Mrs Claus.

I walked heavily down our busiest shopping street. I didn't care who saw the tears rolling down my face. I must have looked very peculiar, with the wind whipping my clothes as I bawled my eyes out.

Just shows. I should never have let myself get attached to someone. I had come here intending to keep myself to myself, to slip through life almost unnoticed. That's the safest way. Instead, I had opened myself up. I had let myself start to care.

They all let you down, in the end.

*

Cod Almighty. The following evening. Effie was treating me. No expense spared. I could order the most extravagant thing on the menu, she said. It was my treat. I deserved it after all the recent ructions.

'You know me,' I said. 'My tastes are simple.'

Effie raised an eyebrow, and it stayed up until the waitress had taken our – modest – order. Effie knew I was being a bit short with her. I didn't mean to sound as I did. What was the point of being in a sulk with everyone? But, try as I might, I couldn't pull myself out of that mood.

I watched Effie take very thin triangles of bread and butter and nibble at them thoughtfully. 'I hope you aren't angry with me for some reason,' she said.

'Of course not,' I said, colouring. 'I'm just tired. That business at the Christmas Hotel wore me out more than I'd thought. And Robert's reaction, of course . . .' I had already told Effie about his weirdness in the greasy café. She was as astonished as I was – or so she said. I knew that, really, she had always thought Robert an untrustworthy type. But that was just prejudice. He was better than that, I knew.

Effie went on: 'You see,' she said, 'sometimes it's hard to get it right. In a friendship, like we've got. When things change or shift slightly . . .' She thought she was being tactful, angling the conversation round to the way she wanted it. I knew exactly what she was up to. But I wasn't going to help her out.

'What's changed?' I said. 'Oh. Here's our chips.'

When our main courses were set before us, and we were fiddling with vinegar and the squeezy plastic tomato, Effie burst out, 'I shouldn't like it to get in the way of our friendship. And spoil things. I wouldn't like it to be – as they say nowadays – an *issue* between us.'

I speared several whitebait with my fork. 'You don't want *what* to be an issue?'

She bit her lip. 'We have actually discussed this. Me and him, I mean. How to negotiate this difficult time. With things changing. With him coming on the scene and everything. And how you might get jealous. Or envious, rather. So, we have actually talked it over. You see, that's because I care. We both care about you, Brenda. Deeply. We both wish you well. And we wouldn't like our happiness to make you miserable or uncomfortable.'

I crunched down hard on my first mouthful of fish. Then I stabbed more on to my fork, wielding it like a harpoon. 'I haven't got a clue what you're on about.'

'Oh,' she said sharply. Then she caught my eye. 'Oh, you. You're teasing me, pretending not to understand. You know exactly what I'm talking about.'

I picked up the fattest chip and dunked it in ketchup. 'I don't! Really! You might as well be talking Japanese. Get to the point! Spit it out, woman!'

The waitress was passing. 'Is everything all right?'

Effie nodded quickly, and waved her away. She leaned closer across the table. 'I'm talking about my new . . . gentleman friend.'

'Oh,' I said. 'Right. I thought you were.'

'You see, it's become rather serious.'

'Serious?' I frowned. 'Really? How long have you known him?'

'You know perfectly well, Brenda. You were there when I first clapped eyes on him. And you were there when he rescued us from the Christmas Hotel. It's only been a matter of days, but I feel I have to tell you that things have moved on rather swiftly. Feelings have been running very high indeed.'

'You make it sound like a fever.'

'Not for no reason.'

I put so many chips in my mouth that it hurt when I swallowed them. 'Anyway,' I said, 'he didn't need to rescue us from the Christmas Hotel. And he didn't *really*. I would have got us out of there, no bother. Even if he *hadn't* turned up. What's his name, anyway?'

'Kristoff.'

'Very exotic.'

'He is.'

'Well,' I said, 'I wish you both every happiness.' I sounded so stiff! I wanted to shake her. I wanted to scream in her face: Don't trust him! I've got a terrible feeling about this! He gives me the willies – just thinking about him!

And I wanted to tell her:

I don't want to be alone, Effie. Don't go running off with him. Don't leave me on my own.

Of course I couldn't say those things.

'He took me dancing,' Effie said. Her face was glowing as she recalled her night out. 'Dancing! Me! He made me put on a proper gown and he picked me up and he was as neat as a pin. He even wore an evening cape. Oh, Brenda, I never thought gentlemen still carried on like that. It was divine. I thought that world had gone. I thought I'd missed out! I'd assumed all my golden chances had passed me by . . .'

'Hm,' I said, laying out my bread to make a chip sandwich.

'Where did he take you?' I imagined that tall, dapper gent whisking Effie around on a sprung ballroom floor. *Come Dancing* kind of thing. She would have been out of her depth, I thought, with a stab of dismay. Surely she couldn't dance. She was so awkward and frozen. He must have regretted it as he dragged her round the polished floor . . .

She beamed and bit her lower lip. 'I'm afraid we were rather wicked and went somewhere quite racy. We went to the nightclub under the Miramar.'

'What?' My mouth fell open, mid-chew. 'Surely not, Effie. You've always said you'd rather die than set a foot inside Sheila Manchu's rancid den of vice.'

'I know. And when Kristoff suggested, light-heartedly, that we retire there for some cocktails and a bop round the disco floor, I was appalled. I felt like I wanted to die. But, oh, I didn't want to seem past it or stuck up. Not on our first date. And so . . . I allowed him to talk me into it. And we went. And do you know, Brenda? I had a marvellous time. It was eighties night.'

'For the over-eighties?'

'The *music*. It was ever so glamorous down there. A Honolulu-style cocktail bar. Plastic lobsters and nets on the walls. Very swish. It wasn't a den of vice at all. I had to admit, Sheila has made it into a very distinctive niterie. She is a very convivial hostess, too. Such a mixture of clientele! And, Brenda, I danced all night long on the arm of the elegant Kristoff Alucard.'

'Well,' I said, embarrassed for her, 'you dark horse.' I smiled – it took some effort to stop that smile going sickly. I couldn't bear the thought of my best friend being made a fool of. That man . . . Surely that was what he was doing. He was sending her up in front of his trendy friends at Sheila's low joint. He had plied Effie with drinks, then got her up on some ghastly, lit-up dance-floor where she must have been dancing around like a madwoman. Jitter-bugging and doing the Twist. Poor Effie. Even now, she showed no embarrassment or shame.

'You don't mind, do you, Brenda?'

That she was out all night, making an idiot of herself at nightspots with a man she hardly knew? 'Of course not,' I said.

'He's sweeping me off my feet. Though . . . he warned me. He won't go too fast. He knows I'm a respectable lady. A pillar of society here. My life has been sedate, if not sedentary. He understands that, and he said, very sensitively, that he will endeavour not to turn my head. He will take it very gently . . .'

I felt I must have been wearing an expression of disgust. I am not prim, but there is something disconcerting about a candid outpouring from someone who is ordinarily more prim than yourself. I crunched up the last of my batter, and turned my thoughts to dessert.

'And,' Effie went on, 'that was when he explained that he's keen not to interfere with our friendship. He knows how we relish each other's company. Two old spinsters together, doing our spinsterish things!' She chuckled and I felt, instantly, as if she had slapped my face. The patronising bugger! Spinsterish things, indeed! And Effie was going along with it. Turning into one of those spineless, silly women, who change so absolutely when a bloke – just any old bloke – shows an interest in them. They turn themselves into whatever the bloke wants, and throw away their old life with everyone in it. A leaden, disappointed feeling stole over me.

'This evening, for example,' said Effie, 'he was offering to take me to dinner somewhere swanky on the road to Scarborough. But then I mentioned we'd already pencilled in Cod Almighty. He backed off immediately. "I know how important your girls' nights out are."'

Girls' Nights Out! I knew for a fact that Effie hated that phrase. She thought it sounded retarded. She had said as much to me as she coolly regarded a hen-night party sprawling about in the road, all L-plates, tiaras and fairy wings.

Effie was grateful to join the everyday, normal world. That's what it was. She would consent to anything. She was flattered and giddy . . . and relieved.

'I wouldn't want to get in your way,' I said dully.

She reached across the table and patted my hand. We both stared down at my hands. My ill-matched hands. I hadn't bothered plucking them for this evening. All of a sudden it was as if they had their own volition: they wanted to reach across the table and throttle the life out of the smug bitch.

It happens sometimes, with different body parts . . . It seems, off and on, that they have a life of their own, their own dreams and desires, which they send up to my brain to flash across the screen. Usually I have to squash them rather firmly. The impulse to choke Effie on the spot for her patronising betrayal took more effort than usual to resist.

'I've told him all about you,' she said, dabbing her thin lips with her napkin. 'I talked for hours and he listened. He's one of those men who really listen, you know. And he said he was intrigued. Really. He said you sound like an amazingly fascinating woman. "Astonishing," he said. "It just goes to show. You look at some people and you think, Just ordinary. Average.

Nothing fascinating there. Even some fantastically glamorous people," he said. "You can think, Ho-hum, not fascinating at all. But others! Well, they can be nothing to look at on the outside. They can be downright odd-looking, at times. But on the inside they can be amazing. Astonishing!"'

I glared at her. 'He must be a very deep person.'

'Oh, he is, he is.'

I shook my head to clear it of an angry buzzing. Effie had cured herself of irony! How on earth had she managed that?

'He says he thinks he loves me.'

After this outburst, Effie lowered her eyes. She was ashamed to meet mine. She had divulged too much.

'He said that?'

'When he dropped me off at my door. Proper gentleman. It was light by then. Nearly six a.m. And he said, "Effie, I know it's too soon. I know it's impossible. Or improbable. But I don't care about that. I don't care about convention. Neither of us is very conventional. And I want to speak my mind. I want to tell you what's in my heart." This is him talking. This is what he said to me, word for word. Well, you can imagine. My heart had just about stopped. I could hear the sea pounding in my ears. I thought I'd drop dead there and then.'

I pictured them: Effie with Bette Davis eyes and her cocktail frock all rucked and sweaty from bopping at the Miramar disco, and him all sophisticated and dashing. His eyes as dark as Bournville chocolate.

I looked at Effie and she was blubbing. Really! Seriously blubbing at the table. 'No one,' she said, clutching that napkin, 'no one has ever said it to me. No one's ever told me they love me. Not once. Never in the world.'

*

For the next few days I was plagued by the pair of them. They were everywhere, insanely happy and smug, clutching each other and swooning about the place. I know I should have been pleased for them, especially after some of the things Effie had told me in the fish restaurant. But as the days went by I felt resentful and cross. I think it was the patronising little wave they would both give when they saw me struggling home with shopping and they were on their way out, all dressed up. They started going to things like galleries and the theatre. 'You don't usually bother with stuff like that,' I accused Effie, and she shushed me. Said something about having her horizons expanded.

Hm.

He was a handsome devil, I'll say that. He seemed to grow more handsome with every passing day: that blue-black hair, greying sleekly at the temples, his skin so delicately pale. And his manners were exquisite. One day, when they had stopped me in the street, he held both my hands and patted them, staring deep into my eyes. 'I would like to thank you for being such a wonderful friend to my beloved.'

Beloved, it was now! He was fast!

'That's all right,' I said awkwardly. I was on my way to the launderette with a huge bag of dirty whatsits. I was furious because my machine had packed up that morning.

Effie was simpering in the background. 'She has told me so much about your lives here,' Kristoff said. His voice dropped lower. 'So many interesting things.'

I shrugged. 'There's nothing very exciting about our lives. You're the most exciting thing round here in ages.'

'I beg to differ,' he responded. 'Effie has told me some incredible things.'

I glared at her. There was no way of knowing what secrets she had offered up to him for the purpose of entertainment. People in love are so silly and selfish.

I hoisted up my jumbo bag of smalls and bade them farewell, but not before they'd trapped me with a dinner invite. At Effie's! That was a turn-up. I'd never been invited even once before. As far as I knew, she never cooked – I'd looked in her fridge once: it was full of those eye masks you wear for migraines.

I accepted, knowing I couldn't wriggle out of it. They were nauseating, but I didn't want to hurt their feelings.

An hour later, slumped on a bench at the launderette, staring miserably at my suds and undies going round, I was wondering whether they had been to bed together. It was a startling, not wholly pleasant idea. Uncharitably, I wondered how Kristoff could bring himself to fancy Effie, him being such a perfect specimen and her such a scrawny mare. But sexual attraction is a funny old thing. Effie had a certain unaccustomed glow about her. She was enslaved by him, all **right.**

'She's smitten,' Leena said, the **following** morning. She was laying out crates of fresh fruit **and veg** under the awning of her shop. 'I saw her this morning. She was up with the larks, buying provisions. You're going to dinner with them tonight, aren't you?' She straightened up, looked at me narrowly. 'How will that be? It must be tough. He's taking your best friend away.'

'Hardly taking her away.' I snatched up a box of masala tea, too savagely.

'As good as. Nothing will be the same now. And who can blame Effie? He's gorgeous! She's made quite a catch there. Who can blame her if she runs off with him?'

'Runs off with him? Is that what she said?' I couldn't bear the idea that she had told Leena more of her plans than she had me. She hadn't told me anything at all. Now she was telling some shop girl that everything was going to change. But, still, I couldn't see it. Effie was tethered to that house, its generations' worth of belongings. She couldn't just walk away from it. It didn't matter whose influence she was under.

'She never said anything about running off,' Leena said softly. 'But I wouldn't be surprised. She's knocking on. She can't waste any more time. Seize the day, I say.'

I'd never noticed before but Leena says the most common-place things. She hasn't got an original thought in her head. I must have been grimacing at her, because then she said: 'Poor you. You'll be lost without your Effie, won't you?'

I pulled myself out of it. 'Hardly. Of course not. Friends come and go. Things change. That always happens. No, I'm very pleased that Effie has managed to snare herself a bloke.'

'I can hear wedding bells,' Leena confided. 'Effie was hinting as much.'

'Nonsense.'

'Maybe that's what this dinner's for. To announce it. Maybe, as her best friend, you're going to be the first to know!'

I was mollified by this idea. Being the first to know. It would be flattering. But it couldn't be true, could it? Effie had once told me that the women in her family – that long line of aunties and witches – had never believed in the institution of marriage. It was Christian and anti-women, and they had never bothered with it.

I had absorbed that information with interest. It was only afterwards that I wondered about the blokes. What did the women do with them, if they didn't marry them? Chuck them away afterwards? Eat them, like the preying mantis does? And if so, had all of Effie's family been born out of wedlock? Quite racy, that, in years gone by. But I had never enquired. The opportunity hadn't arisen. Sometimes Effie was quite reluctant to talk about her unconventional aunties.

'A wedding would be nice.' Leena sighed. 'I like a good wedding.'

I stared at her. It had never been more apparent: Leena was the most boring woman on the planet.

What is it about other people's happiness that makes me feel uncharitable?

He had certainly made improvements to Effie's place, I'll say that for him.

The last time I had been round was on the night of the *Manifest Yourself!* fiasco, and Effie's home had been the usual dusty health hazard: dimly lit, junky and inhospitable. Now that Kristoff had his feet under the table, all of that was starting to change. He had encouraged Effie to put some of her nicer pieces – some figurines and glass lamps – on show, and to hide some of the nastier things. The light was soft and colourful. Throws and rugs were draped artfully here and there. Mr Alucard, it turned out, had an eye for décor.

But had he moved in? That was what I wanted to know. Effie had all these rooms in a prime location. Maybe it was her property the old devil was after. I wasn't clear about where exactly he lived. Effie had given me a vague further-up-the-town answer, wafting her hand, when I'd asked. There was something suspicious about that, I thought.

Still, I couldn't complain about their hospitality. Effie's home had never been welcoming before but now it was glowing with warmth and life. There was a delicious scent of slowly roasting lamb, basted in honey. They had dragged out an old gramophone and a tottering stack of 78s. Ancient, crackling jazz-age ditties accompanied the evening, making us – certainly me – gayer than I really felt.

I had dug out a rather smart jacket and skirt, with boxy shoulders and brass buttons. It had a nautical air and I hope it didn't seem too old-fashioned. Effie surprised me by wearing an Indian-print kaftan with a turban. It was not her usual kind of thing, but it suited her, the way she went floating about. She'd been more adventurous with her eye makeup, too. There was something languid and sensual about her. As she brought out the veg in her best china bowls, I was watching her closely.

Kristoff Alucard was in Edwardian evening dress. He carried it off very well so it didn't look *frou-frou* and overdone, even the ruffles down his skirt front and at his cuffs. The ensemble took me right back to that heady era. I was in London then and Kristoff might have been one of the dashing gents I knew in those days in Russell Square and . . . I frowned, fingering my wine glass. Could it be true? Had I seen him back then? All that time ago?

But my memory's patchy. There's so much of it, that's the thing. People and faces, names and adventures. They collapse into one. They concertina down and I can never be quite sure. Human beings weren't designed for a lifespan like mine.

Or, perhaps, Alucard's.

Effie brought in the roast, a spitting hunk of meat, aromatic and delicious. Her man friend was sharpening the carving knife with an expert flourish.

Oh, Effie, I thought, I hope you're not getting yourself into trouble here. I really hope he isn't what I'm starting to suspect . . .

Soon my qualms vanished because the food was so good and there was quite a bit of booze. Wine came out with every course and Kristoff proved to be quite the expert. He was the type to watch you closely as you sipped the drink he had described and poured for you. Everything had to be done properly. The wine had to breathe, all that malarkey. 'Oh, it'll breathe on the way down!' I had laughed, but he was serious. There were ways of going about things. The correct way to behave. The wine was alive: it needed respect. It had to breathe. He scrutinised my face as I sipped it. I felt I was being poisoned. He was waiting for me to pass out. We drank and drank and drank. I was astonished to see Effie letting herself go so gladly, so easily. She kicked off her new shoes, and Alucard massaged her feet under the table. Her turban was at a rakish angle, and gave her an abandoned, Bohemian air.

What had he done to change her so much?

'I feel privileged,' I said, during a golden lull, much later on. 'It's a real privilege to be invited here, to share in your happiness like this . . .'

During the evening I had changed my mind. Now I felt happy and included. There were no hard feelings and not a hint of jealousy. I was delighted for them.

They beamed at me. Alucard changed the record. More jazz. Later years. Smokier, darker, less hectic music. Sexier, too.

'Thank you, Brenda.' Effie smiled at the head of her long

dining-table and raised her crystal glass to me over the debris of the meal. Queen of all she surveyed. 'A toast to you, Brenda. My very best friend in all my life.'

Moments later, I had to hasten to the bathroom, but I left the dining room complacent and cheery. We were having a lovely time. Everything was going to be fine.

Wines and spirits don't do me any good. I should know that by now. My constitution is . . . well, unconstitutional, I suppose you might say. I had to dash those last few yards of the dark corridor to the loo.

There were gilt-framed portraits of Effie's female forebears all the way down that hall. What a forbidding, pursed-mouthed bunch. As I rushed past them, I felt they were glaring at me, trying to tell me something. They were burning to reach out and warn me . . . of what? You lot are dead and gone, I thought, as I hovered over the toilet bowl, waiting for the worst to happen. You all had your chance. You lived your lives. You spent them in solitude and necromancy, or whatever it was you got up to here. Nasty business. Now, though, you have to leave Effie to have her own fun, make her own mistakes . . .

It was as if they were mithering and muttering on the walls. Agitating against the musty flock wallpaper.

I didn't throw up, but waves of nausea were crashing through me, like the sea at high tide, flung up against the rocks of the bay. I needed to lie down.

Woozily I let myself out of the lav. I was ready to dash past the portraits and not listen to them. But he was standing in the corridor, waiting for me. He smiled broadly when he saw me. 'Are you feeling poorly, Brenda?'

His voice was so rich and thick. It was like that rosemary and honey glaze on the crisp flesh of the lamb. I nodded. 'I'm not used to drinking.'

'Really? I had gained the impression that Effie and your good self were gadabouts, running round the town after dark like the Merry Widows of Whitby.'

I bridled at this. 'We aren't big drinkers. Not at all. And, besides, we aren't always out . . . enjoying ourselves.'

'Ah, yes,' he said. 'So I gather. You also get up to some rather unusual business, don't you?'

He was blocking my way. I wouldn't be able to get past him without expressly asking. Or squeezing by. I didn't want to do either. Where were his gentlemanly manners now?

'Has Effie told you about everything?' I asked.

'Not everything,' he said. 'Not by any means. Enough, though, to intrigue me.'

'Yes,' I said, staring at those emerald eyes. 'You do seem very intrigued.'

'Deadly Machines and simian women,' he said. 'The descendants of an extra-terrestrial. Cannibal pensioners and eternal Christmases. Ghost-hunts. It's all very, very fascinating.'

My eyes were fixed on his. I was frozen to the spot.

'And you, Brenda. What a woman you are.'

'Am I?' And now I felt queasy in a wholly new way.

'I could have spent several lifetimes searching the world for a woman like you. A *unique* woman like you.'

At first I didn't get what he was on about. I blinked. I played his sentence back in my head. I still didn't get it.

He took a step closer. 'I mean it, Brenda.' He drew his lips together, luscious, berry red. 'I've never met anyone like you. Never in my long, long, lonely life.'

And that was when the penny dropped. Right there, in that narrow passageway. Under the glare of Effie's dead aunties. The shock of realisation went straight through my heaving gullet and right into my heart, making that poor, tired organ pound so hard that I was deafened for a good minute and a half.

The next day – drear, drizzly, me with a hangover and severe misgivings – was Jessie's funeral. I felt terribly alone. Effie couldn't understand why I kept myself apart. As far as she knew, the dinner party at her place had been a huge success: I had accepted and celebrated her new relationship. So why, today, did I sit apart in the church, all hunched over in my best black coat with a hat pulled over my eyes? Why, on the endless yomp up the hill, my first trip up those hundred and ninety-nine steps, to the church overlooking the town and the bay, did I struggle along on my lonesome? I could feel Effie puzzling and perplexing at my back, as she strolled along on the arm of the man she loved. Why had I gone taciturn again? Why had I only given them a polite nod, a sickly smile?

Truth was, I couldn't bring myself to be anywhere near that dreadful man. I'd slap his face. I'd end up telling Effie what he'd done. I'd cause an almighty row bang in the middle of poor Jessie's funeral, and that just wasn't on. The old devil would deny it, of course. He'd stand there all cool and say, 'What? Me? Make a pass at her?' And he'd look me up and down – ironic, disgusted. They all would. No one would believe me, least of all Effie. I'd lose her as a friend because she'd think I was trying to poke a spoke in the wheels of her love.

There weren't many people at the funeral. I trogged up that hill in the company of hotel guests, chambermaids and

Christmas elves. Robert led the way up the sharp, curving incline. At first hardly any words passed between us. I kept remembering how he had taunted me in that nasty café. Needless and cruel. What was it he'd said? How big your ears are, your teeth. Like I was a monster who could gobble him up.

As we rounded the headland, the sea was several hundred metres below our feet. A sheer drop. Crashing and booming. It sounded like applause. A slow handclap to accompany the cortège. Dispiriting, bleak. I reflected that I had managed to spoil my new friendships in Whitby. Already. Usually it took longer.

At the top of the hill the church waited for us. They had driven the body the long way round. A pink Cadillac – of all things – was parked beside the stately hearse. We arrived just in time to watch Mrs Claus being hoisted out of it by her elvish lackeys. She was in a huge white fur coat, trying to look solemn, but nothing – not even a burial – could suppress her crazed jollity. I didn't want a confrontation with her today. I scooted past, and into the church, hoping she hadn't noticed me.

What a strange bunch we made, half-filling that small church, coming to pay our respects to Jessie. The vicar was a spindly little man, who licked his lips nervously when he stood in front of the cheap coffin and surveyed us all. I wondered what he was thinking. Even to my eyes, we looked like a bunch of freaks.

He went through his spiel, stammering and coughing, and more people arrived. To my chagrin, Mr Danby and three of his simian assistants, walked in and loped into a back pew. I wanted to shout, 'He's to blame! He's the one who killed Jessie by starting her on those treatments in that diabolical machine!' But I suppose that's hardly the sort of thing you can say in church. Even I – godless Brenda – know that much. I glared at Mr Danby, though, across the backs of the pews. His nasty wet too-wide mouth grinned back in reply.

Music was played after the short service: a very small woman at the organ diddled out an unhymnlike tune. As we filed down the aisle, for our appointment at the graveside, Robert was suddenly beside me. Evidently he had seen my bemusement at the music: 'It's a liturgical rendition of "Yes, Sir, I Can Boogie". It was Jessie's favourite song. She always got up for it on the holidays we took together. She was a proper seventies disco chick.'

I stared up at him. He was handsome in his black suit, his hair combed out of its usual trendy tangle, talking to me in his normal tone. None of the spitting venom of the other morning. We stepped out into a bracing wind, and struggled through the long grass. Under the low chatter of the others, I was delighted to hear him say, 'I must apologise for the other morning. I must have been out of my mind. I didn't mean any of the things I said. I didn't know what I was on about.'

I nodded, surprised, but before I could speak there was a delay in the proceedings: Mrs Claus's motorised scooter had broken down on the gravel path. The burial would have to wait until her elves had sorted it out.

'It was to do with Jessie's death, I think,' he went on. 'And, of course, finding her like that, all frozen. I should never have turned against you, Brenda. I lashed out. I wanted to hurt someone . . .'

'I can take it. I'm quite resilient, you know.'

'And I really do think that . . . because of what goes on at the hotel, sometimes my mind isn't my own. Like the others, I fall under Mrs Claus's influence . . .'

'You still believe that?'

He breathed in deeply, his eyes scanning the graveyard. 'Oh, yes. Up here, away from the tinsel and baubles, I can start to see sense again.'

Then it was time to gather at the grave, to listen and watch Jessie lowered into the black hole. Curious spectacle. Each time I attend a funeral I get nightmares about being buried before my time. Waking up and finding myself buried alive. They are extraordinarily vivid dreams, almost as if it had actually happened to me in some former life. Perhaps it had. Perhaps bits of me had been taken from graves, shaken off, dusted and put to use again. I don't know. Patchy, as I say, my memory. I don't really know where I've been. All I know is, these parts have been mine longer than they were anyone else's, and I put them to the best use I can.

Dreadful thoughts to be having at a graveside.

'Mrs Claus is inviting everyone back to the Christmas Hotel,' Robert whispered, 'for sherry and the funeral baked meats.'

That nearly had me throwing up into poor Jessie's grave. Last night's rich food was still weighing heavy inside me. And the very thought of meat at the hotel – after Jessie's accusations – made me heave. 'I don't think so,' I said. Also, my recent escape from that place was fresh in my mind. If I went in, would I ever get out again? But surely Mrs Claus couldn't misbehave herself in front of the whole funeral party. Today she looked harmless, sitting by the vicar, respectable, even, blubbing at the passing of a true and trusted employee.

In the daytime here *everyone* looked respectable. You'd never think there were such things as magic, evil, disaster and danger. In the clear and logical daylight, it was as if only I believed in such things. And yet, when night came to Whitby, it seemed that the whole place went bonkers.

As we dispersed, Robert patted my arm and said he was due to help serve the funeral tea. He kissed me, and hoped to catch up with me later. I had to agree and forgive him. I needed all the friends and help I could get. I wanted to tell him about Effie and her beau, the situation developing there.

I realised then that I was staring rather hard at her and Kristoff. She pulled a funny face at me. She was irked because I'd been so standoffish all morning. Then I heard Kristoff say he was popping into the church to use the loo, which offered us a few moments alone together. I sidled up to her reluctantly as he slipped away.

'We went to so much effort last night,' Effie said, affronted, 'and how do you repay us? Gallumphing out like that! Dragging on your coat and dashing out into the night – and then, today, giving us the silent treatment! Come on, Brenda, what's your problem? You enjoyed dinner last night. You had a lovely time. You said you accepted our relationship. You said you liked Kristoff. You even toasted us!'

Put that way, her complaints seemed reasonable. In her position, I'd have been cross with me, too. But Effie didn't know the half of it. She didn't know what that man of hers was like. She was an innocent. He was preying on her, making passes at me. He was wicked and she would never see it.

If I told her, she would despise me. I knew that much – I know how these things work. She would think I was trying to break them up out of sheer spite.

'I can't tell you, Effie,' I said. 'Not yet. But . . . I was enjoying myself last night. I was having the most lovely time. I was pleased to see you so happy. I couldn't have been more delighted for you.'

That arched eyebrow of hers went up. 'And then?'

'And then . . . something happened. To change my mind.'

'What?' She was really annoyed with me. 'What happened? I deserve an explanation.'

'I can't tell you,' I said uselessly. I darted away from her. I had made the situation ten times worse. I should have kept my gob shut. I scurried back into the church. I needed the loo, too, to splash some cold water over my scalding face. To sit quietly for a few moments. It was downstairs in the crypt.

And so was Kristoff.

As I stared at my dripping face in the bathroom mirror, I realised I had to confront him, in the cold light of day, and ask him, what he had thought he was doing. What had he meant by those cruelly suggestive remarks last night?

I dashed out, hoping to catch him before he returned to Effie.

But he was taking his time. He wasn't in the gents – I checked – so I scouted out the rest of the crypt. And that was when I found the dark little door at the back. A stone staircase led down into the moist, wormy, earthy blackness, and my feet made quite a lot of noise on the steps. I cried out as I stumbled. I was no good at creeping up on people.

Candles had been lit on an abandoned old altar, and a coffin was laid out, open-topped, satiny plush, all luxurious, in a weirdly obscene parody of the funeral service we had attended above ground. And Kristoff was leaning casually against the altar. He looked mildly annoyed at my sudden entrance.

'You shouldn't be down here, Brenda,' he said, his voice velvety rich.

I felt as if I had been buried alive with him – the thought was almost enough to get me hyperventilating. 'I won't be long,' I snapped. 'I don't want to waste too much time on you.'

'Charming!'

'All I want to know, Kristoff, is what you thought you were playing at last night?'

'I was playing at being your gracious host, Brenda, and I thought I was making a good job of it.'

'You made a pass at me in the hallway! Right under poor Effie's nose!'

He drew himself up. 'I'm sure I did nothing of the sort.'

'You most certainly did!'

'I'm afraid your fevered imagination has betrayed you, Brenda. You are quite mistaken, my dear. Perhaps that is what you wanted to happen, but nothing could be further from the truth.'

'Rubbish!' But my mind was ticking back over those scenes last night. Could I have been mistaken? Could I have made a fool of myself, both then and now? But last night had become a rush of blurred and confusing images already, and I couldn't be sure of anything. 'You kept saying you found me fascinating and intriguing,' I burst out. It sounded pretty pathetic as an accusation, I know.

'Really, my dear,' he sighed, 'I have Effie. Why would I want anything to do with you? Forgive me, but you hardly compare well against Effryggia.'

I blushed crossly. But it was true, I knew. And that, honestly, was what had puzzled me, too. If he had Effie, why was he murmuring sweet nothings to me? I'd put him down as a serial adulterer. The type with no taste or self-control, doing it for kicks.

'Anyway,' he went on, 'I do find you fascinating, Brenda. But not in the way you suspected – or hoped.'

'What do you mean?'

'Professionally,' he said. 'That's how I'm speaking. I find you fascinating, professionally speaking.'

I knew it! My heart set up a frantic tattoo. He was a doctor, a surgeon, a vivisectionist. One of that coldly calculating breed. That was why I had felt his blazing eyes on me – weighing me up, slicing me apart. Wanting to know what was inside me. How I was put together. I have had that kind of unflattering attention all my life. I am used to those stares.

'What are you?' I asked, in a small voice.

He chuckled.

'And what are you doing, mucking about down here, anyway?' I asked, aware again of where we were. I felt claustrophobic.

Kristoff spread his hands and laughed. 'This is my bachelor pad.'

I backed away, stumbled, righted myself and continued backing away.

Kristoff carried on laughing. He didn't move from his spot by the altar.

'What do you want of me?' I gasped, finding myself at the stairs. I'd turn and run at any second. I'd be up in the church in just a few moments. He couldn't come after me there, could he?

'What do I want of you?' He considered. 'Quite a lot, Brenda.

Quite a lot is required of you, dear. But not just yet. The time isn't right. Soon, though.'

I wasn't sticking around for more of this.

I should have. I should have got the truth out of him while he was down there, charging his batteries in his bachelor crypt. But I turned abruptly and fled.

Later that afternoon I was turning over thick clods of earth in my garden. I relished the exertion, puffing out steam and working up a sweat. It would be one of my last chances to tend my flowerbeds before winter stole in. Of course, I kept well away from the rockery.

I felt a prickling at the back of my neck, straightened, and there was Effie.

'Do you think I could have an explanation?' she said.

'Effie,' I said, 'I don't want to talk about it now.'

'Yes, you do, madam,' she said. Then her face softened. 'Is it because you think I've told Kristoff all about you? All your secrets and your history?' She shook her head pityingly. 'Of course I haven't, Brenda. What kind of a monster do you think I am?'

I hung my head. 'I thought the two of you had been giggling about me behind my back.'

'It's rather hurtful to hear,' she said, 'that you would think that.'

'Love changes people. You're so much under his influence.'

'Rot,' she said. 'I'd never betray you, Brenda.'

'But he knows, Effie! He knows all about me. Where I come from . . . what I am . . .'

'Not because of me,' she said. 'I've never said a word.'

I led her indoors and out of the freezing mist that was creeping up the hill into my garden. I would make us spicy tea, and it would be just like before. Before a devilishly handsome man had come into our lives.

'He keeps saying things to me,' I said, as we settled at my kitchen table.

'Things?'

'About how he's . . . intrigued by me. Fascinated.'

Effie raised her eyebrow. 'Really?'

'It's very peculiar.'

'He has some peculiar enthusiasms,' Effie murmured. I was interested that she wasn't suspicious or envious. It didn't occur to her that her boyfriend might have made a pass at me, that he might fancy me. That idea didn't appear to enter her head at all.

'And what's he doing hanging about in the crypt of that church?' I enquired. 'He was skulking in there when I went to the lav.'

Effie cradled her mug. 'He was picking up some of his tools and materials. He's doing historical research down there. Didn't he tell you?'

'He said the crypt was his bachelor pad.'

Effie laughed. 'I think he just about *did* live there before he met me. He's rather obsessed with his work. Tombs and inscriptions and whatnot. Ghoulish, morbid stuff, I call it. I mean, the dead are dead, aren't they? They don't need us poking through their business.' She looked at me. 'Why? What did you think he was doing down there?'

I shrugged lightly. 'I'm not sure. Especially after some of the things we've come up against recently.'

'Darling,' Effie smirked, 'that's as may be. But you really

mustn't go round suspecting the worst of Kristoff. He's a very good man, and he's done me a power of good. He's given me a reason to get up in the morning.'

'Really?' I was surprised. Effie's life before Kristoff hadn't seemed so terrible to me. She hadn't despised it.

'He's a darling, gentle man,' she said.

'Where is he now?'

'Historical research,' she said. 'Up in my attic. He said he couldn't wait to get his hands on my books. All that arcane lore. He's going through all the catalogues and notes I've been compiling.'

The persistent buzzing I'd had in my head for days suddenly exploded into grand, crashing peals of alarm bells. 'He's going through your aunties' books of magic?' I asked. 'You've let him get at them?'

'Of course.' She laughed. 'Why shouldn't I? I hope he has more success than I did. I couldn't make head or tail of the nasty things.'

Suddenly I knew that Effie had made a dreadful mistake.

And I also knew that that was why Kristoff Alucard was paying court to her. He needed those books. He needed access to the precious information hidden somewhere inside them. That was what all this was about.

Effie had been duped. She had been wooed silly. Flattered daft.

And she had let Kristoff steal secrets she didn't even know she had.

I watched him come and go. I peered down at the street from my highest window. It became something like an obsession with me, keeping tabs on Effie's bloke. I would watch him leave her shop at the strangest hours: midnight, five a.m. seven o'clock at night. There was no pattern to his behaviour. He seemed to come and go at will, looking mightily perplexed. Often he had with him one of those thick, leatherbound books from Effie's collection. To all intents and purposes, he was doing precisely what Effie had claimed: the kind of historical research that had him stomping through town at all hours of the day. He was searching for something, using fragments of clues from Effie's books to get to it.

'I don't know what it is,' said Effie, sharply. 'And, what's more, I won't ask him.'

'But don't you think he's behaving oddly?' I said.

She shrugged. I bit my lip. After almost a week of study and tramping about, he had stopped taking Effie out. Things had gone quiet on that front. 'Well,' she said, 'it was exhausting.' This was as we had morning coffee in the Walrus and the Carpenter. 'We couldn't have carried on at the same rate. Gadding about like youngsters. No, perhaps this is a more sedate period when things settle down. It can't be excitement all the time.'

I was wondering whether, in terms of our friendship, Effie and I were back on an even keel. Here we were, back in our old routine, coffee and shopping, with nothing coming between us. Certainly not fellas.

I didn't believe what she was saying, though. 'Sedate period'. 'Settling down'. It didn't look very sedate to me, whatever Alucard was doing. These days, he seemed excitable, clutching those vile books to his chest, dashing about. But it was an excitement that had nothing to do with Effie.

That afternoon we bumped into him as we headed back across the bay. The mist had crept in early, but it wasn't so thick that he could brush past without noticing us.

'Oh!' he exclaimed. 'I'm so sorry. How rude of me!'

Effie was quite piqued. She had shouted across the road at him several times. People had seen. Now she felt foolish. 'Where are you off to now, Kristoff?' She sounded weary.

Poor Effie, I thought. The shine's soon gone off the affair. She was so listless and pale. I wondered if she might be anaemic or something. Love does funny things to people. Neglect does even worse.

'Ah, you know,' he said jauntily, 'more hunting about. More looking into the deep, magical past of this place.' He grinned wolfishly and I saw that he wasn't his usual spruce self. His hair was awry, greasy and lank. He wasn't as suave as usual either: he was wearing an anorak and carrying an old string bag of Effie's books.

'The magical past?' I asked, frowning. 'I didn't know that was what you were looking into.' But, of course, it had to be that, didn't it? What else had Effie's aunties been interested in?

'I think I'm on the brink of something,' he said.

'Really?'

Effie was openly sceptical now. 'Go on, then. Tell us what it is. We can't hang around all day in this freezing fog.'

'I'd rather not say just yet,' he whispered, 'in case I'm wrong. But I'm almost sure I've found it. The clues in the books have led me to just the right spot. This is it! The whole reason I'm here in the first place! Almost at my fingertips . . .'

I heard Effie's sharp intake of breath: that remark had stung her. He didn't notice.

'Well,' she said, with a wave of her veiny hand, 'you'd best get on with it, hadn't you? We wouldn't want to hold you up.' She was dismissing him as she would a small child, sending him out to play.

Kristoff didn't need telling twice. He grinned, then vanished into the mist.

'He'll be off up the steps,' she said, 'poking his nose round that church again. And the abbey. That's where he seems to concentrate his searches.'

'But what for?' I said. We started walking again, heading for home. 'What is it he's looking for?'

She shrugged as if it meant nothing to her. As if she couldn't have cared less. But that was a lie and we both knew it.

Effie invited me in. 'Come and see what he's been looking at.'

'Hm?'

'While he's out I'll show you what he's been reading. Some of his notes are about the place, too.' Effie was worried. 'I don't like it, Brenda. Remember when I said there were nasty, frightening things in some of those books?'

I followed her upstairs.

In just a few days, Effie's home had fallen back into moribund disarray. The worst room turned out to be the one that Kristoff had taken to working in, at the top of the house. The oldest books were concentrated there and a battered dining-table was spread with a selection of them. Slips of paper held open pages, and there were crumpled notes written in Kristoff's strange, nearly legible hand.

'Not much of this is in English,' I said, peering at the books, stirring through the loose notes. I found myself reluctant to touch anything, not so much for fear of being found snooping but because there was something horrible and tainting about them.

'Remember that stuff I read about creatures controlling us from other worlds?' Effie said. 'And some of the illustrations of those weird, crablike beings with tentacles and angel wings?'

I nodded, although that night I'd thought Effie had hit the sherry rather hard.

'He's been scouring those books. Old gods, he says, and old rituals.'

'I don't like the sound of it,' I said. Then I glanced at Effie. 'This must be horrible for you. He seemed like Mr Perfect.'

'He still is Mr Perfect,' she snapped. 'I'm just not sure about his hobbies.'

We rolled up our sleeves then, and set to work examining the texts. I had to put aside my physical disgust at touching those books. As before, they reminded me of the ones that had lined the walls of my father's laboratory.

Some time later, as evening wore on, and the light in the upper windows turned a pretty shade of apricot, I gave a falsely hearty laugh, which broke the silence. 'You'll never guess, Effie, but I've been fretting and worrying for days because of your Kristoff.'

'Really?' she said, turning pages carefully. 'And why's that? What's there to worry about?'

I chuckled. 'You know what I'm like. I see monsters and nefarious schemes everywhere. But . . . I did think he had you under his influence. Like a demon lover. He had swept into your life and taken you over absolutely . . .'

She smiled at me. 'To be honest, that's rather how it feels. Not that I'm complaining. I just assumed that that's how love is.'

I laughed again. 'And you'll never guess what I'd started to suspect. You'll think I'm ridiculous. But it was the way he went about, all regally. And his clothes and the pallor of his skin. And the way I found him skulking in that crypt and he seemed so at home there. And then I thought, Well, of course, none of that can be true, can it? Because he's out and about in the daytime. He isn't afraid of the sunlight. So, of course, I'm thinking nonsense, I decided. And I was relieved – so relieved!' I gave another fake-sounding laugh.

Effie was staring at me. 'What on earth are you on about?'

My face fell. 'He's a vampire, isn't he?'

Effie smirked. 'All that, for such a simple question! Really, dear. You should learn to spit things out.' She tutted at me. 'But, yes, of course he is. I thought that was pretty obvious.'

Her pallor! I thought, with a rush of sheer horror. Her listlessness and the changeable moods. He'd had a go at her!

'And you,' I said, very quietly, 'has he bitten you?'

'Oh,' she said, 'not really. It's early days, you know. I mean, I might look like a silly old woman who's lost all her sense. I might seem desperate to you, but I do have my self-respect, you know. I haven't given him my all. Not yet.'

'But *has he bitten you*?' I insisted. 'Are you . . . undead, Effie?'

She was scandalised. 'Of course not! You'd be the first to know, Brenda. Do you think I'd keep something like that from you?'

I shook my head. How could she be so blithe about it?

She laughed. 'I thought you'd worked it out days ago. It's obvious. Think of his name, what it spells backwards.'

'Oh!' I've always been useless at anagrams and crosswords,

things like that. You need a certain kind of analytical mind for such things. Same as doing research in mouldering books like these. I couldn't make much sense of them. 'So, he's Dracula, then? That's what you're saying?'

Effie rolled her eyes at me. 'You're so *slow*, Brenda. Sometimes I don't know why I bother.'

Now that the secret was out, Effie was looking like the cat that got the cream, like a much younger woman who had managed to snag a famous pop star or a footballer. Maybe in her family of witchy old women snaring the Prince of the Undead counted as much the same thing.

'So how come he can go about in the daytime?' I asked.

'The same way he puts lots of garlic in his food, wears a crucifix – upside-down, of course – and has a reflection in the mirror. Those are all very old-fashioned ideas. He's not stuffy and stuck in the past at all. He's updated himself.'

I was impressed. I was amazed, too, at how sanguine Effie was. 'Sanguine' was an unfortunate word. I pictured him nibbling at her, drawing up bright beads of blood, her waving him away, laughing like a schoolgirl. What had Effie got herself into?

She had surrounded herself with monsters. She had invited him over her threshold, and welcomed him into her life. And next door she had me. Her best friend. We were the two people closest to her and we had these monstrous, unnatural pasts, stretching back through recent centuries. Poor Effie. Did she ever wish she knew some ordinary people?

'I know what you're thinking, Brenda,' she said, 'but you mustn't worry. I have nothing to fear from Kristoff. He really does love me, you know.'

I tried to smile, wholly unconvinced.

'He has a different relationship to time from the rest of us. He doesn't see me as I see me, or you, or anyone else. He doesn't see this sagging flesh and the wrinkles. That's just the envelope, how I am on the outside at this moment. Because he's lived so long – much longer even than you – he has learned to see in four dimensions, rather than three. He can see time itself within me, through me and behind me. He sees all the Effies I have been, right back to the cradle. All those much more youthful and vital versions of me, stretching out behind me. And that's what he loves. All of me, going back into the past.'

I was mollified by this – a little. It sounded rather nice.

'And my female forebears,' she said, 'he can see them, too. Their genetic influence on me, and everything they have passed down.'

Everything that had made Effie who she was, Kristoff perceived and understood. It made sense to me that his burning eyes could see all those things. That he could somehow *see* time.

Then I wondered what he saw when he looked at me. I wasn't a consistent, coherent being like Effie, with a long line of ancestors. I wasn't integral in that way. What did he see? What shape was I in four dimensions? Was I even more monstrous than I am in three? He said he was fascinated by me. Intrigued. Now I realised that he must know far more about me than I did. He would have seen everything at a glance.

A chill crept over me.

Both Effie and I jumped in our rickety chairs when we heard the door bang downstairs.

I was meant to be here, in this town, at this time. I've always known that. It is as if all my long life until now has been a prelude to coming here. To my purpose here.

It was that night, as Effie's new fancy man stepped back into her house, that I started to find out what was expected of me in Whitby. Kristoff Alucard was in possession of some of the answers. And as he trod up the staircases and headed towards us, in his makeshift study, I knew that the truth of my destiny was closing in on me.

'Look natural,' said Effie, breathlessly.

'What?'

'Look as if we weren't going through all his things.'

Too late. He slipped into the room like a shadow. He glanced at us narrowly, suspiciously.

'I was having a tidy round . . .' said Effie, in a rush.

'Nonsense.' Alucard sighed. 'You needn't make up stories for me, my dear. Naturally you wish to know more about my recent activities and researches. The texts belong to you. It is only right that I keep you informed. Forgive my reticence, my dear. But I had to be sure.'

Effie glanced at me. 'Sure of what?'

'I have found it,' he said. His voice was trembling. 'Your books gave me the few extra pointers I needed. And now I've found it!'

'Tell us!' cried Effie. 'What is it? Treasure? A . . . weapon? A golden chalice?' She was ransacking her memory for mythical objects.

'The Bitch's Maw,' he said, in a low, thrilling tone.

A few bells rang in my head, clamouring for attention. I gripped the corner of the table. I knew he was speaking the truth. I had heard that name mentioned before, in this very house. During the seance, just a couple of weeks ago, that name had issued from the lips of Brian the psychic. My father had mentioned the Bitch's Maw.

And we had been warned. We had heard dreadful things coming through the ether. But what had we done about it?

Nothing. That was the truth. We'd had enough to be getting on with, it was true. We had been set upon by all manner of strange events. But we hadn't done a thing about the place my father had referred to as the Bitch's Maw. Something about the misogyny of the term had made me flinch. It wasn't something I had wanted to dwell on.

But here it was again.

Effie sat down heavily. 'That again!' she said. 'I shouldn't be surprised. What was it we were meant to do, Brenda? Watch over the souls exiled from hell? What did Brian say? That hell is bursting at the seams?' I nodded at her. 'Well,' she said, 'I thought he was talking nonsense. Rambling and ranting about nothing.'

'The Bitch's Maw is real,' Kristoff said. 'It has been here for almost a thousand years. It connects this town with the nether regions, and it can never be destroyed. So, it needs watching. It needs to be guarded. That is what your forebears did, Effie. It was their function here.'

'Rubbish,' she said. 'No one ever told me about it. Great Aunt Maud never said a word about any gateway to hell.'

'Gateway is a good word for what it is,' said Kristoff, gently. 'It's hidden from prying eyes. It's invisible, until the correct phrases are said. All the clues are in those books, Effie, especially those left behind by Great Aunt Maud. And if she didn't tell you about your duties here, there must have been a reason for that. She must have been taken from you too soon . . .'

'A fishbone,' Effie said. 'It was a sudden, undignified death.'

'In this more rational age,' Kristoff sighed, 'it would have been hard to convince you, anyway, of the Maw's existence. And, throughout your life, it has been neglected. The entrance to hell has been untended—'

Now I butted in: 'You – you're one of the damned,' I told him. 'Are you one of those who escaped through this gateway thing?'

His eyes burned, and he looked offended. 'Certainly not. I am earthbound, just as you are, Brenda.'

'Then . . . why are you here? What do you want with the Maw thing?'

He cast an eager, hungry gaze over the splayed texts. He looked as if he wanted to reach out with those slender fingers, those pointed nails, and rake through the pages, rip out that secret knowledge and devour it in one go. Then he grew calmer. 'I am working for someone else.'

'Oh, no!' Effie gasped. 'Not a Higher Power! Not one of those terrible creatures!'

Kristoff seemed alarmed. 'Certainly not. I am being employed by a rather more lowly, humdrum organisation. The Ministry of Incursions and Other Wonders.'

'MIAOW,' I said. 'You're working for MIAOW?'

He nodded, produced a plastic wallet and flashed a neat ID card at us.

'You're telling me Dracula's working for the secret service?' I said.

He shushed me. 'Don't use that name. It sets off alarms at all sorts of levels. Best stick to my other names.'

'I don't believe it,' I said flatly. 'What can they possibly be giving you to get you to work for them? You're a free spirit, Prince of the Undead! You don't need a salary, a pension, a career! What's got into you, man?'

He looked away. 'Is it any more remarkable than the Bride of Frankenstein opening a bed-and-breakfast?'

'Hm,' I said. '*Touché.*'

'Needs must,' he said. 'We've all had to retrain, professionalise ourselves, haven't we?'

'Brenda,' Effie broke in, 'I didn't even know that MIAOW existed.'

'They've dogged my steps for years,' I said, 'and I'd assumed they were leaving me alone now.'

'It's true,' he said, 'that your file at the Ministry is rather thick. They've kept tabs on you, Brenda, but they don't regard you as a threat. They would never do you any harm. Rather, they're interested in you. And, of course, in your ultimate destiny.'

'Hm,' I said.

Effie was staring at him rather closely. 'So, really, you came here for Brenda's sake. It's true, isn't it? You're here in the line of duty.'

'Of course,' he said stiffly. 'But—'

'And you only stuck around because of her and this destiny business and—' She flailed out then, with both hands, sweeping a number of the precious books to the floor. 'You only got close to me for the sake of these tatty old things. These books of pure evil. That's what you courted me for, wasn't it? You never wanted me at all!' She was doing battle with herself, trying not to break down in front of him. I was paralysed with mute horror.

'Effie, you mustn't believe that,' Alucard said urgently. 'You must never think that.'

'But I do, Kristoff. How can I believe you? Think of the horror you've unleashed throughout your life. I was kidding myself. I'm a crazy old woman. How could I ever have thought that a demon like you would be capable of love? A monster! A devil!'

'No,' he said. 'Effie, that's not true.'

'I think he's sincere, Effie,' I said. 'I'm not the most perfect judge of character, but I think—'

'And you!' she rounded on me. 'All this nasty stuff is right up your street, isn't it? Monsters and demons, things coming out of the past and up from hell. Why, you must be in your element, lady! I suppose it all makes you feel rather special, doesn't it?'

I opened my mouth to reply but the ferocity of Effie's attack had knocked the wind out of me.

'Brenda *is* rather special, Effie,' said Alucard. 'She's unique. But you are special too, and vital to the success of my mission here. With the knowledge acquired by your aunts, you have shown me how to find and open the Bitch's Maw.'

'I've hated those books all my life,' Effie said bitterly. 'I've hated everything to do with magic and all of that. I turned my back on it. But it gets you in the end, doesn't it? That world reaches out to you, and gets you eventually . . .'

But I was staring at Alucard. 'Open it? That's what you want to do?'

He nodded. 'I think I can.'

'But why on earth would you want to?'

He licked his lips carefully and, for the first time, I saw his glinting fangs. 'Because then I can seal it. For ever. And that is my mission.'

Out we went, gallivanting again in the silvery moonlight. It made me excited – it always does, all the frost and the satiny dark

– but that night dread weighed on me too. There was a tingle in my extremities and a ringing in my ears.

Effie and I wrapped up warm. She lent me an elegant wrap thing that only just went round my shoulders. She was muttering to herself the whole time, as we prepared for our trip to the abbey and the mystery of the Bitch's Maw.

'You don't seem best pleased by any of this,' I said quietly.

She put on her good sheepskin gloves and glowered at me. 'Would you be?'

'It seems to me that we're equally mixed up in it.'

'Perhaps. But . . . Oh, really, I thought I'd found a nice, uncomplicated man-friend. I thought I was having a proper relationship at last, like other people do.'

'But you are!'

She shook her head dolefully. 'I feel a bit used, to tell the truth.'

'Ladies?' He had slipped into the hallway, and was standing at a tactful distance from us. Now he was wearing a dark cloak with a red silk lining and he was looking every inch the part. We were ready to embark on the last phase of his mission.

Just look at me and Effie, I thought, setting off into the night, tagging along on the heels of this – this abomination.

I know. It comes to something, doesn't it, when even I get to call someone an abomination? But that's what he was, wasn't he? Or what he used to be. I don't know why or what had changed his nature. I don't know how he had calmed down, cleaned up his act and 'professionalised', as he put it. But he had gone from a ravening, corpse-sucking demon lord to a smarmy secret agent. I'm not sure I wanted to know how that had happened.

As we left the building through Effie's dingy shop, he gave my shoulder a staunch pat, as if we were brothers in arms. I stepped aside as Effie locked and bolted the door and refused to meet his eye. I hated him insinuating that we were made of the same stuff, that we were bonded somehow. I was, in principle, against everything Alucard stood for, yet he spoke to me as if we were alumni from the same old School of Monstrosity.

We marched through the mist-shrouded town centre and Effie kept shtum. Her heels scraped loudly on the cobbles and I was wondering how she expected to climb up to the abbey in shoes like that.

'A long time ago,' said Alucard, 'I met your father.' I glanced at him sharply. 'On a number of occasions, actually.'

I breathed out slowly. I wasn't sure I believed him. 'Is that a fact?'

'I found him charming. If a little egocentric. But, then, why shouldn't he be? He had created life from scratch. Imagine that!'

'Indeed,' I said drily.

'I was pleased to make his acquaintance,' Kristoff said. 'Over the years I have met a great many of the great, the good and the downright wicked. Your father stood out, you know. Oh, yes. He was remarkable.'

'When was this?'

'Oh, I don't remember exactly.'

'So, is it true, then,' I said, 'that you lot spent much of the nineteenth century hanging around together and having bloodcurdling adventures? Wolfmen and lizardwomen, mummies, zombies and . . . my dad?'

He chuckled: an oily, uncanny sound. 'Our paths crossed on a number of occasions. Monster team-ups, we liked to call them.

You know, Frankenstein Meets the Wolfman Meets Dracula's Daughter, kind of thing'

I whistled. 'You must have had a whale of a time, running about in central Europe, being mobbed by torch-waving peasants, getting bumped off and being resurrected all over the place.'

I looked at Alucard, and he was smiling.

'I wouldn't have wanted to be involved anyway,' I said. 'All that supernatural nonsense.'

'Really?' Alucard said. 'I can't help but think you must have been lonely, Brenda. All those years alone, abandoned on these islands. A reject. Herr Doktor's terrible mistake.'

I flashed him a look. 'All right! Don't go rubbing it in.'

Of course, I had thought these things a million times and I really didn't feel as sorry for myself as all that. Not any more. But in Kristoff Alucard – this man-beast gone legit – I had come across the closest thing I would ever get to someone from my own time and background. I felt like wailing and gnashing my teeth at him. A dreadful wave of self-pity and loss came over me as we crossed the bay and headed for the steps.

Town was dead. It was as if we three were the only living things abroad. And some of us were hardly living.

'It can't have been easy for you,' he said, as we turned on to the path that would wind us round the headland and above the rooftops. Eventually it would take us right to the top, overlooking all of Whitby. 'None of it could have been very easy.'

'No,' I said. 'It hasn't been.'

'From the little I saw of your father, and from the little I know, I'm sure he would have been very proud of you.'

The steps are very steep, pebbly and noisy to climb. Effie was crunching ahead, and my own large feet were slithering along in the shale. I was out of breath already, feeling my age and all my fleshy heaviness. Of course Alucard was gliding along beside me as he talked. Patronising sod.

'I don't care,' I said. 'I really don't care what he would have thought of me. I've never needed him for anything, and I don't need his approval now.' I gritted my teeth as the crash and swelling boom of the sea filled me with rage. I fought to control my temper, hunched my shoulders forward and tried to increase my pace. I started counting the steps. I thought superstitiously that good things would come if I counted them all.

Kristoff Alucard's words had put me right back in the past.

At the beginning. Lying on that makeshift trolley. Coming to life, I suppose you would say. Opening these eyes. Stirring these limbs. And slowly becoming aware of the world about me. A nasty, confined, slimy sort of world, the basement laboratory on that island. But as yet I knew no other. I drew in a huge breath and my lungs ached, crackled, wheezed. Then I saw my prospective husband staring down at me from that window, high up in the wall. My beautiful Intended looked so eager and gleeful. He was delighted to have witnessed my birth.

But my father wasn't glad.

His hawk-like face was overcome with disgust. His sharp nose wrinkled in dismay as visions of horror rose before him. It was at that moment that Herr Doktor had realised he couldn't bear the thought of my husband and me breeding. My fiancé's delight appalled him. He saw visions of our dreadful children: of our kind slowly populating the world. He realised the sacrilege he had created in setting himself up as God. And so, seconds after my birth, he had decided to mend his ways and murder me.

I mean, we never even knew, did we? We never got a chance to find out whether we were compatible, whether we could breed or not. We were never given much of a chance to do anything.

Kiddies. That would have been something, wouldn't it?

My father, it seemed, couldn't imagine anything worse. He wanted to ensure that the world would not suffer the vile offspring of this monstrous woman. He wouldn't risk opening a door into a world that could never be closed. Who knew what might come tumbling out?

So my father did what he felt was the only decent thing. He murdered me. Out came the scalpels and knives once more.

My husband wailed and screamed to be allowed in to save me from my father. Only minutes into this life, I was fighting to stay alive.

But I was murdered.

Or so my father and my husband thought. They left me to it, lying in my own blood. They tore off to pursue each other. Monster and creator locked in combat unto death. And I was left behind.

And now Alucard was telling me I should care. I should be thrilled that my father would have been proud of me.

No. I think he would have been proud of his handiwork, his cleverness and skill. He'd have been cock-a-hoop that this body – this child of his intellect and nimble surgeon's fingers – has lasted so long. But proud of me for myself? I doubt it.

My father never could, never would and never actually did give a fuck for me.

'I won't talk about the past any more,' Alucard said gently, as we approached the top of the hill. 'I can tell you don't like to.'

We paused in the shadow of the church. We caught our breath and watched the endless glimmering of the North Sea. 'There isn't time to get caught up in the past,' I said. 'Just look at now. Look at the present. It's so huge. There's quite enough of that to be going on with.'

'You're right,' he said. He cast a furtive glance across the graveyard to where Effie was picking her way through the long grass, stiff-backed and frosty.

'I do have feelings for her, you know,' he said suddenly. 'It wasn't just a pose, or a means to an end.'

'Well,' I said, 'good. I suspected as much.'

He nodded, and seemed a bit lost. 'It hasn't happened for a long time. I thought my feelings had evaporated. I'm so corrupted and congealed inside. And there she was! But . . . I've messed it all up.'

'I'm sure you haven't, Kristoff. Effie will come round. She just feels a bit less special than she did a few days ago. You made her feel wonderful, you know. You really did.'

He smiled at that. He wasn't used to feeling unsure. I decided that what I liked about Alucard – despite everything – was that there was none of that posturing male-ego rubbish about him. He didn't need endless flattery. It was enough for him to hear that he had given pleasure – sheer, unadulterated pleasure – even if only for a short while.

I envied them both just then.

I thought, Where's *my* fancy man?

But it wasn't the time to dwell on such things.

'Come on,' I said. 'Let's find this gateway. Are you sure you know what you have to do?'

He nodded. I suppose he's always been pretty efficient.

'I'm word perfect,' he said, and struck out, determined, for the ruins of the abbey.

He knew where he was going. He had checked and rechecked the notes and cryptic hints left by Effie's female relatives, and now he knew which corner of the great ruins he should head for.

Effie and I fell back, letting him lead the way through those opened chambers. I had never really been so close to the place. Something had kept me away. The atmosphere surrounding it, perhaps. Now that we were wandering through the middle of the building, I felt as if I was inside the skeleton of a vast creature, its stunted ribcage rising brokenly to the sky.

Perhaps I had never visited the ruined abbey because it reminded me too much of myself.

Alucard flitted ahead, sure of his purpose. His black and scarlet cloak billowed behind him as he moved like a whisper among the rubble and long grass, cutting rather a dash.

Were we scared? I'm not sure. Effie and I exchanged a few glances, but not many words. All that I was sure of was the rightness of our being there. We were both in no doubt that we were meant to be at this point, at this time. It had been on the cards for ages. I'm no good at spotting constellations and all that, but the stars looked brilliantly propitious through the shattered abbey roof.

He had stopped at a ruined tower and motioned us over. A tiny doorway was concealed behind a scrub bush, which he cleared with a ripping sound. 'Just inside,' he said. 'It was the cell of an abbess over a thousand years ago. It's she who guards the way. It was she who opened the gateway in the first place.'

'An abbess?' said Effie. 'Well, it just goes to show.'

We struggled in through the hole, and had some difficulty standing up in the confined space. Alucard lit a match and suddenly there was a real whiff of sulphur. Effie pointed this out, and we all laughed uneasily. A short tunnel opened up ahead. It smelt rancid and wrong – like bad milk or vegetables, rather than old stone and earth.

'It should be just a few yards down this way,' Alucard said.

His voice was shaking! He was nervous! I thought.

'Look, I've got to start this chanting business now. I need to concentrate.'

'How long do the invocations last?' Effie asked.

'I don't know,' he said. 'I haven't rehearsed.' He started then, inching forward into the darkness, holding aloft his weirdly long-lasting match, which sputtered and spat. The words he spoke were ancient and alien-sounding. They came out in long strings and stanzas, sometimes sounding like poetry, at others like demands, commands and earnest prayers.

I felt Effie draw away. She was slipping backwards down the passage and through the nun's cell. Alucard noticed too and, not breaking off from his spell-saying, gave me a look and a nod to fetch her back. All of us had to be there.

I caught up with Effie. She was leaning against the stone wall outside, breathing raggedly under the milky moonlight. 'I had to get out for a bit,' she said. 'I hate being around magic. I couldn't stand it when I was a child. This is bringing everything back.'

I nodded. 'We all have to be there, though.'

'I know. I'll just get my breath.' She gazed at me searchingly. 'Do you trust him?'

I didn't know. But it seemed we were in too deep now to back out. We simply had to trust him, and I told her so. 'I believe he wants to seal off this gateway,' I said.

Effie straightened up and tugged on her sheepskin gloves again. Then, like a rabbit in the middle of the road, she froze.

'What is it?'

'Look!' she gasped. 'Who on earth is that?'

Across the top of the hill, silhouetted against the bright night sky, a figure was moving through the abbey's bonelike remains. He was bustling towards us, all businesslike, and as he grew nearer we heard him whistling a jaunty little air.

'He's coming straight for us . . .'

He was a short, pale-haired man with rounded shoulders and stubby arms, carrying a hefty suitcase.

'Danby,' Effie said. 'It's Mr Danby.'

Sure enough, he was close enough now for us to see his smug, ghoulish face, with its too-wide, simpering smile. As he stepped up to us he clicked his heels and gave a silly salute. 'Ladies! An auspicious evening, no?'

Effie frowned. 'I don't know what you're talking about.' She spoke with the kind of hauteur that would have frozen any mortal in an instant. But it seemed Mr Danby was made of sterner stuff.

'I wonder, given the solemnity of our mission this evening, if we might draw a veil over the recent unfortunate goings-on at my boutique? I hope perhaps we can have a truce and learn to work together.'

'A truce!' Effie spat.

'Why would we have to work together?' I asked.

He sniggered. 'You will learn shortly. But come now, let bygones be bygones and all that. Surely if I can sweep my feelings under the carpet, then you two ladies can, too.'

'Our friend Jessie died as a result of your jiggery-pokery,' Effie ground out.

'Surely not,' he murmured. 'No, that is not at all true.'

'And I had a hellish experience in your Deadly Machine! And, what's more, we know what you were up to! Feeding your old mother on the life essences and whatnot of all your poor victims!'

'Well,' he said quietly, and tapped his battered leather suitcase, 'my mother is a remarkable woman. She needs careful looking after. She deserves the best.'

We didn't know what he was talking about. He sounded loopy.

'Has Alucard begun his invocations?' Danby asked. 'Would you like to lead the way, ladies?'

I couldn't think of anything nastier than squashing ourselves into that claustrophobic space with Mr Danby right on our heels. But we went, and he was squeaking with interest as we scuttled up the passageway to stand with Alucard.

'I have brought her,' Danby interrupted loudly.

'Brought who?' I asked. 'What are you on about?'

Kristoff stopped chanting and held the match close to Danby's pale, sweating face. 'Good,' he said. 'Thank you, Danby.'

A terrible chill went through me. This was a plan we knew nothing about. These men had organised something behind our backs.

'I don't like this,' Effie whispered.

'Me neither.' My voice was rather gruff, as if I might lose my temper at any moment and batter our enemies into submission.

Danby laid his suitcase on the dry, sandy ground and opened its clasps and straps. We crowded round to see, quietened by his solemnity.

'He has brought the guardian,' Alucard whispered. 'The one who controls this gateway.'

'In a suitcase?' Effie scoffed.

Danby flipped open the lid.

There, in a nest of tiny blankets and satiny sheets, lay a tiny nun. She was as withered as a sun-dried tomato. Her habit was minuscule, and she was glaring up at us with such malignity that we all drew back. She was like a wrinkled, evil, holy, fairy. She sat up, stretched, coughed and looked furious.

'This,' said Mr Danby, 'is my mother. The abbess.'

'The original abbess.' Alucard sighed. 'Welcome home, my dear.'

'That?' Effie pointed a shaking finger at the little woman. 'That's what the Deadly Boutique was all about? Keeping that thing alive? That dreadful homunculus?'

'Effie,' I warned. 'Don't!' I knew that the creature wielded awesome powers and that my friend was overstepping the mark.

'All my efforts, for a very long time, have been dedicated to keeping the abbess alive,' Mr Danby said, clasping his sweaty fingers together. He watched, enraptured, as the nun dusted herself down and hopped out of her suitcase. She surveyed us and tutted loudly.

'We have found the hiding place of the gateway,' Alucard said portentously.

'It wasn't hard to find,' she said, in a harsh, grating voice, much too big for her tiny frame. 'Not once you were in possession of the books.' I felt Effie stiffen beside me.

'We have come to the Bitch's Maw, as appointed,' Alucard said. 'I have uttered the spells, and I have drawn you here, Reverend Mother. Show us the Maw.'

She nodded. There was a weaselly, canny look about her that I didn't like one bit.

As we watched, the tiny nun raised her skinny arms and closed her eyes.

Almost instantly the dark rock of the wall behind her turned translucent orange. It pulsated as if it was molten: lava held in check behind melting glass. Then it brightened, turned brilliant white, and the silhouette of that midget hag was burned into our retinas.

When the brightness died down we could see a circular entrance before us. It was covered with inscriptions and seemed to lead off into an unimaginable distance. As my eyes grew accustomed to the light, I saw a lush forest inside the tunnel ahead. It was a primordial, verdant land, of a kind that no one here has seen for many hundreds of years.

'This is the way,' said the nun. She glared at us appraisingly. 'What were you expecting? Fire and brimstone?'

'To be honest,' said Effie, 'yes. Things have a dismaying habit of turning out exactly as badly as you expect.'

The midget nun cackled. 'Very good! I like her, Alucard. Now, what is it you require of me?'

Kristoff Alucard licked his ruby lips. This was the tricky part, we knew. 'I have been sent,' he began, 'to close the Bitch Maw for ever. To seal it off from the world.'

The nun looked appalled. 'But whatever for?' She blinked in astonishment. 'Sent? What do you mean "sent"? Who can send you anywhere, Alucard? Who would dare? Since when did you do any man's bidding?'

He straightened himself to his full height. 'None of that is any of your business, Reverend Mother. All that matters is my mission.'

Her face crumpled in concentration. 'This isn't what I was expecting.' She shot an evil look at her quaking son, Danby. 'You idiot. Seal the Maw, indeed! As if such a thing were possible. You should have warned me, Danby. You're useless!' Danby was quaking in his elegant shoes, as far away from the hole in the wall as he could get.

To me, that forest was delicious. It had a fresh, fecund smell: the most inviting scent I had ever experienced. A cool breeze wafted out and everything seemed to be covered with a light morning dew. I could feel myself teetering forward, preparing unconsciously to fling myself into hell . . .

Effie grabbed my arm. Wherever we were going, we would go together.

'The people of this world don't want the gateway to exist,' Alucard said. 'It's far too dangerous to allow the denizens of hell to come and go as they please . . .'

'You talk as if there are thousands tramping about,' laughed the nun, 'all coming to Whitby on their holidays. Illegal immigration from the underworld! The numbers are highly exaggerated, you know.'

'Even one is too many,' Alucard said. 'Even you and your sniggering son. Or Sheila Manchu. Or the proprietress of the Christmas Hotel.'

I was holding my breath. Mrs Claus! Sheila Manchu! Of course they were damned. Of course they had escaped through the Bitch's Maw.

'They don't cause many problems,' the old nun said. 'They seek merely to live a quiet life in this small town. They do not want to be in hell, and hell has no need of them. As someone put it recently, hell is bursting at the seams.'

'I can't allow it,' Alucard said, preparing to spring. 'I am pledged to protect mankind from the denizens of hell.'

'What? Really? How ridiculous! You, who feasted on them, who made this world a sensual playground – made everyone submit to your fiendish appetites?'

'That is in the past,' said Alucard. 'I work for the Ministry now.'

'Oh, the Ministry,' said the nun. 'I've had that lot after me before. Do you mean MIAOW?'

Alucard nodded tersely.

'How ludicrous,' said the nun. 'They've castrated you, Count.'

'Perhaps.' He looked at Effie. 'But things change. People change.'

The abbess followed his glance. 'You've fallen in love with the witch?'

'Witch?' gasped Effie.

'I have.'

'You do not deserve to love,' said the nun. Then, with a wave, she hexed him.

We had barely time to realise what was going on. A vast wave of power emanated from her tiny form. Like an invisible fist, it reached out, grabbed Alucard and shook him as if he were a rag doll. He cried out once, sharply, with infinite regret, and was flung into the Maw.

He went spinning and dwindling through the air to vanish in the far distance and that swaying canopy of trees. Effie screamed. She collapsed beside me and I had to hold her up, though I was pretty startled too. Beside us, Mr Danby quivered with laughter.

'A lackey for the Ministry, indeed!' cursed the abbess. 'My dear, you're better off without that old fool. I've always thought he was weak. You do not need him.'

'You've – you've sent him to hell!' Effie sobbed.

The abbess cackled. 'In a fashion, that's true. But he can't stay there – no soul. Like your friend Brenda. They'll hunt him down and drive him out . . . eventually.' She was convulsed with laughter.

I patted Effie, trying to console her. But it was hopeless.

'Oh, never mind him,' said the abbess. 'He might have been sweet so far, but he'd end up reverting, you know. One day you'd wake up with your delicate throat ripped out and a raging thirst. Forget him.'

'I want to go home,' said Effie.

'You may,' said the Abbess. 'Our work here is almost complete.'

'What work?' I said. 'We've done nothing but send poor Kristoff away.'

'He has been put out of the way, yes. The plot to close the gateway to hell has been halted. The Bitch Maw will remain open for the foreseeable future.'

'And spill hellish inhabitants into Whitby for as long as it amuses you,' I added tartly.

'Of course,' said the abbess. 'That's as it should be. That is why I am in this town. And why Danby is here, to keep me alive. And why Effie, her female relatives and their books of old knowledge are here. And finally, Brenda, it is why you are here. You have work to do among the damned.'

I stared at her. I knew that what she was saying was true. I knew this was my destiny at last. The buzzing in my ears was a fanfare now.

'Some will need your help. Some will be out of control. Some you will have to do battle with. But you will come across them all, Brenda, one way or another. You must be waiting for them when they emerge from the underworld.'

'Why?' Effie asked, still choked at the loss of her beau. 'Why should we do anything for you?'

'Because there is no one else,' the abbess said. 'Only you stand between your precious world and the demons absconding from hell. Only you can sort them out.'

'Oh,' said Effie, in a very tired voice. 'Splendid.'

The abbess waved her arm, and the glowing Maw with its primeval forest faded. I thought about Alucard, trapped in there somewhere, in one of those ghastly realms. He'd be all right, wouldn't he?

The wall was black stone once more.

'Pop me back in my suitcase, Danby,' we heard the nun say in the darkness. He set to work diligently, ignoring us now, tending his precious mother.

It was time to go.

Effie and I found ourselves wandering back across the top of the hill. We linked arms against the cold and the dark. We were shivering with terror and trying to conceal it. We didn't say much. 'Poor Kristoff,' Effie said, at one point. 'Poor, poor Kristoff.'

We didn't want to talk about it yet. Any of it. The main thing was to get ourselves down those hundred and ninety-nine steps and home. We could think about it, and the implications, later, when we were safe. Not here, not yet.

'Kristoff will be fine,' I said. 'He'll escape – you'll see, Effie.'

Effie was struggling to regain her composure. 'But what else will escape, Brenda? Who will escape from hell next?'

We were cutting across the church graveyard at the top of the steps. It wasn't the nicest place to be, after everything we had been involved in. But we were impatient to be home.

We skirted the graves, treading lightly, hearts pounding.

One was covered with fresh flowers. Jessie's, of course.

The carnations and roses were stirring in the breeze.

Actually, when we looked closer, they were doing more than that. They were being dislodged. Beneath them, the freshly turned earth was juddering and heaving.

Effie and I drew back, clutching each other.

We stared, frozen, as two hands emerged from Jessie's grave. They were hairy, dirty hands, clawing desperately at the night air.

What were we supposed to do? Run screaming from the graveyard?

Effie and I looked at each other calmly. Then we stepped forward, took hold of a shaking forearm each – and *heaved* . . .